LATE EDITION

LATE EDITION

FERN MICHAELS

WHEELER
CHIVERS

This Large Print edition is published by Thorndike Press, Waterville, Maine USA and by AudioGo Ltd, Bath, England.
Copyright © 2010 by MRK Productions.
The Godmothers Series #3.
Fern Michaels is a Registered Trademark of First Draft, Inc.
The moral right of the author has been asserted.
Wheeler Publishing, a part of Gale, Cengage Learning.

LIBRARY OF CONGRESS CATALOGING-IN-PUBLICATION DATA

Michaels, Fern.
  Late edition / by Fern Michaels.
    p. cm. — (The godmothers series ; #3)
  ISBN-13: 978-1-4104-3580-4 (hardcover)
  ISBN-10: 1-4104-3580-6 (hardcover)
  1. Female friendship—Fiction. 2. Large type books. I. Title.
PS3563.I27L38 2011
813'.54—dc22   2011020585

BRITISH LIBRARY CATALOGUING-IN-PUBLICATION DATA AVAILABLE
Published in the U.S. in 2011 by arrangement with Zebra Books, an imprint of Kensington Publishing Corp.
Published in the U.K. in 2012 by arrangement with The Kensington Publishing Corp.
U.K. Hardcover: 978 1 445 86560 7 (Chivers Large Print)
U.K. Softcover: 978 1 445 86561 4 (Camden Large Print)

Printed in the United States of America
1 2 3 4 5 6 7 15 14 13 12 11

In Loving Memory of a dear friend,
Susan Manning

PROLOGUE

Malibu, California

At dusk they gathered to speak to the dead. With Sophie acting as their spiritual guide, the official leader of their weekly séances, the four women — Teresa Amelia "Toots" Loudenberry, Ida McGullicutty, Mavis Hanover, and Sophia "Sophie" Manchester, lifelong friends of more than fifty years — took their seats around the old wooden dining table left behind by the former pop star who'd lived in the beach house before Toots purchased it almost a year earlier.

Sophie had read somewhere that once wood was charged with an unnatural entity, it acted as a conductor. When Toots remodeled the house, they'd kept the table for the sole purpose of conducting séances. Using a purple silk sheet for a tablecloth and a drinking glass as their tool for communication should a spirit decide to join them, Sophie did what she always did before they began. She said her prayer.

"Oh, great one, bless this dump and those who inhabit it, living or dead."

Toots kicked her on the shin beneath the table. Sophie cast a wicked eye at her best friend, as if to say, "I'll kick your rear end later."

Sophie took her bottle of holy water and spritzed it around the table. She flicked a few extra droplets in Toots's face just to tick her off.

She sat back down in her chair, tucking the small bottle of holy water inside her pocket. "We are here to communicate with the other side. We are friendly. We mean no harm." Sophie said this at the beginning of every séance she conducted. Who knew what kind of evil lurked in other dimensions?

"Let's place our fingertips on the glass. Very gently," Sophie instructed.

When the tips of their fingers were lightly touching the glass, Sophie scanned the others. All three had their eyes closed. Good. They were learning. She closed her own.

"If there is anyone who wishes to make contact, we are willing to allow you into our . . . *realm*," she said in place of the word *home*. She really wanted to say *home*, as it sounded so much more inviting. Couldn't have a spirit believing they weren't welcome. "Come into our *home*," she added, suddenly changing her mind.

No air circulated in the room, yet the candles she had lit earlier flickered, as though a slight breeze had passed through the room. Sophie opened her eyes, shocked at what she saw.

Hundreds of tiny white lights, *orbs* they were called, spun around the room so fast, it was hard to follow the movement.

"What the hell?" Toots blurted in total amazement.

"Shh," Sophie cautioned. "I'm not sure what's happening."

Mavis and Ida stared at the bright dots dancing around the room. Moving, it seemed, at the speed of light, the orbs whirled around the room, then shot off to who knew where, only to have another hundred or so take their places. After several minutes of shock at what they were seeing, they heard a soft drone begin to fill the room, low, as if the sound were coming from a distance.

Bees, Sophie thought. It sounds like a swarm of bees. Seconds passed; the noise grew louder. Toots, Ida, and Mavis looked to Sophie for guidance. The noise became louder and more distinct as the small circles

9

of light darted around the dining room.

Voices. It sounded like hundreds of people trying to talk at once. Sophie jerked to attention, trying to identify the interpreter, or whatever it called itself. Her hearing as sharp as a sword, Sophie went from her normal olive-colored skin to white in less than a second.

"Walter!" she whispered, knowing it couldn't be, yet she'd clearly identified his voice as one among many. Maybe she was cracking up, losing touch with reality. Maybe it was time to give up the ghosts, move on to something more . . . *earthbound.*

The others gaped at her. "Sophie," Toots said in a normal tone. "What did you just say?"

"Nothing." Sophie shook her head, hoping to clear what she *thought* she heard. She scanned the room, still jam-packed with the translucent balls of light, trying to distinguish exactly where this so-called voice was coming from.

"Liar," Toots said in a low tone.

"Shh," she said. Sophie leaned closer to the table, wrenching her neck into a position so precarious that it actually made a popping sound.

"Are you okay?" Toots asked. She moved her chair closer to Sophie's. "Something isn't right. We need to stop this right now."

Hearing the alarm in Toots's voice jolted Sophie back to reality, or as much as one could, given her current circumstances. "I'm fine. Listen." She leveled her gaze at the door leading to the kitchen.

The high-pitched garble in the room thundered in their ears, sounding like thousands of hoofbeats pounding against the earth. Straining to discern a male voice in the earsplitting loudness, Sophie cleared her throat before she spoke. "If you wish to make yourself known, do so or leave this room!"

In the blink of an eye, the room temperature dropped at least twenty degrees. Shivering with fear yet wanting to clarify what she'd thought was a voice from the past, Sophie drew her strength from Toots, who'd placed her hand on top of hers. Sort of like their secret handshake.

The anomalies began to disappear one by one, until there was only a handful of the translucent balls of light hovering several feet off the floor. After several seconds, the voices stopped, and the only sounds in the room were coming from the women themselves, their quickened breaths, in and out.

One by one, the orbs of light began to take on form. Each vaporous cloud became distinguishable by its gender, its clothing, and, lastly, for some of them, a face of sorts.

Before she totally lost her cool, Sophie counted the spirits. Thirteen in all. That had to be a bad omen. Clearing her throat again, Sophie spoke to the ghostly apparitions floating above the table.

"Identify yourselves!" she commanded with more power than she felt. The only female, or what Sophie designated as a female, swirled below the others. The misty image wore a flowered-print housedress with a V neckline. Several tissues leaked from her large bosom. Long wisps of white hair touched the flounce of her outdated dress.

"Oh my God," Toots said. "It's . . : *Mrs. Patterson?* But . . . how? She's not . . ."

Sophie careened around so fast, her neck popped again. She'd be in a body cast if this kept up.

The old woman, void of the dentures she wore in life, smacked her waxen lips together. *"Dead?"* A cold mist passed through her lips when she spoke. *"Then where's Snuffy? Is she dead, too?"* The old woman looked at Toots as if she knew the answer to her question.

Scooting their chairs across the hardwood floor, the four gathered closely around one another as quickly as possible.

In a raspy voice, Toots demanded, "Is this for real? If I remember correctly, Snuffy was Mrs. Patterson's cat."

Sophie nodded, asking, "Who the hell is Mrs. Patterson?"

"My neighbor in Charleston, but I'm not sure she's actually dead," Toots whispered.

Ida and Mavis hovered side by side, hands gripping one another. Sophie and Toots examined the hazy, mistlike woman levitating just above the table. She didn't appear to have any legs. The male entities continued to linger a few feet above and behind the single female.

As suddenly as she had appeared, the ghost of Mrs. Patterson disappeared. In her place, one of the male ghosts zoomed over so quickly, Sophie wasn't sure if what she thought she saw was actually happening. At least she wasn't until she saw Ida's features change from astonishment to total and absolute fear. Ida's lips moved, but there was no sound. She shook her head, and her lips kept moving, but she remained completely speechless.

The male spirit bobbed above the table. His features were nebulous, yet his clothes were clearly outlined while still being transparent. Dark slacks and a fitted suit jacket shimmered against the flickering light from the candles.

"It's . . . *Thomas!*" Ida placed a hand over her heart, as though she were in pain.

Sophie responded succinctly and without fear. She stared at the creepy form of matter that had captured Ida's attention. "Now's your chance to ask him exactly where he bought that tainted meat."

Just as one would expect, Ida took a deep breath and proceeded to slither out of her chair, landing in a dead faint.

The spirit began to twirl, becoming cylindrical in shape, then shot toward the ceiling. A hollow sound, which Sophie could have sworn was laughter, reverberated through the room. The remaining orbs whirled around in every direction, reminding Sophie of shooting stars.

As fast as they had come, the other eleven orbs disappeared.

Sophie removed the bottle of holy water from her pocket. She proceeded to dump its contents in Ida's face. Within a split second, Ida jolted back to reality.

Sputtering, wiping the remains of the holy water off her face with the back of her hand, Ida sat up, leaning against the chair's legs. "I believe Thomas has returned from the grave to haunt me."

Toots spoke, fright making her words shaky. "You may be onto something."

For once, Toots, Mavis, and even Sophie nodded in agreement.

CHAPTER 1

The beach house, Malibu

Sophie Manchester sat on the deck, staring out at the Pacific and watching the reflections off the waves as the sun rose behind her. She rose, turning to the east, and watched a giant ball of fire floating above the mountains. Vibrant yellow, orange, and a dozen hues of pink, it appeared like a rosy blush-colored wine splashed across the sky. She crushed her third cigarette out in the giant shell she and Toots used for their ashtray, then began pacing back and forth across the ocean-facing deck. The view was out of this world, but it could have been the Taj Mahal for all the attention she paid it. Haunted by last night's events, she wondered if she'd opened a door that was meant to remain closed. She'd heard Walter's voice; she would know it anywhere. The question was, should she continue to experiment with the unknown? There was no way

17

in hell she would admit it, but she was now truly frightened of the ability she had to make contact with the other side. It was one thing to get through to Hollywood's dead stars. It was a totally different ball of wax when it came to ex-husbands and neighbors who might still be alive. Madame Butterfly had told her many years ago that she had a special gift, but Sophie had always shrugged it off as a bunch of mumbo jumbo. She wasn't so sure anymore.

Mavis, all 146 pounds of her, carried out a tray filled with an ungodly amount of healthy food, a carafe of fresh-squeezed orange juice, and four steaming mugs of coffee.

Placing the food-laden tray on the patio table, Mavis said, "I knew I would find you out here smoking those nasty old cigarettes. Are Toots and Ida up yet?"

"I heard Toots stirring around when I woke up. Nothing from Ida," Sophie said flatly. "She's probably still in shock after last night."

Ever cheerful, Mavis observed, "Well, that was quite an experience. I don't know that any one of us will ever get over it." Mavis proceeded to empty the tray, placing the plates and cups on the table. "I've made steel-cut oats with fresh blueberries, and

18

sliced pineapple with whole-grain toast, minus the butter, of course. I do believe you will like this fresh sugar-free strawberry jam I made last week. I saw this recipe on the Food Network, one of Paula Deen's shows, but I made a few healthy substitutes. She uses so much butter, it's a wonder that sweet little woman hasn't suffered a major coronary from all that unhealthy cooking she does. Though I do enjoy her show."

Sophie rolled her eyes, grabbed a mug of coffee, and carried it back to her lounge chair, where she sat down and lit another cigarette. "Why do you watch her if her show cooks nothing but fattening, unhealthy food?"

Mavis sat down at the table and stirred blueberries in her oatmeal, then took a healthy sip of orange juice before answering Sophie. "She's such a dear woman. She reminds me of Toots. You know, sweet and silly, a little bit on the ornery side but with an air of sophistication. I would love to go to her restaurant in Savannah, Georgia, sometime before I die. Plus, I would have a chance to see those old graveyards from as far back as the eighteenth century. I think I will add that to my life list. What about you, Sophie?"

Sophie blew out a funnel of smoke and

took a sip of coffee. "Actually, there are a few places I would like to see before I cross over into another world," Sophie said. One evening, when they'd all had too much time on their hands, they'd each made a list, calling it their life list, of things they wanted to do before they passed on.

"Good. We all need something to look forward to in our old age, something fun and exciting."

Sophie crushed out her ever-present cigarette before lighting another. She remembered last night and found that the place where sarcasm usually dwelt had become the home of fear. "Never hearing from . . . Well, let me put it this way. I want to make it my number one priority to guide Walter's ghost straight into the fiery pits of hell. That's going to the top of my life list."

Mavis shook her head. "That is so sad, Sophie. You need to revamp your list."

Sophie rolled her eyes. "I could say the same about you. This new fascination you have with graveyards, reading the obits like they're great works of literature. Is that something on your life list?"

Mavis ducked her head, took a large spoonful of oatmeal, and practically shoved it down her throat. "That isn't on my list."

"Oh. Then explain why you're so fascinated with the obituaries." Sophie took a drink of coffee. "I'm waiting."

Mavis stood, gathering up her bowl and the plate of fruit. "I certainly don't want to sound rude, Sophie, but that isn't any of your business. It's just something that . . . well, I'm curious about. How long people lived, whom they left behind."

Sophie inhaled, then blew the smoke out, where it swirled above her head like a halo. "I could understand if it were *family.* But these are strangers. You need to find another hobby."

At that moment, Toots stepped outside, saving Mavis from having to reply. Spying the coffee, she helped herself to a mug. "What're you two arguing about this early?" Toots sat down in her deck chair, reaching for *her* ever-present pack of cigarettes. She lit up and blew the smoke out in one giant puffy cloud.

"Mavis's morbid fascination with the obits. It's her new hobby," Sophie said.

Mavis snatched the tray off the table so quickly that her mug of coffee tipped over, sending the brown liquid flying through the air, then landing on her charcoal gray blouse. Sophie just then realized that Mavis seemed to be wearing a lot of different shades of gray lately. Maybe she was in mourning for all those strangers she spent so much time reading about.

"I'm going to pretend we never had this conversation. Now I have work to do." Mavis rushed through the open doors, her willowy blouse flapping like wings.

"Stuck-up!" Sophie shouted to her back. Since Mavis had lost all that weight, she'd become a bit conceited, but, Sophie granted, Mavis was entitled since she'd literally worked her tail off to lose almost a hundred pounds. If asked a year ago, Sophie would never have believed Mavis could be so dedicated, so disciplined, but she'd proven her wrong. The same with Ida. Her life had been defined by her fear of germs. Had Toots not stepped in, who knew what Ida would be doing right now? Though Ida's OCD wasn't as severe as some cases, and all the girls suspected her of playing this up to the nth degree, none of them wanted to see her suffer in any way.

"You shouldn't be so hard on her," Toots said. "She's come a long way."

Sophie rolled her eyes. "I know that. I just don't understand this newfound fascination with the obits, that's all."

"What about our newest . . . ah . . . hobby?" Toots was almost hesitant to bring up last night. It'd scared the guff out of all of them. "Séances? That's not your everyday hobby."

"It isn't a hobby at all. You, of all people, should know that. It's a . . . gift," Sophie informed her.

"A gift? I thought this was entertainment, something for Abby's column for *The Informer*," Toots replied. Abby was Toots's daughter and the editor in chief of a Los Angeles–based tabloid that, unbeknownst to Abby, Toots had bought a year or so ago. Toots took a sip of her coffee, then tossed the remains over the deck. "Mavis makes the worst coffee."

Sophie reached for a slice of pineapple from the platter Mavis had left on the table. "Her food stinks, too. I need something real. Like a ham-and-cheese omelet with a side of greasy hash browns. This healthy stuff will be the death of me."

Toots nodded in agreement. "Stop trying to change the subject. I want to talk about what happened last night."

Sophie swallowed her pineapple, took a drink of coffee, then lit up. "I was as shocked as the rest of you. I think I've opened up a portal for our dead husbands. I did some heavy-duty research on the Internet last night, after I went upstairs. I know it sounds nuts, but I don't have any other explanation. You got any bright ideas?"

"Isn't that supposed to be evil, like a place for demons to come and go? Take over someone's personality, their soul?" Toots asked.

Sophie shook her head, her dark brown hair wrapping around her face. She tucked the loose strands behind her ears. "You're talking about demonic possession. I don't believe we have anything like that going on here. It's like I said, I think our exes are coming back to . . . I'm not sure what they're coming back for. Maybe they just want to frighten us. I don't have any other explanation."

Toots was quiet for a moment. "I suppose if Leland should decide to . . . make his presence known, I'll have to explain why I didn't bury him with his expensive bottle of scotch. The old coot was cheap in life. I doubt that's changed in death. Maybe he's stuck in between, you know, waiting for whatever it is they wait for to help them cross over to the other side. Or in his case, he might be waiting for a U-Haul to bring his fortune to his grave site."

Toots took a deep drag from her cigarette. "In his case it might be that he'll return for all that money he left behind."

Sophie laughed, but her heart wasn't in it.

24

"I suppose if Walter and Leland crossed paths, they could . . . Hell, I don't know. Maybe Walter's looking for Leland's bottle of scotch that you were supposed to bury with him. Could be his liver's been revived."

Coffee spewed from Toots's mouth as she uttered a hearty guffaw. "Only you would think of something like that at a time like this." She wiped her mouth with a tissue from her jeans pocket.

All traces of humor gone, Sophie inquired, "What is that supposed to mean? 'At a time like this'?"

"You know what I mean. This séance ordeal. Last night. Do you suppose there is a connection of some kind, something we're missing?" Toots asked.

"I thought of that, and I'm coming up as empty-handed as you are. I think we need to try another séance tonight. We'll try to duplicate last night's séance as closely as possible. Same time, same candles. We'll wear the same clothes, the whole deal."

"Something tells me Ida isn't going to be game for this a second time," Toots said.

"Then we'll just have to make sure she is game," Sophie shot back.

"Explain exactly how we're going to do this. I doubt that Ida will ever want to sit in on one of our séances again. Now that she's seen Thomas, and before you say anything, no, I cannot believe these words are coming out of my mouth, but it is what it is, so how do you propose we convince her to come to another . . . performance?" It amazed Toots how she accepted these . . . peculiar entities as part of their normal, everyday life.

"We could threaten her. With something extremely germy," Sophie said, a huge grin on her face.

"That's a terrible idea, especially after all she's been through!" Toots lit another cigarette. "Just what kind of germs are we talking about here?"

"Something the seagulls would ignore." Sophie laughed. "Maybe an unusually smelly dead fish. A dirty diaper. I see people tossing disposable diapers into the water all the time."

"That's beyond disgusting. I can't believe we would even consider doing this to poor Ida given what she's been through this past year. I don't know if she'd be able to withstand something so vile," Toots said.

The sliding glass door opened. "Poor Ida, what? I heard what you said! What are you two up to?"

Sophie and Toots had the grace to appear chagrined.

"We aren't up to anything," Sophie said hastily.

Normally, Ida wasn't an early riser, so neither Toots nor Sophie had expected to see her out on the deck at sunrise. It was obvious that Ida had had a rough night. There were dark circles beneath her eyes, her impeccable pageboy was a mess, and she still wore the same navy slacks and mauve blouse she'd had on the night before, only they were wrinkled, as though she'd tossed and turned in them all night.

Ida reached for a mug of the now-cool coffee Mavis had left on the table. She took a sip, made a face, then took a seat in the chair opposite Toots.

"You look terrible," Sophie said cheerfully.

"You're not much to look at, either," Ida complained. "I haven't slept a wink. This has been one of the worst nights of my life." Ida made a dramatic gesture of sweeping her hand out in front of her as though she were a game-show model about to reveal the grand prize behind door number two.

Toots and Sophie looked at one another, then quickly glanced away.

Sophie, who was never at a loss for words, said, "I thought the night Jerry dumped you for Toots was the worst night of your life."

Years earlier, Ida had been dating Jerry,

who at the time she'd thought was the love of her life. As soon as he laid eyes on Toots, he'd immediately dumped Ida for Toots. Ida made a habit of reminding Toots of this whenever the urge hit her.

Toots tried to suppress a giggle. "I did you a favor, and you know it." Jerry had been a skinflint and a lousy kisser to boot.

"You certainly remind me often enough," Ida snapped back.

"I'm not the one who's always doing the reminding, if memory serves me correctly," Toots said. If they all lived to the ripe old age of one hundred, Ida would still remind Toots of this so-called indiscretion that had happened so many years ago. Toots and Jerry had shared a brief marriage; then he'd kicked the bucket. He'd been husband number five or six. After eight marriages, it was hard to name them in numerical order. Someday she would do so. She'd match up all her marriage certificates with the death certificates. Maybe she would start a scrapbook. Scrapbooking seemed to be all the rage these days. At least she could claim she'd never been divorced.

"Stop it, both of you. I'm sick of hearing about Jerry. If my memory serves me correctly, and we all know I have the memory of an elephant, Toots said he was a dud in the sack, as well. So, once and for all, Ida, why don't you thank Toots for the favor and be done with it."

Uncharacteristically, Ida flipped Sophie the single-digit salute. The three of them burst out laughing, which eased the tension immediately. They laughed until tears streamed down their faces. Exhausted from their unexpected hysterics, the trio suddenly became quiet. The only sounds were the occasional cry from a seagull and the noise of the ocean as its waves caressed the dampened, bone-colored sand. A mild breeze carried the scent of wood smoke, doubtlessly left over from a beach bonfire the night before.

Ida looked Sophie directly in the face, her tone as serious as ever. "Can you explain what happened last night? I . . . I don't know when I've been so frightened."

Sophie glanced at Toots, who shook her head and shrugged her shoulders, as if saying she hadn't a clue how to answer.

"You saw Thomas's ghost. What's to explain?" Sophie asked.

Exasperated, Ida threw her hands up in the air. "And you think I'm just supposed to accept that like it's . . . like it's *normal?*"

"I'm afraid I must agree with Ida. Seeing all those famous stars is one thing. Seeing people we know, especially our dead spouses, well, that's a bit much if you ask me."

"I didn't ask. I don't know what's got your panties in a knot. You didn't see any of your dead husbands," Sophie singsonged. "Yet."

"*Yet* is the right word. Where is this leading? Are we so bored that we have nothing better to do than stir up a bunch of unnecessary trouble just to entertain ourselves?"

Sophie considered her question. "Yes, I think that's exactly what's going on. We're bored, but we've found a way to entertain ourselves. We aren't hurting anyone." Sophie paused then, considering her words. "Except ourselves, and we're all okay, aren't we?" she challenged.

"When put that way, I suppose we are. But what if, what if we've opened a portal that's not supposed to be opened?" Toots asked. "As in a portal to hell?"

Sophie lit another cigarette, inhaled, then blew out the smoke like Puff, the Magic Dragon. "If that's the case, then we're screwed."

Toots shot Sophie a killer look. "You're so ugly, I swear. It should've been you instead of Ida that caught that pervert sniffing all those undergarments."

"Never would've happened. I'm not quite the rounder as Ida. I can go without a man."

"Then maybe you're interested in Ms. Goldstein yourself," Ida said, lifting her perfectly sculpted brow but smiling as she did so. Ms. Goldstein was the district attorney responsible for trying the case against the three con artists.

"Kiss off, Ida," Sophie snapped back.

Mavis took a deep breath. "Can you girls ever speak to one another nicely? I don't think we've ever had a conversation that didn't involve one of you talking mean or hateful to the other. I think all of you are very disrespectful to one another."

"We are," Toots said. "But I wouldn't want any other way. It's all in fun, and as far as concerned, none of us mean to hurt another. That ramrod-straight Leland fit when the word *shit* came out of uth. He used to call me potty mouth. glad I planted him, God rest his l."

the norm, they all cracked up en Miss Prim-and-Proper Ida. ook her head. "Well, it was just

Later that evening, they all scrambled around the table in the newly remodeled kitchen, ready to dig into the piping hot pepperoni pizza that Giorgio's, their new favorite pizza joint, had just delivered. Mavis, still as pleasant as ever, had set the table as she normally did, with the everyday dinnerware, forks, knives, and royal blue cloth napkins. Apparently she'd forgiven Sophie her morning's indiscretion. It was apparent Ida had spent the afternoon napping, as her under-eye circles were gone, and her hair was smoothed to perfection. She had changed into a pair of black slacks and a pearl-colored top and appeared more herself. Toots had spent the afternoon proofreading an article for *The Informer*. Sophie had prepared for the evening's scheduled séance. She'd set up the video and voice recorders just in case.

They had just learned that the jury had

reached a verdict in the trial of the State of California versus Patel Yadav, Mohammed Dasgupta, and Amala Malik, the trio charged with identity theft, fraud, and numerous other crimes. Ida had had the misfortune of getting involved with Patel, who'd posed as Dr. Benjamin Sameer, medical director at the Center for Mind and Body. He'd almost bilked her out of three million dollars, but fortunately, or unfortunately, depending upon how you looked at it, Ida had caught the charlatan in the act of sniffing her racy red and black panties. She'd stopped the financial transaction in the nick of time. The case was being covered on truTV, and now there was a verdict.

Toots positioned the small television set where they all had a bird's-eye view. She bumped the volume up several notches before sitting down at the table.

"You should've used the paper plates, Mavis. This is just more dishes to wash," Toots complained as she reached for a generous slice of the cheesy pizza with large pieces of pepperoni. Tonight, they couldn't wait to clog their arteries.

"Oh, I don't mind," Mavis said sweetly. "Gives me something to do. I'll need to work off this meal, anyway."

"One slice won't ruin your svelte figure.

Let's listen," Ida said, nodding toward the TV set.

With an evil grin that lit up her dark brown eyes like a bottle of good whiskey, Sophie said, "Yeah, I can't wait to see Ida's lover on the news."

Toots reached for her royal blue napkin. "Enough! You can't keep your nastiness to yourself, can you? This case is already a joke as it is. What's your take on it, Ida?"

Ida, always trying to play the role of elegant lady of the manor, dotted her mouth with her napkin and placed it on her lap before speaking. "I think that dirty old man deserves to be laughed at. I hope they give all three of them the maximum sentence. I've never been so embarrassed in my lif[e] And to think, I thought he was a ge[ntle]man."

Ida sliced a piece of pizza or[ ] and shook her head. "I can't [ ] to tell that old prosecutor[ ] incident. Personally, [ ] cheap thrill of sorts[ ]

Sophie, never [ ] to add her t[ ] she has a cru[ ] your age. Mayb[ ] lesson. Ever thin[ ] the other side?"

it
I'm
one
had a
my mo
I'm so
cheap so
As was
laughing, e
Mavis just sh

a thought. A passing one."

For the next few minutes they gorged on pizza and drank a good bottle of Cabernet Sauvignon from a local winery.

They all focused their attention on the TV. When the snazzy, pink-lipped reporter's face filled the screen, Mavis bellowed, "She's the one I watch on the news every night," as if that were the grandest thing in the world. Of course the local news media would be covering the trial. Los Angeles loved a trial, especially one that involved a panty sniffer posing as a doctor who happened to cure a very wealthy woman of obsessive-compulsive disorder.

"Shhh," Sophie called out. "Let's listen to what she has to say."

"Dominating tonight's news, a case that has held Californians captive for weeks. Patel Yadav and his two partners in crime, Mohammed Dasgupta, who has been referred to as Patel Yadav's adopted son, and Amala Malik, who had a romantic relationship with Mohammed, were all present in the courtroom today as they faced a jury of their peers. After a two-week trial, the three were found guilty on all counts in the indictment. The sentencing hearing has been scheduled for next week."

The news anchor said a few more words

about the trial, and Toots couldn't help but notice how her eyes sparkled when she mentioned that Patel had also been caught with a drawerful of female undergarments. She implied he'd had a thing for them, yet didn't elaborate on exactly what kind of thing. Maybe the reporter would do a feature on men and the "things" that turned them on. Give the male species another kick in the pants. Men. They were true creatures of habit. Perverted old bastards.

Mavis grimaced at the reporter's apparent delight in her subject matter.

Sophie gaped at Ida, a sly grin causing the corners of her eyes to appear to spread out like a fan. "I remember the day you came home from the pervert's place, or, to be more precise, the real Dr. Sameer's house. You said something about there was more to the story. Something about telling us later. Do you recall saying that?" Sophie questioned Ida as though she were a government agent contemplating using enhanced interrogation techniques.

Ida's eyes bulged. "Sophie, has anyone ever told you that you have no class or manners?" Ida held a hand out in front of her. "Don't answer that. Of course they have. I'm sure I have. You're nosy, too." Ida tilted her chin up a notch.

"Toots, don't you remember Ida telling us there was more to this story? That someday she might tell us? I have a pretty good memory. I know that's what she said."

Toots wiped a string of cheese off her plate with a fingertip. "Well, it does seem like there was more to the story, I agree. But I'm not sure I even want to know what it is. I might get sick or something." Toots's last words were drawn out, her acquired Southern drawl even more pronounced than normal.

Enjoying the attention, Ida cast an evil grin at Sophie. "How much is it worth to you?"

As Toots threw her head back and roared with laughter, Mavis reached down for Coco, who'd been hovering at her heels. Sophie waved both of her middle fingers out in front of her as if they were the answer for everything. More laughter.

"I wouldn't give you jack, Ida. You should know better than that. I'm saving my five million dollars for something worthwhile. Your *sex*-apades aren't worth it. I'm betting even *The Enquirer* wouldn't give you an Indian nickel. It's not like you're famous or anything."

Ida took a deep breath. "If you're all so concerned — no, if you're all that *nosy* — I

37

guess I'd better tell you what happened firsthand," Ida said. "So you'll get the truth the first time. I'm sure any paper would love to get their hands on this story. So now, before I reveal anything, I need each of you to promise me something." Ida glared at the three of them.

Their heads bobbed up and down like apples in a tub of water.

"And just like we've been doing since seventh grade, I want you to seal this with our secret handshake. Is it a deal or not?" Ida asked, her tone more serious than it had been minutes before.

One by one, each woman placed a hand on top of Ida's. When the four hands were placed on top of each other, they tossed them high in the air, shouting, "When you're good, you're good."

"Now that you have our sworn secrecy, it's time to spill the beans," Sophie announced.

"All right. As you all may recall, I was quite upset when the taxi dropped me off that day. I tell you, I was in utter shock! That man took me for an idiot, but thank goodness I came to my senses," Ida said before getting to the really juicy details she'd promised.

"Okay, so you were in shock. Now tell us

what actually happened," Sophie insisted.

Mavis adjusted Coco on her newly slender lap, Toots refilled their wineglasses with the last of the Cabernet Sauvignon, and Sophie drummed her fingers across the tabletop. Ida was queen of the moment.

"Well, you all know what I caught him doing. That much is public knowledge. At least no one can accuse me of wearing granny panties."

"Didn't he steal and sniff those lacy red and black ones you found in his pile of lingerie?" Sophie questioned, a huge grin on her face.

"Yes, they were red and black, and before you ask, they were clean."

Sophie smiled, sneering. "So Patel must've been disappointed when he realized you hadn't left your . . . scent behind."

"Ugh, that's enough, Sophie! We don't need to know that," Mavis said.

"She's right. Be quiet, Sophie, so Ida can finish the story. I don't want to spend the rest of the night discussing this sick, perverted man," Toots said.

"Sure you do," Sophie teased. "Okay, finish the story so Toots's virgin ears won't fall off."

Toots gave Sophie the finger.

"I'd been so upset the night before, at dinner. I assumed Sammy, uh . . . Patel was going to propose. He'd laid the foundation. What was I supposed to think? I thought we were going out for a romantic dinner. Then we wound up at the house."

Impatiently, Toots spoke up. "We know all that. Just tell us what you were so ashamed of."

"You're almost as bad as she is," Ida complained, nodding toward Sophie. "I remembered calling Russ, my banker, asking him to transfer three million dollars. That should have been a warning sign, but I wasn't listening with my brain."

"When do you ever?" Sophie interjected.

"Shut up! For Pete's sake, you're the one who wanted to hear this personal story so badly. Yet you can't keep your mouth closed for more than three seconds. Go on, Ida. I'll jap-slap her if she interrupts you again," Toots threatened.

"Thank you," Ida replied. "I should've known something was off when I asked for his banking information and he had it written out on a slip of paper ready in his pocket, as if he knew I was going to lend him the money. I remember being a bit disappointed when he accepted my offer. Of course, in hindsight, I know that was my instincts trying to tell me something, but I was too enamored of that idiot to listen.

"Once I got over the initial shock of seeing *him*" — Ida shook her head, disgusted — "sniffing his collection of unmentionables, I ran back into his bedroom. I remember being shocked and so thirsty I could've drunk an entire gallon of water. I was trying to gather myself, decide what to do next, when Sammy, Patel, whatever he calls himself, came into the room. He called out my name. I recall thinking I was screwed." Ida smiled at the expressions on her friends' faces as they cottoned to her play on words, then, chuckling to herself, continued with her story.

"When I came out of the bathroom, he was lying on the bed, naked as a newborn babe. The next thing I saw . . . was his *thing*. He'd been fondling himself." Ida had the good grace to blush.

Laughter bubbled up from the three women.

"What came next?" Sophie questioned. "Get it?" she added.

Ida shot her a twisted smile. "Do you want to hear the rest or not? If you continue to interrupt me, I'm not going to finish the story."

"Leave her alone, Sophie. This is starting to get really good," Toots said.

Ida resumed her tale. "It was obvious he'd been vigorously entertaining himself while I was in the bathroom. Looking back, I'm sure it was the panty sniffing that got him all hot and bothered, certainly not anticipation at being with me. As soon as he saw me, he told me to undress . . . and, of course, I did. I stripped down. Fortunately, I only got as far as my bra and panties. I . . . oh, this is so embarrassing." Ida paused, her humiliation no longer as funny as it seemed a minute ago.

For once, Sophie kept her trap shut. Mavis rubbed Coco between the ears. Toots simply waited while Ida composed herself.

"He asked me to . . . finish him off, and I almost died right there on the spot. I would rather have French-kissed Aaron Spelling's ghost. I told him to 'relieve himself,' and the SOB did . . . well, almost, and right in front of me! He asked me to *watch*. I was so mortified, I ran out of the bedroom, outside to the deck, where that nasty Mohammed gaped at me like I was a Playboy Bunny. I was so ashamed, but I stood there and let him rake his eyes up and down. I was not going to give him the satisfaction of knowing how humiliated I was. That little tramp Amala finally went inside for her robe, which I gratefully slipped on before I went back in to retrieve my purse and, of course, to put my clothes back on. The rest you know." Ida exhaled. "You have no idea how glad I am that that's finished."

Sophie perked right up. "Did old Patel ever finish, you know, get his rocks off?"

Ida's face looked as though she'd sucked a lemon. "Do you have to be so graphic? Really."

"I was just curious," Sophie shot back.

Before Ida could reply, the telephone rang, jarring them all. Toots answered on the third ring.

"Abby, I'm so glad you called," Toots said loudly, letting the others know it was Abby so they wouldn't say anything that could be overheard. "You can't imagine what . . . well, never mind," Toots said into the receiver.

Ida, Mavis, and Sophie waited with bated breath for Toots to finish her phone call.

"Yes, of course. I'll tell her," Toots said, then clicked off. "Abby says to tell her three godmothers hi, and she loves you all."

Toots returned to the table.

"Don't ever tell Abby about this . . . thing. I would die if she were to think of her godmother as a . . . floozy," Ida pleaded.

"Abby knows you're loose," Sophie said matter-of-factly.

"Sophie, enough. I wish you would learn to filter your words. You're just mean," Toots said.

"I should never have told you about this. Sophie, you're not going to let me live this one down, are you?" Ida's eyes filled with tears. "I should go back to New York City. At least I won't be known as the former lover of a . . . pervert."

Upset, Ida shoved her plate to the side before downing the last of her wine. Ida blew her nose on the royal blue napkin. "I shouldn't allow myself to get so wrapped up in a man. It's not like you all haven't reminded me of this often enough. If this is what it takes to help me swear off men for a while, then it's what I'm going to do." Ida's expression grew serious. "Toots, should I go home?"

"Maybe we should make a quick trip to Charleston. Bernice keeps asking when I'm coming home, and I keep telling her soon. I can't put her off forever. And you . . ." Toots glared at Sophie with a wicked grin. "You have got to take that old bag and leave her in the drawer once in a while. I know it's hard, but you're gonna have to try. For all our sakes. Especially Abby's."

Sophie's olive skin turned maroon. "Don't you use Abby that way! She would be

44

ashamed of you, Toots. I'm surprised that you would stoop that low. Yes, I am an old bag at times, and yes, I will *try* to tone it down a bit. For Abby. Just so you know."

"Good. Then it's settled. We're going to Charleston — that is, if you all want to. I can't force any of you," Toots said. "However, if you'd rather stay here, this is your home, too. We've been friends for more than fifty years. I refuse to allow that slimy crotch sniffer to disrupt our lives any more than he has already. For all his perversity, that aside, he is the one responsible for curing you of your obsession with germs. We have to keep that uppermost in our minds."

Toots stood and headed for the sliders that led to the deck. "Now I am going to smoke. Sophie, would you care to join me?" she asked before slipping outside.

CHAPTER 3

"Do you really want to go to Charleston?" Toots asked as she passed the lighter to Sophie.

"Sure. It's not like I have anything better to do. Well, I can perform one hell of a séance, but I suppose I can do that anywhere. I'm not sure about Mavis, though. Have you noticed how she's been dressing lately?" Sophie took the lighter from Toots, lit her cigarette, and inhaled deeply.

Amazed, Toots asked, "How did we go from a trip to Charleston to Mavis's wardrobe?"

"You know me. I say the first thing that comes to mind. She's been wearing all that ugly gray and black. You would think she's in mourning." Sophie paused, then directed her gaze to the deck doors, through which they could see that Mavis and Ida were busy in the kitchen. "I still can't believe Ida's actually touching dirty dishes. She's come a long way, but don't you dare tell her I said that." Sophie sucked nicotine into her lungs as though it were pure oxygen.

"And if you continue to insult her the way you've been doing, she'll be right back where she started when we came out here."

"Nah, she won't. She likes herself too much now. Which is a good thing, but if you ever tell her I said that, I will kick your saggy ass all the way back to Charleston. You won't need to charter a private jet." Sophie puffed heartily, the end of her cigarette glowing like a bright orange beacon in the evening's dusky pinkish gray and violet sky.

"How would you know if I have a saggy ass? Have you been spying on me while I shower? Maybe Ida hit the nail on the head. Maybe *you* should ask Carla Goldstein out on a date."

"If I weren't so relaxed right now, I'd smack you," Sophie said, then added, "Right on your saggy old ass."

"Then go for it," Toots suggested.

"Oh, for Pete's sake, I'm teasing. You, of all people, should know that half the crap that comes out of my mouth is just that. A bunch of crap."

"If I didn't know that, I wouldn't have been friends with you all these years. For two old broads, we've been through a lot, especially this past year. Who would've thought we'd wind up in California, chasing ghosts?"

"That's why I say, 'Never say never.' "

"You must admit, this is way off the map. Ghosts. Panty sniffers. Not your average senior citizens' twilight years," Toots observed caustically.

"*Average* isn't in my vocabulary. I'm surprised it's in yours. Average number of marriages, average number of fortunes you've inherited. There is nothing average about you, Toots. Hell, you broke average way back when."

"I'm not sure if I should be insulted or if that's a backhanded compliment, coming from you."

Sophie stubbed her cigarette out, lit another. "You can take it any way you want. Bottom line, Toots, there is nothing average about you at all. Come to think of it, there really isn't anything average about the rest of us, either. Oh, we might've had average lives up to a certain point, but not one of us even comes close to the average senior citizen now. I don't want to spend my last years wearing diapers and dropping my teeth in a glass for someone else to clean the spinach stuck to them. What about you,

Toots? Are you happy now?"

Toots raised her eyebrows in amusement. "What in the world has got into you today? Why so philosophical all of a sudden? And to answer your question, yes, I am happy, and I realize we're not average senior citizens. We never will be. It's not in our genetic makeup. I don't want to be like anyone else. Simply being myself is good enough for me."

They could hear the crash of the waves on the beach as the tide swept out into the unknown. Seagulls cawed, swooping low to catch their evening meal. Soft laughter from a group gathered around a small fire dribbled up to the deck. The pungent odor of marijuana wafted its way past the deck and onward.

"You ever smoke pot?" Sophie asked.

"Yes, I tried it a couple of times. Did nothing except make me stink. Why? Are you thinking about joining that group on the beach?" Toots motioned to the young men and women clustered around the fire.

"You want to?" Sophie teased. "Sure give 'em a scare."

"No, though don't let me stop you if that's what you want to do. I'm content right where I'm at."

The sliding doors opened. Mavis carried a

tray with a pot of coffee, cups, sugar, and cream. Ida trailed behind with a store-bought apple pie, a stack of paper plates, plastic forks, and paper napkins.

"You must've read my mind, Mavis. I was wishing for a cup of coffee. I believe I have what is known as a slight buzz from the wine," Toots said.

Mavis placed the tray on the table, poured four cups of coffee, then added sugar and cream before handing Toots a cup.

"I could really get used to this," Toots said. "What about you, Ida? At home I serve Bernice her morning coffee, plus fix her breakfast. She likes Froot Loops almost as much as I do."

Ida took a cup of coffee and sat in one of the deck chairs that overlooked the beach. "As you all know, I can get used to just about anything. I'll be fine once Patel is locked up. With any luck, it won't follow me around the rest of my life. I don't want to be known as the woman who slept with a panty sniffer. No one has mentioned all those other stars he bilked out of millions. I wonder why."

Patel Yadav had ripped off a half dozen stars, older actresses who, like Ida, had fallen prey to his con, yet there hadn't been a lot of press concerning that. The theft of

Dr. Benjamin Sameer's identity had been the major story as his clinic had been one of the top clinics in the country for every phobia known to man, and then some. His success rate was almost 100 percent. With Hollywood brimming over with all sorts of psychos, it was no wonder the story had become national news and remained a cable favorite until being knocked out of the headlines by the story of a group of Republican congressmen who had been caught red-handed "partying" with a group of transvestites at a fund-raiser to support the party's position on bartering for medical care.

Sophie took the cup of coffee Mavis held out to her. "I would guess they have some powerful publicists, who've worked diligently to keep their clients' names from making headlines. It's too damn bad that prosecutor learned about his sick fetish. Otherwise, your name might not have made headlines. It sure as hell clashes with your OCD, I'll say that. Maybe Oprah will come knocking on your door. She likes exploiting anyone and anything that makes the news. She had a show on the other day about people who hoard everything. They say that's a sickness, too. Call it hoarding. This woman found a carcass of a poor little kitten in all of her junk. It looked like it'd been stuffed. I felt sorry for the cat."

"That's terrible! I couldn't imagine not knowing where Coco is, or having so much stuff that I couldn't find her. Poor woman. She needs help," Mavis said. She cut four slices of pie and placed them around the table. Sophie took two plates, handing one to Toots.

"Once Patel is sentenced and shipped off to prison, maybe Oprah's hoarder will hook up with the panty sniffer via snail mail. They could end up on that new show, *Prison Wives*. That would truly be a case of 'it's a small world,' " Sophie said.

"Where in the world do you come up with such nonsense?" Ida asked. "Maybe you should consider writing a novel."

"Not my style. I was never good at spelling. Abby's the writer in the family."

"True. Well, it was just a passing thought," Ida said idly as she stared out toward the Pacific.

For the next few minutes, all four women sipped their coffee, and enjoyed the sweetness of the sugar and cinnamon in their apple pie. They were lost in the moment, with thoughts known only to themselves.

Bubbles of creamy waves gushed onshore; the sky had darkened to a deep shade of blue. Tiny stars, small pinpricks of distant light, twinkled one by one as they made their first appearance in the evening sky.

"I miss Charleston," Toots said out of the blue.

"I miss Maine, too. Phyllis, my neighbor, assures me that her kids and grandchildren are taking very good care of my home. I'm glad it's not sitting there empty, just gathering dust."

"Well, I wouldn't take that stink hole condo I shared with Walter all those years if you handed it to me on a gold platter. I'm glad I sold it. Maybe someone else can make good memories there, because I sure as hell never had any. I should've pushed Walter down the stairs while I was still young. Maybe I would've met someone and had a family of my own. I always wanted kids, but I guess it worked out for the best. I could've ended up with a clone of Walter."

"Good Lord, Sophie, what has gotten into you this evening? Is there something going on that I don't know about?" Toots asked.

Ida and Mavis remained silent as they observed the interchange between their two longtime friends.

"No, I was just thinking about last night, that's all. Walter, Thomas. Maybe tonight one of your husbands' ghosts will make an appearance. That's the only *strangeness* going on that I know about."

"It is odd, no doubt about it," Toots chimed in. "Isn't it about time to start another séance? You said we needed to duplicate last night's scenario. I'm ready if you all are."

"Then what are we waiting for?" Sophie asked. "I've got everything set up. All we need to do is put on the same clothes we wore last night. You never know."

"I refuse to wear dirty clothes," Ida said.

Mavis adjusted Coco on the usual spot on her lap. "I can change, but most of my clothes are the same. I don't know that this will matter, but if you insist, I'll go upstairs and change now."

"Okay, I'll do the same," Sophie added. "Toots, are you willing?"

"Of course. Let's get started. I can't wait to see who appears tonight," Toots remarked. "Boring we are not."

Mavis and Ida followed Toots and Sophie inside to prepare for the night's performance.

Twenty minutes later, all but Ida wore the same clothes they'd had on the previous evening, when they were visited by ghosts of husbands past.

54

As was becoming the norm, Mavis lit the candles while Sophie spread the purple silk sheet on top of the wooden table. She used the same drinking glass they always used. Almost a replica of last night, right down to the time of day.

They all sat down in their respective seats. Once they were seated, Sophie began with her usual prayer. When several minutes passed and nothing happened, Sophie tried another method, something she had been reading about but up until now hadn't had the courage, or rather the nerve, to try.

"Let's all hold hands," Sophie announced. "I'm going to try something different."

They reached for each other's hands and waited for Sophie's instructions. Taking a deep breath, Sophie stared at the doorway leading to the kitchen, just as she had last night. "We want to talk to whoever is out there. If you hear this, make a rapping noise."

The room went silent. When nothing happened, Sophie repeated herself. Still, nothing happened. Sophie was ready to resort to what worked when the drinking glass flew off the table, shattering as it hit the wall opposite from where Sophie was sitting. Momentarily stunned, Sophie, along with Ida, Toots, and Mavis, stared at the wall;

then all eyes went to the pile of broken glass on the floor.

An event that might change their perspective on what they'd undertaken was about to occur. Moisture gathered in the palms of her hands as Sophie gave Toots and Mavis a reassuring squeeze. Fear hung in the air like dust in a musty old attic.

Ida whimpered, pulling her hand away from Mavis's. In a loud whisper, she said, "I can't do this." She ran out of the room so fast Sophie didn't have a chance to react.

"Shh, it's okay. We can do this ourselves," Sophie said, hoping to reassure Toots and Mavis. Wanting to let her friends know she was still in control, she pulled her chair closer to the table, releasing their hands as she did so.

After another cleansing breath, Sophie tried to make contact with the ghost *or* ghosts again. "Whoever is here with us now, are you responsible for shattering this glass? If your answer is yes, make a rapping noise, once for yes and twice for no."

A knocking sound came from beneath the table. Once.

Sophie eyed Toots, who had a death grip on Mavis's hand. "Okay, so you broke our glass. Are you friendly? If you're friendly, rap again."

One sharp rap came from under the table.

"Okayyy," Sophie said. "Were you married to someone in this room? If so, prove it." Succinct, and to the point, she hoped this spirit had a sense of humor.

The room was still, not even the flames on the candles made the slightest flicker. It was as though the air had somehow become thicker, visible like fog.

Ever so slowly, the purple sheet began to wrinkle, as if someone were grabbing it and slowly tugging on it, similar to the magician's trick of yanking a tablecloth while the dishes remained intact. Mavis, Toots, and Sophie were transfixed as they saw the sheet lift up like a tent. When the edges of the purple silk sheet elevated to the top of the table, the three women gasped, their breaths coming in shallow pants.

Sophie held herself together. This was remarkable. She glanced over at the video recorder. The bright red light shone like a beacon, indicating it was on and running. The voice recorder hummed along, too.

The purple silk sheet rose above the table, swirled back and forth like a matador's cape, then dropped directly into Toots's lap. "Oh my gosh!" she cried out.

"It's okay. Stay calm," Sophie said to Toots. "So you're one of Toots's many husbands? There have been *so many.* Is there any way you can distinguish yourself?"

Toots wasn't frightened enough not to be insulted by Sophie's questions to this . . . spirit.

Suddenly, the candle flames doubled in size, then extinguished themselves. Darkness filled the room, along with the scent of melted wax. Toots tossed the sheet off her lap as though it were on fire.

"Be quiet!" Sophie cried. "We don't know what we're dealing with!" Prepared for the unexpected, Sophie whipped a Bic lighter out of her pocket. She relit the candle on the windowsill behind her.

Sophie reached for the sheet, placing it back on the table in a pile. "Are you angry with Toots?"

Again, the purple silk sheet sailed from the tabletop. Only this time it floated like a magic carpet around the dining room, zooming around the table, then dropping on the floor in front of Toots's chair. Mavis placed her hand across her chest while Toots stared as though she were in a state of shock. Sophie genuflected.

As suddenly as it started flying around the dining room, the sheet dropped to the floor, after which there was a bloodcurdling scream.

CHAPTER 4

Ida was sitting in the bathtub, soaking her aching bones. This séance stuff was too much for her to deal with. She'd been through so much since Thomas's death, and the last thing she needed was a bunch of wild ghostly apparitions chasing her around the house. Maybe it was time for her to go back to New York, call it quits. Ida's fingers were starting to prune, so it was time to get out of the hot water and get into bed. She might even consider taking one of those sleeping pills that so-called excuse for a doctor had prescribed for her. She flicked the drain button with her toe and stood up. She was reaching for the thick, fluffy bath towel when she looked at the mirror above the sink. It was completely fogged up, yet the words *I was poisoned* formed in wet drips on the mirror.

Ida let out a bloodcurdling scream.

Heavy footsteps bounded up the stairs,

stopping when they reached her bedroom door. A loud banging ensued.

"Ida, what the hell is going on in there?" Toots asked, fearful for her friend, causing her heart to skip a beat. Mavis and Sophie were right behind her.

"What's wrong? Is she trying to scare the daylights out of us just to tick us off?" Sophie asked.

Toots banged on the door again. "Ida, if you don't answer me or come out of there, I'm going to call nine-one-one, and they'll drag your ass out dressed or not."

They waited for the bedroom door to open, anything to let them know Ida was alive and well.

Sophie raised her voice several octaves higher. "If you don't open the door, I'm going to kick it down and drag your flabby ass out and tie you to that Hollywood sign in the hills. Then the world will know you wear padded bras because your tits are the size of fried eggs." Sophie always went for the humor. Sometimes it worked, and sometimes it didn't. Without further ado, Sophie raised her foot high in the air and kicked the door, doing nothing more than injuring her foot on the solid oak. "Open this damned door now!"

"Oh, stop it! I have a key for all the

bedrooms on top of the door frame." Toots raced down the hall, where she ran her hand across the top of her door frame. A soft whimpering could be heard from behind the door to Ida's room, which remained locked. Finding the key, she quickly returned and unlocked the door, then, seeing no one in the bedroom, rushed to the bathroom just as Ida, wrapped in a large bath sheet and looking like she had seen a ghost, opened the door.

When Ida saw Toots and the others, she turned her back on them and walked back into the bathroom, where she dropped onto the floor in a heap.

"Follow her," Toots said.

Ida and Sophie trailed behind Toots, all three stopping when they entered Ida's bathroom.

With a shaky finger, Ida pointed to the words etched in the steam still running down the mirror.

I was poisoned.

One by one Toots, Sophie, and Mavis read the words, each expressing shock at what she saw.

As was the norm, Sophie was the one to break the silence. "So it wasn't that tainted meat that killed Thomas, after all. Good grief, Ida, it seems to me Thomas has come back from the grave to tell you he was murdered! Toots, what about it?" Sophie asked. Ida had yet to utter a single word.

Mavis stationed herself in the doorway, almost afraid to say anything for fear of upsetting poor Ida any more than she already was.

"Do you think I should call nine-one-one?" Mavis asked.

"Hell no! I'll take care of this," Sophie informed her.

Toots was shocked by what she saw. Huddled in the corner where she had collapsed, the giant bath sheet still wrapped around her, Ida was as white as a sheet. She had a haunted look in her eyes, her lips were blue, and her teeth were chattering as though she were freezing.

In a voice that was barely a whisper, Ida said, "I think they killed him."

"What the hell are you talking about now?" Sophie asked, not immediately connecting what had just been said with the frightening words oozing down the foggy mirror. Then Sophie followed Toots's gaze to the mirror and finally understood.

"If what this mirror says is true, then someone murdered Thomas. All this time, poor Ida thought he died from tainted meat. This is serious stuff, nothing to laugh at,"

Toots said.

"Yes, and I can just see it now. We call the police and tell them Ida's former husband was poisoned. They are really going to believe us, especially when they find out he's been dead for almost a year. I wonder what they'll think when we tell the cops that a ghost wrote this on a foggy bathroom mirror. Can't you see how bad that makes all of us look?" Sophie asked.

"She's right. "Should we call Chris?" Mavis asked, referring to Christopher Clay, Toots's stepson, who was a local entertainment lawyer.

"No, I don't think that would be a very good idea." Toots stooped down to the floor, reached for Ida's hands, and gently tried to pull her into a standing position. "Ida, you need to get yourself together. We can handle this. After all, we are the godmothers." She said the last few words in an attempt to humor Ida.

"Let me take care of this," Sophie said. "Get your dirty, rotten ass off the floor, and quit acting like a wimp! I've had it with you and your prissy-ass ways. First, it's the OCD and all the germs. Second, you wind up doing the horizontal mambo with that old, perverted fake doctor, and now, when we're at the point of phenomenal success with our séances, you have to screw it all up by letting the spirit of your ex-husband scare the shit out of you."

With her usual tactlessness, Sophie grabbed Ida's hands in her own, pulled her to her feet, and guided her into the bedroom. With a none-too-gentle shove, she pushed her down onto the bed.

"You have the subtlety of a tsunami," Toots said. "You all know I'm not one to run away — chicken poop I am not — but I think it's time we left, time to go to Charleston. I think we've all had the scare of our lives tonight. Once we're in a place where we all feel safe, I really believe we need to call the authorities in New York and tell them our suspicions. I don't think we need to mention any spirits or ghosts. We'll figure something out. Sophie is a good liar, so she should be able to come up with something."

They spent the rest of the evening soothing Ida and preparing for their trip to Charleston. Toots called Abby, explaining to her that they were making an unscheduled trip back home. She told Abby that she was going to contact Chris about house-sitting the beach house while she and the godmothers were gone. But if for some reason she could not reach him before they left tomorrow, she would call Abby and ask her to contact Chris to see if he would mind house-sitting for a few weeks. Abby said she would be more than happy to take care of it, telling her not to worry, that she and Chris could handle things while she was gone. With nothing more to do than pack their bags, make a few phone calls to, among other things, arrange for a chartered flight back East, and try to drown out the events of the evening with a few stiff drinks and more than one pack of cigarettes, they called it a night.

Tomorrow was another day.

CHAPTER 5

In spite of all the events of the evening, once the four friends had calmed down and gone to their separate rooms, Mavis couldn't wait to boot up her computer and check for new orders, but she didn't want what appeared to the others to be her odd behavior to arouse any more suspicion than it had already. Lately, Sophie had been giving her an eagle-eyed stare every time she saw her wearing dark colors. Unbeknownst to the others, Mavis had been working with a Web design company for the past couple of months, and her new Web site was up and running. A retired schoolteacher turned entrepreneur, or so she liked to think of herself, Mavis hoped she'd found a need that she could fill while making a little bit of extra money in the process. Though she received Social Security and a small pension from her years of teaching English, Mavis hated being so dependent on Toots for almost everything. She owed her life to Toots. Literally. It had been almost a year since Toots had sent her a plane ticket to visit her in Charleston.

She had been a hundred pounds over-weight and lonelier than she had wanted to admit. Mavis could never forget the shopping trip Toots had arranged for her when she arrived. Catherine, a petite woman who used to dress such stars as Doris Day, had a shop specifically intended to provide attractive clothes for plus-size women. Mavis fit the bill. The woman dressed her bulky frame, and once they'd landed in this wonderful land of movies, sunshine, and sand, Mavis had started dieting, because she knew her life depended on it. It had been close to a year, and she was one hundred pounds lighter and a perfect size eight. She had never intended to get into the fashion business. She'd been a high school English teacher her entire life. However, when she started losing weight, her clothes hung on her like a sheet. Handy with a needle and thread, Mavis took in her clothes; then, when she lost even more weight, she started remaking the clothes herself. Toots, ever the bearer of gifts, had bought her the best sewing machine on the market, and here she was, designing, making, and selling her new clothes over the Internet. Surprised at how much she enjoyed designing and creating eye-catching outfits, she beamed with every outfit she finished. They never failed to elicit a compliment from the girls. *If,* and it was a big *if,* her line of clothes was successful, she'd already made contact with a factory, and she'd even found a source of high-quality material that would put her mourning clothes right up there with those of some of the big-name designers. Ralph Lauren, Anne Klein, and Gloria Vanderbilt, watch out!

She'd taken to reading the obituaries with her morning coffee after she decided a romance with George wasn't what she wanted, especially knowing he needed that vacuum construction device, VCD, to have sex. Herbert, her dearly departed husband, had been her one true love. She wasn't looking for a romance but tried to keep an open mind. One just never knew about these things. She'd seen dear Toots through eight marriages. Mavis seriously doubted she'd live long enough to marry that many times. Toots was a lovable person. No wonder she'd had so many husbands.

Mavis was excited as she logged on to the Internet and clicked on the URL that was exclusively hers. She knew Sophie suspected she was up to something, but Mavis wanted to keep it under her hat for a while. She needed to see if her enterprise was going to be a success or just something to while away the hours. She'd always been content living day to day when she was in Maine, watching her soaps and eating junk food. Now she felt as though she was being transformed with each pound she lost. And with every pound shed, she'd discovered she wanted to *do* something. Make her mark, even if it was just a tiny blip on the World Wide Web.

A few months ago, she'd read an obituary that brought barrels of tears to her eyes. Knowing it was the right thing to do, she'd dressed in her latest design, a charcoal gray skirt that flowed over her hips like silk, topping it off with a light gray blouse and matching jacket. If asked, she would tell you this was her best design so far. Ida had complimented her, wanting to know when and where she'd purchased the stellar suit. Mavis had told a tiny white lie when she'd said she didn't recall. It was too soon to reveal her plans. She would know when the time was right. If she had any success at all, she would share her new business with the girls.

For now, she thanked Pearl Mae Atkins. It was Pearl's obituary that sent her to her first funeral, if one wanted to call it that. Poor Pearl's obit had said there was no one left; she had died at home alone in her sleep. The obit had said there would be a five-minute memorial service at Chasten's Funeral Home. With no one to say a final good-bye, Mavis had felt compelled to make sure Pearl didn't pass into the other world without someone to wish her a safe journey. She'd secretly made arrangements for a taxi to pick her up and wait while she attended the service, then return her home. The girls would laugh at her if they knew just how sad she'd felt. On the way, she'd had the taxi driver stop at a convenience store, where she'd purchased all the long-stemmed roses that sat in a dirty white bucket next to the cash register. Had time permitted, she would have ordered the biggest, brightest floral arrangement that was within her budget, but the roses were the best she could do.

Other than the funeral director, no one else had attended Pearl's quick send-off. Mavis had cried for the lonely old woman she had never met in life and placed the handful of roses inside a coffin that she knew had been used at many showings before Pearl's. When it was time to bury her, the expensive-looking coffin would be replaced with an old pine box. Sadly, this happened to all the lonely Pearls of the world who had no one to give them a proper send-off.

Clicking her way to her Web site, Mavis was thrilled when she saw she had sixteen orders for her latest designs for Good Mourning, her new line of clothes. After sending Pearl off, Mavis had become obsessed with reading the obits. There were many more like Pearl who had no family, no friends, not a single soul to care how they were laid to rest.

For whatever reason, Mavis had felt compelled to try to change this for as many as she could. She didn't want to ask Toots for help. She would simply ask how much she needed and write a check. Mavis wanted to do this on her own. That was when she'd come up with the idea to sell her clothes. She began attending large and small funerals, where there were often hundreds of people in attendance. She watched them, saw what they wore, and knew that most of the women's clothing would be shoved to the back of the closet or donated to charity. Mavis knew Toots had given away her mourning clothes after each of her husbands died. Why couldn't people keep the clothes they wore for their loved ones' final send-off, but wear them over and over?

Couldn't the clothing hold a special memory of those that had passed? They didn't have to be black and ugly, like most of what she saw when she attended funerals. She knew then what she would do to commemorate the Pearls of the world.

Mavis started spending most of her nights staying up late, sewing her clothes. She'd designed her own label, which read GOOD MOURNING BY MAVIS. She had three styles, three colors, and thirty-six pieces ready for shipping. She started with her own size eight, then added tens, twelves, and fourteens. She had done her homework, discovering that the average-size woman wore a size twelve. From there she'd set up an account with FedEx. They would come to the house and pick up her orders in the boxes they'd provided. She'd also set up an account with PayPal in order to collect payment for her sales. Mavis was still amazed at the Internet. It had truly opened her up to a new world. Without it, she certainly wouldn't be working on a project that just might turn out to be something more wonderful than she'd ever dreamed. If only Herbert could see her now.

For the next three hours, Mavis packed the FedEx boxes with her designs. She'd been smart to go with average sizes, she thought, as she carefully folded the last size twelve and placed it in tissue paper before stuffing it inside the box. She stuck the addressee label on with all the FedEx info, then placed the box in a large plastic container she would drag to the end of the drive at precisely eight thirty tomorrow morning. She put away all evidence of her new business before going to bed. She was tired, but in a good way.

Mavis was happier than she'd ever imagined.

CHAPTER 6

It was three in the morning when Toots finally reached Chris on the phone. He agreed to stay at the beach house while they were gone, explaining that an old chum from law school had popped in unexpectedly, so Chris was thrilled when Toots offered him the chance to house-sit. He said his friend from Illinois would be stoked at the thought of hanging out in Malibu.

With that taken care of, Toots e-mailed Bernice with a to-do list. She gave her the details of their chartered flight, telling her she'd hired a limousine service to pick them up from the airport. As usual, Toots, aka LAT Enterprise, would stay in touch with Abby and *The Informer* through e-mail. Abby wouldn't be the least bit suspicious, Toots hoped.

At nine o'clock in the morning, they left the beach house to make their ten o'clock charter. Toots was tired but knew she could sleep once she was on the plane.

Mavis took her sewing machine along. None of them could figure out why, but Mavis never asked for much, so allowing her this bit of eccentricity was more than fair. Sophie, never wanting to be left out, brought along her cameras and her EVP, electronic voice phenomena, just in case she decided to hold a séance while in Charleston. Toots took nothing but the clothes on her back because Charleston was her home. She had everything she needed there, and then some. Ida packed four suitcases, each one for a specific item. One for her lingerie. The second held her shoes, the third her toiletries, and the fourth her clothes. Toots had hoped like hell this number and orderly thing wasn't about to become an OCD issue in another form, but when Toots asked Ida if she could peek inside her luggage, instead of being neat and orderly, her things were tossed in just like anyone else's would be. Ida was good to go.

They were all quiet on the flight from the West Coast to the other side of the country. Ida read a romance novel; Mavis had several articles of gray clothing in her lap and was stitching away. Sophie chomped on nicotine gum like her life depended on it, and Toots simply enjoyed being surrounded by her three best friends in the entire world. Life was good, she thought before nodding off.

A slight bump jarred them to attention as the jet landed at Charleston International Airport. Coco barked at her beauty sleep being interrupted. Mavis let her out of her carrier and kissed the top of her small brown head. "You're such a good girl," Mavis said, stuffing her gray material in a large bag one might use for knitting.

"If I don't smoke soon, I'm gonna die," Sophie said.

Toots stretched, unfastened her seat belt, then peered out the small window. "You'll live for ten minutes without a smoke. It's good to be back home. I've missed this old place."

"How long do you think we'll be here?" Ida asked as the plane taxied to a stop.

"I'm not sure. However long it takes," Toots answered. "I have a few business matters to take care of. Then I need to spend some time with Bernice. Poor old gal, she's been lost without me to order around. Why do you ask? I thought we were all in agreement on this. We'll stay as long as we want to."

The plane came to a complete stop on the tarmac. As they waited for the ground crew to secure the plane, they gathered their small bags and Coco's carrier. They waited for the pilots to unlatch the door leading to a small set of folding metal stairs.

"I was simply asking. I may need to go shopping while I'm here, that's all," Ida retorted, her newfound bossiness almost a pleasure. Almost. God forbid she turn into another Sophie.

Toots started speaking before Sophie had a chance to comment. "I can't wait for you all to see my place again. In the spring, it's the most beautiful place on earth. The azaleas and camellias are blooming. The night-blooming jasmine smells like heaven. Then, of course, there are the dogwoods, the magnolia trees. It's my favorite place in the world this time of year," Toots gushed on. She was so happy to be home, even if it was just for a short period of time. Her gardener, Pete, one of her best male friends, would no doubt, when he learned of her return, have the gardens in tip-top shape. The dead leaves would be trimmed from her two giant angel oaks, and the shrubs clipped to perfection.

"It sounds perfect. Maybe someday we can all go to my home in Maine. While not as lavish as Toots's plantation home, it's quite beautiful this time of year. Wild black-eyed Susans, lilies of the valley grow wild. Then there are the daisies. They're a sight to behold. They grow wild all over the state." Tears filled Mavis's eyes. She dabbed at them with her knuckles. "Oh, dear, I think I'm suddenly homesick."

Toots squeezed her hand. "Anytime you want to go home, just say the word, and I'll make it happen."

Mavis nodded. "Thank you, Toots. You're really the best friend a woman could have. I'll be fine. This talking about Charleston's beauty reminded me of home, that's all. I plan to return one day. I'm just not sure when that day will be."

Sophie was the first to leap off the plane. She practically jogged to the small general aviation airport across the tarmac, where a large plastic ashtray had been placed next to a cement bench. Toots, Ida, and Mavis, who carried Coco, trailed behind. Toots scrambled through her purse, searching for her cigarettes and lighter. She wanted a cigarette badly but wouldn't tell that to Sophie if her life depended on it. She wasn't about to give her the satisfaction. The private jet Toots had been able to charter this time did not allow smoking; none of those that did allow smoking, which she had arranged for on previous trips, were available at such short notice. Sophie had complained like crazy. Toots wasn't that much of a smoker that she couldn't go without a cigarette for a few hours — though she would've given a hundred bucks for a piece of Sophie's nicotine gum just to calm her nerves.

The limousine and driver she'd hired were waiting in the general aviation area. The pilots told her they would arrange for the ground crew to have their luggage taken to the limo. All she had to do was fish through her wallet for tip money. She handed the pilot and his copilot each a hundred-dollar bill. She knew they'd been paid handsomely, but a little extra never hurt.

"Thank you," they both said in unison. The taller of the two, a nice-looking young guy in his early thirties, said, "When you're ready to return, call me. I'll try to make sure I'm on the schedule." He reached inside his wallet for a business card.

"Only if we can smoke," Toots replied, stuffing the card inside her purse.

Both pilots laughed, the tall one speaking. "We'll see what we can do." With that, they made their way to a lounge reserved exclusively for pilots, while Toots lit up outside with Sophie. Ida raced inside to the ladies' room, and Mavis walked Coco in a grassy area on the side of the building, where two other dogs scampered about, looking for the perfect spot to take care of business.

"Hurry up. I don't want to keep the limo driver waiting," Toots said as she dropped her smoke into the plastic ashtray.

"You've been gone for months. What's the rush?" Sophie asked. "Surely you can wait another ten minutes."

"Oh, zip your lips! Mavis and Ida are waiting." Toots pointed to the pair waiting just outside the exit.

"Okay, okay!" Sophie said.

When they were all seated inside the limo with their baggage and Mavis's sewing machine, the driver headed for the interstate. Toots's home was within a half hour's drive.

They were subdued on the ride, even Coco, each of the old friends wondering what, if anything, this trip would bring.

CHAPTER 7

Toots was excited as the limousine driver drove through the wrought-iron gates. Her heart raced with exhilaration as he drove along the winding path leading to her house. Giant oak trees dripping with Spanish moss canopied the short path, and just as she'd envisioned, the gardens were flush with spring's blooms. The azaleas were every hue of pink under the midday sun; the camellias, red, white, and orange, exploded from verdant stems, like wild arms reaching out from the earth and begging to be touched. The scent of night-blooming jasmine lingered in the dewy afternoon air. Toots pushed the button to lower the window. She could almost feel the fragrance of her gardens as she closed her eyes, allowing the slight breeze to caress her face. *Home. There is truly no place like it,* she thought.

"What are you doing?" Sophie asked.

Brought out of her reverie, Toots turned

to her friend. "If you must know, I'm reminding myself that I actually live here, surrounded by all of nature's splendid wonder, and that it's all mine."

Chastened for once, Sophie just stared at her.

Mavis broke the silence. "I know just how you feel. Maine in the autumn, I refer to it as Mother Nature waving good-bye. All the reds, yellows, and oranges, so vibrant. But then comes the cold, stark winter, with its ice storms and freezing temperatures. I have to say, the older I get, the less fond I am of Maine's harsh winters. Something in between would be very nice. A little bit of all the seasons."

"Yeah, New York sucked in the winter," Sophie cut in, "and stank in the summer. Always smelled like sour milk."

Toots eyed Sophie with shock and wonder, her comments never ceasing to amaze her. "Remind me never to visit New York during the summer or winter," Toots remarked sarcastically.

Before Sophie had a chance to come back with another snide remark, the driver pulled up to the front of the house. Toots sprang from the vehicle like a bird from a cage, running to greet Bernice, who stood on the front porch, her arms open wide. Toots practically fell into them.

Now this *is home,* she thought, squeezing her dear friend in a tight hug.

"Damn woman! You trying to kill me or what? You found someone out in California to take my place?" Bernice asked, her gravelly voice filled with humor.

"Good God, no! You could never be replaced. Let me look at you," Toots demanded, then stepped back. Bernice, she observed, hadn't changed one little bit. Nearing seventy-one, she still had a few good years left. She was petite, with a bit of a hump on her back from osteoporosis, her white hair was cut almost as short as a man's, and her piercing blue eyes still didn't miss a thing. Bernice had a heart of gold. She and Toots were closer than most sisters, which made her homecoming even better. Toots had missed her friend much more than her house.

Ida, Sophie, and Mavis, who held Coco close to her chest, waited at the bottom of the steps while Toots gushed over Bernice.

"Stop standing there and staring! Come inside." Toots motioned, then turned back to Bernice. "I don't suppose you have any sweet tea with mint? I'm as thirsty as a desert thorn."

Ida, Sophie, and Mavis followed Toots inside.

"You know damn good and well I do," Bernice called over her shoulder. "Just because you've been living the high life in California doesn't mean we've followed suit here in the South."

"I've been home ten minutes, and you're starting in already. Bernice, pour us a glass of tea while I tip the driver. He has our luggage stacked by the front door. I'll be right back."

Toots raced out the door, grabbing a handful of twenties from her wallet. Outside, she held the wad of money out for the driver. "I'll double this amount if you bring the luggage and sewing machine inside and take them upstairs." She counted out five twenties.

Apparently he knew a deal when he saw one. "Just tell me what goes where," he said, "and I'll take care of it."

After the luggage and Mavis's sewing machine were placed in the appropriate bedrooms, Toots handed the driver a hundred-dollar bill. "Thanks," she called to his retreating back.

He waved, returned to the limo, and drove away. She stood there watching until his taillights could no longer be seen.

Breathing deeply, Toots drew in the fresh air, the familiar smells and sounds. The chirping of birds, the occasional sound of crickets rubbing their legs together, frogs croaking, sounds she hadn't realized she'd missed until just then. The sounds of home.

She opened the door and walked down the long hallway leading to the kitchen. It was still her favorite room. Her red cabinets were intact, and her much-loved fireplace still dominated the room. Toots opened the drawer where she always kept a supply of PayDay candy bars and extra cigarettes. Yep, it was fully stocked. Good old Bernice. Maybe. Shoot, she hadn't checked the pantry.

Before she joined the rest of the gang, who'd moved to the large enclosed patio in the backyard, which overlooked her two angel oaks and a variety of greenery, Toots parted the wooden doors. Yessiree! She counted six extra-large boxes of her favorite cereal, Froot Loops. Mavis would have a hissy fit, but too bad. It was time for Toots to indulge her sweet tooth. She'd had enough healthy meals in Los Angeles to last her a lifetime.

Then Toots joined the group. "I had the driver take our luggage upstairs. I'm ready to relax and catch up." She reached for the pitcher of tea, poured herself a glass, and reclined in her favorite white wicker rocker.

"Okay, Bernice, you've had time to get reacquainted with Abby's godmothers. Tell me what's going on here. Did Dr. Pauley call? He said he wanted to see Mavis, check her blood pressure while we're here."

"If he's like me, then he won't recognize her. I thought you'd traded her in for a newer model. Damned diet worked a miracle, if you ask me. No telling what Doc's going to think. He phoned this morning. I told him you'd call." Bernice laughed. "I can't wait to see the expression on his face."

Sophie couldn't keep quiet any longer. "Bernice, if you'd had to live with Mavis for the past several months, you wouldn't laugh. I've never eaten so healthy in my life."

Bernice smiled at Mavis. "If I could look like her, I'd want to eat whatever she does."

They all laughed, continuing to relax while Bernice filled them in on the local gossip. What store had the best price on beef. Then there was the new bakery called The Sweetest Things that had opened last Saturday. Bernice told them she had stood in line for two hours, hoping to purchase a dozen of their cupcakes, which supposedly were to die for. What she hadn't counted on, she explained, was the man in line in front of her, the size of a small house, who had suffered a massive heart attack while waiting in line and died right there on the spot. Bernice wasn't sure if he'd had heart troubles or what, but after witnessing the man's death, there was no way in hell she was going to buy even one cupcake from that place. She told them the news traveled fast. The next morning, the place was empty.

"I'll have to scope the place out," Toots said. "I need a liberal dose of something sweet."

Bernice filled their glasses with fresh tea. "I don't think I would do that if I were you. People are talking. Some say that building is . . . Well, they're saying it's haunted. They think the young girl that owns the place is some kind of witch or something. Said she has these weird-looking eyes." Bernice's eyes darted from Sophie to Ida, then to Mavis, stopping when they reached Toots. "They say it's bad luck. I'm guessing the place won't last the rest of the month."

Toots contemplated Bernice's story. "Where is this bakery located?"

"Three doors down from the Dock Street Theatre," Bernice said.

Toots's head snapped up so quickly, she felt her neck crack. A pensive shimmer shadowed her eyes. Awkwardly, she cleared her throat. "Do you know the girl?" Toots asked.

"Nope, and I don't want to. I heard she'd inherited the place. Whoever she is, she's brought bad luck with her."

Toots shifted in her rocking chair. Suddenly, she felt hot, as though she were burning from the inside out. Close to what a hot flash felt like. But it had been years since she'd experienced one. For them to return at this stage in life was nearly impossible. She reached for her glass of tea and downed it. After she rattled the ice cubes at the bottom of the glass, she tipped it back again. Crunching on an ice cube, Toots took the few seconds to compose herself and her thoughts. This was just plain weird.

"What gives?" Sophie asked. "You look like crap. Is there something in the water that I should know about?"

Sophie looked at Toots. Toots nodded. Searching for an explanation for her sudden reaction would bring up the ghostly visits at the Malibu beach house. Even though *The Informer*'s column "Ghostly Encounters" was now one of its most popular features, Toots still didn't like discussing her experience with . . . *strangers?* But Bernice wasn't a *stranger!* Next to Abby and Chris, Bernice was as much a part of her family as the godmothers. Hating this feeling that set her apart, Toots did what she always did when her hand was forced. She simply told the truth.

For the next hour, Toots, with numerous interruptions from Sophie, explained what had happened at the beach house. She even went as far as telling Bernice about their weekly séances. Had she bet money on Bernice's reaction, she would've lost.

Toots was sure Bernice would tell them they were crazy, and most likely those apparitions they saw were nothing more than hallucinations from too much booze. She didn't tell her about Ida's experience with the bathroom mirror. That could wait for later.

Bernice watched Toots. She was frightened of something, truly frightened. All that Marilyn Monroe confession stuff, well, she figured Abby's column was just a crock, and left it at that. The Bing Crosby and Aaron Spelling stuff, she'd attributed that to just more Hollywood bull. Now she wasn't so sure. Pure, raw fear glittered in Bernice's clear blue eyes when she finally spoke. "This is why you returned to Charleston, isn't it?"

CHAPTER 8

Toots was totally dumbstruck. Trying to maintain control of her newly fragile nerves, she swallowed back fear, unlike any she'd ever known. Even the experience the other night at the beach house hadn't caused her such total and complete panic. The question was, *why?*

"What's that supposed to mean?" Toots asked, her words sounding wobbly and unsure.

Bernice took a deep breath. "You've come back to . . . I don't know, take care of things. Ghostly things. You know, like they do on television."

Had she?

Toots didn't have an answer. Other than a strong feeling of homesickness, there'd really been no emergency, no rush for her to come home. Well, there had been that ghostly husband thing, but she wasn't going to tell that to Bernice just yet, either. Yes,

90

she had some business to attend to, but it wasn't anything that couldn't have been handled through FedEx, fax, or e-mail. Maybe there *was* a purpose for her deep longing to return home. Maybe, just maybe, she was needed here, too, just not in the way she'd expected.

The five women were silent. When they could no longer stand the stillness on the enclosed patio, they all started talking at once.

"I brought my equipment," Sophie stated.

"I think we need to check this out further," Mavis suggested.

Ida shook her head. "I don't know what to think."

That left Toots, who still couldn't come up with a proper reply, at least one that would explain Bernice's statement.

Bernice stood up and grabbed the pitcher of tea. "I'm going to refill this and add a little something extra. You all can discuss what I said as soon as I turn my back."

Even though she'd not spoken a word since Bernice's proclamation, as the unofficial leader of the group, Toots felt compelled to take charge. After all, Bernice was *her* housekeeper.

"Sophie, tell me your thoughts. I know you're just dying to," Toots cajoled, hearing the shakiness in her own voice and not liking it one little bit.

"I think Bernice is right," Sophie declared. "You wanted to come home for a reason, and it just might be it's your new calling in life. We could be like those Ghost Trackers on television."

Toots looked as though she'd been sucker punched, because that very thought had just that minute crossed her mind.

Would Sophie have known her thoughts *if* she wasn't a mind reader? They were exceptionally close, but mind reading? That was too extreme even for Sophie. Lord, she needed to take a vacation. Maybe a stiff drink. Something to bring her back to her normal reality, though her reality, at least in the past year, had been anything but normal.

"I'm not a mind reader, you kook. I just know you, Toots. That's why I'm always one step ahead of you. Business is just an excuse you're giving yourself to justify this trip. Am I right or what? You're more into this ghostly stuff than you care to admit," Sophie said to Toots.

Heaving a sigh of relief, Toots tried to maintain control, act as though nothing were out of the ordinary, which was totally not true. "You're always right, Soph. This newfound interest in the dead has me more intrigued than anything I've been involved with in a long time, even *The Informer.* You, of all people, should know that. I wanted to see Bernice, and, yes, I do have a few business matters, though they could have been handled through the mail, but I decided I'd rather do them in person. So if that makes Sophie a mind reader, then so be it."

Bernice returned, carrying a bright red tray with a matching pitcher and tall glasses decorated with red and white polka dots. "I've made Long Island ice tea this time around. I'll warn you, I didn't skimp with the hard stuff."

Toots removed a glass from the tray, set it on the table beside her, then took another, handing it to Sophie. Mavis passed, and Ida practically swallowed the entire glass in one gulp. Bernice helped herself, leaving the tray on a large wicker table next to the floor-to-ceiling windows overlooking the gardens.

A minute or two passed before anyone spoke. Toots took control as the alcohol warmed her insides and relaxed the tightness in the back of her neck. Fortified with false courage, Toots said, "Okay, tell me about the bakery."

"Well, you know the stories about the Dock Street Theatre," Bernice said. "It's three doors down from them. Not the best place for a bakery, but who am I to say what's best for anyone? Hell, I have trouble deciding which brand of coffee to buy from week to week."

Sophie slurped her drink like a horse at a trough. "What's the Dock Street Theatre? Never heard of the place."

"You tell her," Bernice said.

Toots took a sip of her drink and placed the glass on the table beside her. "It's local folklore. In the early eighteen hundreds, the Calder family built a hotel in Charleston. They called it Planter's Hotel. After that went broke, it was turned into a theater. It's been said by more than one person that a couple of ghosts wander around the old place. Supposedly one of them was a famous actor named Junius Brutus Booth, or you might recognize his son's name, John Wilkes Booth, the assassin who killed President Lincoln. The other ghost is some nameless prostitute the locals refer to as Nettie. It's said she worked at the place when it was still a hotel and was standing on the porch one day, when she was struck by lightning and killed instantly. I certainly don't believe any of this malarkey, but it is what it is.

"Bernice, you said the man at the bakery was the size of a house? It doesn't take much to deduce he suffered a heart attack from his lifestyle. I seriously doubt the location of the bakery had anything to do with his sudden death. He could've been waiting for a heart transplant, for all we know. Maybe this was his one last visit to a bakery before turning over a new leaf. As a matter of fact, I think we should visit this place first thing in the morning. I, for one, would love to have a praline. They do have pralines there, don't they?" Toots asked Bernice.

"We're in Charleston, for crying out loud! Car dealerships have pralines. So I would guess a bakery would have them, too," Bernice mumbled.

"I mean *real* pralines. Not those artificial, prepackaged ones that are made in New Jersey," Toots said.

"You can find out for yourself first thing in the morning. Pete made sure to fill up your Lincoln and the Land Rover, so you're good to go. I'll stay here, thank you very much."

"Why don't we have a séance here? I have all of my things, and it's not like any of us have any plans tonight," Sophie suggested, perking up at the idea.

Toots caught Bernice's shocked look and smiled.

"I live in Charleston, remember? This place is about as ghostly and haunted as you can get. Séances? I've been to more than you can shake a stick at. I say bring it on." Clearly, Bernice had imbibed too much. Toots knew she was afraid of her own shadow, but she wasn't going to bring that up right now.

"Ida? Mavis? What about it?" Sophie asked.

"I'll pass. I have some sewing I want to catch up on," Mavis said. "And I have a few e-mails I need to take care of, too. I might need to make a trip to FedEx tomorrow, Toots. Do you think you could take me to town if I need to go?"

Toots and Sophie both raised their eyebrows. "Sure, whatever you need. Why FedEx? Can't you just drop a letter in the mailbox?"

"I may have a few packages to send up north, that's all. I said I would send some things, and, well, I just don't want them to be late if at all possible." Mavis stood up, smoothing imaginary wrinkles from her navy slacks. "Did the driver take my sewing machine to my room? I just hate being without it."

"Does this have anything to do with all that gray material you've been lugging around?" Sophie asked.

Startled by Sophie's question, Mavis

answered, her words rushed. "Not one thing. I don't even know why you would say something so silly. Now, I am a bit tired, and poor Coco, well, it's time for her dinner. Bernice, do you have a can opener I can use? I thought I packed one, but I'm not sure. I'll just run upstairs for a can of food and her bowls. I'll be right back." Mavis zoomed out of the room at the speed of light.

"WTF? What's crawled down her skinny spine and bit her on the ass?" Sophie asked.

Bernice quickly refreshed their drinks, then followed Mavis. "I'll be right back."

Toots nodded, taking a sip of her drink. "Mavis is up to something. I wish I knew what it was."

"Whatever it is, it has something to do with her morbid obsession, reading the obits. She's been acting strange lately. Grabs the paper before anyone has a chance to look at the headlines. She hasn't been reading *The Informer,* either. That's not like her. She's always supported Abby's work. Think we should spy on her?" Sophie smiled, her eyes lighting up like a Roman candle on the Fourth of July.

"You're a sneaky old woman, but I don't have to tell you that. Yes, I think we should spy on her. Not too much. Just a little. I'm curious why she needs to go to FedEx. Mavis never sends packages, says it's not in her 'budget.' " Toots made air quotes. "I'll give her anything she wants. All she has to do is ask."

"Me, too, but I believe Mavis wants to get by on her own, at least as much as her pension and Social Security allow. You've been good to all of us, financially and otherwise."

Ida had remained silent. Sitting in the corner, she finally chose to make her presence known. "I think we need to do what we came here to do, then get back to LA. It seems we, rather *you two,* are getting sidetracked. Aren't we supposed to be finding ghost stories and Hollywood gossip for *The Informer?* Well?" Ida asked. "Am I right?"

Sophie jumped up like the Energizer Bunny. "Where does it say the stories have to come from Hollywood? At least the ghost stories. If it ends up Thomas really was murdered, don't you want to find out? I would think a ghostly encounter, no matter the freaking location or who it is, would be newsworthy to *The Informer. The Enquirer* sure as hell gets around, and *The Globe,* too. Maybe that's the secret to their success? We've been trying too hard to focus our . . . research . . . in one location. The beach house. *If,* and this is a big *if,* what *if* we could have séances wherever there's been a sighting? Why can't we do that? I'm not talking about traveling around the world, just within, say, each of our home states. As much as it ticks me off to admit it, we're all going to go to our respective homes. Eventually, we have to. Why not kill two birds with the proverbial stone? Maine, New York, South Carolina. I'd bet my last Marlboro we could find something worthy to print. And speaking of Marlboro, I'm going outside to smoke." At that pronouncement, Sophie swirled out of the room like a cloud of dust.

"I'm going to join her," Toots announced and followed Sophie outside, where she sat on the steps leading to the back door into the kitchen.

Two seconds later, Ida plopped down beside them. "Don't blow smoke in my face," she said.

The two lit up and smoked three cigarettes apiece before going back inside.

CHAPTER 9

Los Angeles

Abby sliced the New York strip in half. Poor Chester deserved a special treat after sitting patiently in the car for three hours without a peep.

"Here you go, boy. Medium rare, just the way you like it." She scooped the steak into his dog bowl and freshened his water. She stood at the kitchen sink, staring out the window. She wasn't hungry but forced herself to take a few bites, anyway. What was that saying? Something about sleeping and eating when you can because you never know when you'll have to be on a stakeout? Abby chuckled at her play on words.

She'd finally finished all the remodeling on her little ranch house. Abby had done most of the work herself on the weekends and nights when she wasn't out chasing a story. She was quite pleased with her life at the moment but knew it could change on a dime. To date she still hadn't met the new owners of *The Informer,* and, truly, at this stage of the game, it didn't seem to matter. She was acting editor in chief, and so far her decisions hadn't caused the paper to go bankrupt. Her boss seemed pleased with her work. Sales had almost doubled since she'd started her column, "Ghostly Encounters." Maybe it was the public's newfound fascination with ghosts, or it could be that most of her encounters just happened to be with dead movie stars. Whatever, she wasn't about to question it.

Life was good.

Which always, *always* brought forth an image of Chris Clay, her best friend. Sort of. He just didn't know it yet. She didn't plan on telling him so anytime soon, either. She'd known Chris since she was a little girl, as her mother, her flamboyant, outrageous mother, had married Chris's father, Garlan Clay. He'd died while Chris was still in law school. Her mother had continued to share her life with Chris, always including him in their small family events. It'd taken Abby by complete surprise when she realized she cared about Chris more than as a mere stepsibling. They really hadn't grown up together. Chris was away at boarding school, and when Abby started high school,

Chris went away to college. They'd been more acquaintances than anything. Until her mother had a wild idea and decided she wanted to live a bicoastal life. She'd issued several invitations that always included Chris. While on a stakeout of sorts, Abby and Chris had wound up at Pink's, a ratty diner in LA famous for its hot dogs. He'd kissed her fingertips that night, one by one, and Abby had fallen completely, totally in love. She just hadn't told Chris yet. There wasn't any rush. At twenty-nine, she still had a few years before her biological alarm clock sounded. For now, she was content to enjoy the occasional dinner, a drive to the beach, or one of Sophie's séances at the beach house, which Chris attended, albeit reluctantly.

Abby considered driving out to the beach. Chester would love to go for a run; but Coco was gone, and it would break poor Chester's heart if the Chihuahua wasn't there. Besides, Chris was house-sitting for her mother, and he'd invited a college buddy to hang out. She didn't want to interfere with their "guy time."

She forked a last bite of steak and rinsed her dishes before putting them in the dishwasher. Chester pushed his bowl aside with his big paw, his way of telling her he was finished.

"Okay, boy. I know what's next." Abby opened the kitchen door that led to her fenced-in backyard. Chester would spend the next hour or so watching squirrels. Watching but, for some unknown reason, never chasing. She'd lucked out when she'd found Chester at a local shelter. He'd been a Christmas gift to herself. Her sweet baby love, she liked to call him when no one was around. And he was her love. Her friend and protector. Wherever she went, Chester followed. He went to work with her daily, and since the fire at *The Informer* building, he'd become quite the watchdog, as most German shepherds were.

With the evening stretching out before her, Abby finished up in the kitchen and changed into a hot pink sleep shirt with an image of Tinker Bell splashed across the front. She clicked the TV to her favorite channel, Lifetime. When she saw the current movie was the same one as the night before, she grabbed her briefcase off the sofa and pulled out her laptop.

Once a reporter, always a reporter. Just because she wasn't at the office didn't mean her workday had ended. Abby was constantly searching for material for *The Informer.* It was a weekly, and if she wanted to stay on top of the game, she couldn't let the competition get one up on her. She booted up, clicked on her e-mail client, hoping to find the next headline from "an unnamed source." She was three columns ahead for "Ghostly Encounters," courtesy of her godmothers, so she was safe for a bit. However, as editor in chief, it was up to her to provide leads for the reporters. It was one of the reasons she and Chester had spent three hours staking out Lobo's, one of Hollywood's newest hot spots. Supposedly, Simon Cowell and Paula Abdul were seen making out like two teenagers there the past three nights. Abby, quite well known to the stars as a tabloid reporter, had thought it would be in her and *The Informer*'s best interests if she remained hidden in her yellow MINI Cooper. Her parking place had afforded her a bird's-eye view of the only exit. If the two former *American Idol* judges were there as a couple, Abby was going to catch it on film. Three hours had produced nada. She'd given up her stakeout and gone home. Tomorrow was another day.

She answered e-mails pertaining to a few leads she was chasing, hoping they would turn into more than just leads. An e-mail from an address she didn't recognize caught her attention. Opening the e-mail, Abby felt her adrenaline kick in big-time. She scanned through it once, then again before hitting FORWARD. Chris needed to read this. Reaching for her cell phone inside her well-worn briefcase, she pushed the number two on her speed dial.

He answered on the first ring. Abby's heart rate sped up at his "hello."

"Chris, it's me. I just received a very interesting e-mail. I just forwarded it to you. Read it and give me your advice. I'll hold on."

Abby heard Chris chuckle. "Good evening, Abby. How are you?"

Smiling, she spoke. "I'll tell you after you read that e-mail I just sent. I'll hold."

Chris's sigh could be heard over the phone. Abby heard him rustle around, heard a few clicks, then the automated "You've got mail" voice.

Locating the e-mail, Chris said, "Okay, give me a minute."

Abby waited while he read the e-mail. A few seconds later, he came back on the line and asked, "Do you still have the contact info for Special Agent Gaynor? He needs to see this ASAP."

"Somewhere. Hang on a second." Abby rifled through her beat-up briefcase, searching until she found what she was looking for. "I have it. Who calls? Me? You?" Abby wanted to make the call herself, but there were times a tabloid reporter had absolutely zilch in the clout department. This was one of those times.

"I'll take care of it," Chris said.

"Are you sure? I don't want to mess with your guy time. Mom said you had a friend at the beach house this week. I can imagine house-sitting for her was at the top of your list."

"Hey, it's Toots. I'd do just about anything for her. My buddy is passed out in Sophie's bedroom. Three drinks, and he was a goner."

Abby laughed into the phone. "Okay, I'll send you the contact information in an e-mail." Abby paused, wanting to say something else, something cutesy and fun, but nothing came to mind. "Call me as soon as you learn anything, okay?" She hoped she didn't sound desperate, but in a way she was. She needed to see Chris but didn't have the guts to tell him straight up that she missed him. It was still too early for that kind of talk. She'd waited half her life. She could wait a little while longer.

"I'll not only call you. What would you say if I invited you and Chester to dinner tomorrow night? You can meet Steve. I've told him all about you. When I said you were hotter than Meg Ryan, he drooled."

Abby's smile spread across the universe. Yes! Life was good. So very good right now that she could actually taste it.

"Well?" Chris asked again. "Or did you have plans?"

"He really drooled?" Abby couldn't help but ask. "Is he hot?"

Chris's laughter was so loud, she had to pull the phone away from her ear.

"I'll let you be the judge of that. So does this mean you'll come?"

"Sure, Chester could use the exercise. Want me to bring anything?" she asked.

"Nope, just you and Chester. Eight o'clock work for you?"

"Perfect," Abby replied.

"Maybe I'll have heard from Agent Gaynor. I know how much you want to find that SOB you used to work for. There are a few others who also wouldn't mind getting their hands on him."

"It's been almost a year. The FBI has been so close, but every damn time they think they've got him, the jerk disappears into thin air. This e-mail, if it's legit, just might be their chance to snag him, charge him with whatever the hell they can. I would love to see the look on that smug, phony play-

CHAPTER 10

Back home in Charleston, just like clock-
work, and despite jet lag, Toots awakened at
her normal time of five thirty. She had a
busy day ahead of her. First and foremost
she planned to travel to the new bakery to
find out what, if anything, was going on.
Knowing Charleston was full of superstitions, folklore, and numerous tall tales,
Toots seriously doubted there was any merit
to Bernice's stories of witches and evil.

After taking a quick shower, she dressed
in a pair of khaki pants, a white blouse, and
her favorite navy blue loafers. She pulled
her dark auburn hair up in a topknot, added
a touch of peach blush, mascara, and her
favorite coral lipstick. Ready to face the day,
she raced downstairs to make a pot of coffee for Bernice. For as long as she could
remember, this had been their morning
routine. Toots always had the coffee brewing and a large box of Froot Loops, whole

milk, and loads of sugar ready for their breakfast. Since Mavis had been on her healthy diet, losing one hundred pounds, both she and Sophie had gone along with the regimen to lend their moral support. Showing once again that no good deed goes unpunished, they had almost died from sugar withdrawal each and every day when Mavis served up oatmeal and fresh fruit for breakfast. Now that Toots was back home, it was time to hit the Froot Loops and the sugar. Healthy breakfasts be damned.

Downstairs, Mavis was already in the kitchen, preparing oatmeal with sliced strawberries and whole-wheat toast. "Good morning, Toots. I thought you would sleep in today, this being your first day home."

"No, I told you girls last night I plan to investigate the new bakery. You want to go with me?"

"No, I can't. Would you mind if I borrowed one of your vehicles to drive to the post office or FedEx, if they have one close by? I have several packages that I need to get in today's mail."

"Of course not. Sophie seems to think there's a big mystery surrounding you and your packages. Is there?" Toots asked.

Mavis looked down at her bowl of oatmeal, unable or unwilling to meet Toots's gaze. "No, not at all. Remember I told you I had promised I would send all those packages up north?"

"Yes, I do, but I still think something fishy is going on with you. Sophie does too."

Bernice chose that moment to enter the kitchen, putting a stop to their conversation. "It's been a long time since I walked into the kitchen and found a pot of coffee brewing. How long do you plan to be home this time?"

Mavis appeared glad for the reprieve and continued slicing strawberries.

"As long as it takes. Why?" Toots asked.

Bernice poured herself a cup of coffee, removed the half-and-half from the refrigerator, then added three heaping spoonfuls of sugar. "I don't know. I just thought after all that ghost talk last night, it might've scared you off. Are you really going down to that bakery?"

Toots rolled her eyes. "Of course I am. Now I'm going to finish this coffee and leave. Mavis, if you want to borrow the keys to the Lincoln, Bernice will give them to you with directions to the post office, FedEx, whichever. Sophie and Ida are still upstairs sleeping. I have no clue when they'll be down. Just make sure they have some breakfast."

"Well, I can see that you're back to your same old bossy self," Bernice quipped.

"Yup, and you'll be lucky to keep your job if you start sassing me," Toots said with a smile.

"You've been saying that for thirty years," Bernice snapped.

"And I'll be saying it for thirty more if we're lucky. Now I'm out of here." Toots grabbed her purse off the counter, scooped up the keys to her Land Rover, and headed for the garage.

Bernice flipped her the bird.

It felt good to Toots to be back in her own vehicle. While she loved the sporty red Thunderbird she had purchased in Los Angeles, it was just a toy car. What was even better, she knew Charleston like the back of her hand and could get anywhere with no need to study maps, use a GPS, or get directions. In addition, though morning traffic in Charleston was heavy, it was nothing like the traffic in Los Angeles. Twenty minutes later, she found herself parking her Land Rover in front of The Sweetest Things, the bakery Bernice thought was spooked. The Sweetest Things. She liked that name, thinking it was very appropriate. Inside, the sweet smell of dough rising, sugar bubbling, and melting butter teased her senses like a drug.

It had been so long since she'd had real sugar, her body might react in strange ways. The bakery appeared empty. Had it not been for the sweet, tantalizing smell wafting throughout the small shop, she would have thought it was closed.

The thought had no sooner entered her mind when a woman of no more than thirty appeared from the back of the kitchen. She was small and slender, with short blond hair worn in a spiky do; her bright blue eyes were the color of the sky. A cheerful grin greeted Toots. "Hi. My name is Jamie. Can I help you?"

"I've been dying for some sweets and was told to come here." Damn! Talk about putting your foot in your mouth. Toots remembered a man had just died while waiting in line for his sweet treats. She hoped she hadn't offended the young woman.

"You came to the right place. I've been baking for five hours and need to take a break. How about you pick something out? I'll pour you a cup of coffee, and you can join me. On the house."

That was the last thing Toots had expected. It didn't look as though people were beating down the doors. Why the offer of free sweets and coffee, she had no clue, but she was going to take Jamie up on it. Plus, she wanted to find out exactly what had happened to that man who died while waiting in line. The poor woman looked beat, like she could use a break.

"That's a lovely offer, dear. But you don't look like you have a lot of customers. Why would you give away all these lovely desserts?"

The young woman poured two cups of coffee and filled a plate with a variety of pastries before coming out from behind the counter to sit down at the small table in front of the window. "I don't suppose you've heard what happened here?"

Yes, she had, but she wanted to hear it straight from the horse's mouth. A small white lie was in order. "No, I haven't. I've been in California for the past several months."

"I guess that's a good thing," the young girl said. "Otherwise, you might not be sitting here eating these pastries or drinking this coffee with me."

"I can't imagine why you would say that. This place is adorable." And it was. Decorated in shades of pink and red, the shop looked like something right out of *Willy Wonka & the Chocolate Factory.* Colorful and sweet. Toots placed her hand beneath the table and crossed her fingers. It was her second lie in less than five minutes.

"I know this isn't the most popular area in Charleston, especially for a bakery. When my grandmother died, she left this building to me. I spent the last six years working in the bakery department of a large chain grocery store. I'd always wanted to have my own bakery, and when Mimi died, I figured it was finally my chance. My assistant and I spent days preparing all the baked goods. I'd spent weeks decorating, ordering, just doing all the general things required to open a new business.

"I blew my advertising budget to hell because I had so much positive input from the locals. On opening day, we had a line wrapped around the building, and I was in my heaven. Then the worst thing possible happened. While a man was waiting in line, he suffered a massive heart attack and died. I have to admit he was a hundred pounds or more overweight, and I'm sure the heart attack would have happened no matter what, but Charleston being Charleston, word spread quickly that my bakery was" — Jamie paused, a slight smile lifting the corner of her lip — "to die for. Haunted. With all the local superstitions and folklore, that was all it took to ruin me. I've heard some are even calling me a witch. I've had a few tourists come in, but that's about it. I've got enough money to keep the place going for another month. After that, it's all she wrote. So now you know my sob story. What's yours?" Jamie took a sip of coffee.

Bells went off in Toots's head. Her gut told her this was the right thing to do, and before she changed her mind, she formed a quick financial plan. Rightfully, she should check with Abby first, but then those days were over, she reminded herself. No longer accountable to anyone other than herself, she could make a snap decision if she wanted, and the hell with it.

"Have you ever thought of getting a partner?" Toots asked, her voice laced with excitement.

"Yes, I have, but I don't know of anyone who's willing to toss their money into a bakery, especially now, in these terrible financial times. Though it'll break my heart, I think I'm going to have to chalk this up to experience and move on."

Not wanting to reveal her plans before she'd given them five minutes' more thought, Toots asked, "Have you been to a banker? I have a good friend in town who is president of the Bank of Charleston. Maybe I could put a good word in for you."

Jamie shook her head; a smile that didn't

reach her eyes showed pretty white teeth. "My credit sucks. There is no way a bank would lend me a plugged nickel."

Toots looked at her watch. Five minutes had passed. It was time to make a decision. There was one final test, and if it worked, her decision was made.

"Do you make pralines here?" Toots asked.

"Actually they're one of my specialties. I just made a batch. Hang on, and I'll get you one." Jamie raced back to the kitchen, returning a minute later with a plate piled high with pralines.

She held the plate out for Toots. Not needing an invitation, Toots took a praline off the plate, sank her teeth into the rich, sweet, sugary confection, and her decision was made.

"I think you've just found yourself a partner," Toots said.

CHAPTER 11

Four hours later, Toots parked the Land Rover in the garage. She was barely out of the vehicle before Sophie and Bernice practically pounced on her.

"Where in the world have you been? We've been worried sick about you," Bernice said.

Toots got out of the car, slammed the door, and walked inside the house without saying a word. Sophie followed her inside like a bad odor.

"I'm here now. That's all that matters. And besides, it's none of your business. You all are the nosiest bunch of old women I've ever seen," Toots remarked.

"We thought maybe you'd had a heart attack!" Sophie informed her. "People die when they go to *that* bakery. If you weren't my best friend, I'd kick your ass right now."

After Toots had a few seconds to gather her thoughts, she decided she couldn't put off the inevitable. "Where are Mavis and

Ida? There's something I need to discuss with all of you."

"Mavis went to FedEx. Then she said something about stopping at Catherine's clothing shop. Ida went with her. She said something about looking for a salon so she could have her hair done and a manicure and pedicure. I expect they'll be gone the rest of the day," Bernice said.

Being her usual sarcastic self, Sophie spoke up. "Please, *please* tell me you haven't found your ninth husband. If that's the case, I'm going to have you committed to the nearest nuthouse."

Toots shot daggers at Sophie. "Do I look like an idiot?"

"You want the truth or a lie?" Sophie asked.

"What I want is to smack that smirk off your face right now," Toots said.

"Go for it," Sophie singsonged.

"Seriously I need to talk to you all. I did something today, and I want your opinion."

"I hope you didn't have a bikini wax," Sophie said smartly.

"You have an ugly mind," Toots responded, though she couldn't help but smile when she recalled Ida's telling them about the time she'd had a bikini wax. "I met the young woman who owns the bakery. Her

119

name is Jamie."

"And that is supposed to impress me how?" Sophie questioned.

"If you could keep your big trap closed long enough, I might be able to tell you," Toots said. "The young woman is about Abby's age. Apparently she inherited the building from her grandmother and sank every dime she owned into the business. When that obese man died in front of her store, her business went from what might have been fantastic to a few stray tourists here and there.

"She invited me for coffee and pastries. By the way, she makes the best pralines I've ever tasted. That alone should draw a crowd. Long story short, I went with my gut instinct — as you know I'm famous for doing — and offered to buy half of the business. I am now half owner of The Sweetest Things." Toots looked at the two women, saw the expressions on their face. Shock and awe.

"Have you been drinking?" Bernice asked.

"I think she's been smoking pot," Sophie announced, almost beside herself.

"Do you realize what you've done? You'll lose every dime if you decide to make it public that you are part owner of that wicked place. I heard she was a witch,"

Bernice said, her voice rising to near hysteria.

"I knew you would say something like that," Toots commented. "That woman is no more a witch than you are. She's had some bad luck because of horrible circumstances, but that's no reason for her to throw the towel in. If you tasted one of her pralines, you would know exactly what I'm talking about," Toots said with a smile.

She watched Bernice and Sophie, the looks on their faces. Stunned didn't begin to describe their expressions. Their mouths hung open like treasure chests waiting for more booty to be shoved in. Toots figured their tongues would start flapping again momentarily.

Bernice was the first to regain her composure. "Surely, you're not going to throw good money after bad. I know you like sugar and all that bad crap, but this is even off the scale for you, Toots. First you buy a tabloid newspaper. Now you're telling us you're buying a bakery, and it's probably haunted. The owner is a witch, and you think you can make it work simply because you like her pralines?"

"I agree with Bernice," Sophie said. "You're out of your freaking mind. Or you've just got so much money, you don't know what to do with it. I'm inclined to believe that it's a little bit of both. What do you think Abby will say when you tell her you've bought a bakery? It even sounds stupid!"

"And this is coming from the woman who does séances and talks to dead people? Give me a break! Why do you think I was gone so long? What do you think I did? Just run to the bank, make a withdrawal, hand it to the woman, and say, 'Here, have at it'? Well?"

"Yes, actually I do. As I recall it, your gut instinct hasn't always been right," Sophie remarked.

"When?" Toots challenged.

"Let me think." Sophie tapped a mani-cured nail against her temple. "Wasn't *it you* who invested one hundred thousand dollars in those charcoal underpants? I remember when you wrote me about that over twenty years ago. You said they would be the next Wonderbra or better. What did you think? That you were going to save the world from obnoxious odors?" Sophie laughed out loud.

"It was only a hundred grand. It wasn't that big a loss. And for the record, I just saw an infomercial the other night that was advertising charcoal underwear, so there!"

"And what was that deal with the flying

car? Didn't one of your husbands invest a bucket load of money in that scheme?"

Bernice perked up at that. "I remember that. Even though I don't like to fly, it seemed like a good idea at the time."

"Yes, I believe that was George. If I recall correctly, he thought of himself as George Jetson when that flying-car deal came around. *I* didn't invest the money. It was his to do with as he pleased. So is there anything else you want to rub in my face?" Toots asked.

"I'm sure I'll think of something," Sophie replied.

"Well, while you're busy *thinking,* I'm going upstairs to take a shower and change. I'm going to make dinner tonight." With that, Toots turned on her heel and walked through the kitchen, into the dining area, and up the stairs into her own room. Had she made a mistake? Was she just another old lady with too much money who didn't know what to do with it? No, she didn't think so.

She truly believed Jamie and her bakery could be very successful. Yes, she had invested in a few things here and there, but only because of her desire to help others less fortunate, and so what if she lost a few thousand dollars along the way? It was her money to lose. Though she had to agree with Sophie, the flying-car deal had been a bit out there.

She quickly showered and changed into a pair of black slacks and a bright red top. She loosened the topknot and let her hair cascade around her shoulders. She went over to her dresser and looked in the mirror. Not bad for sixty-five. She dabbled a little blush on her cheeks, a little gloss on her lips, then slipped into a pair of comfortable sandals and was back downstairs within twenty minutes.

Bernice and Sophie were sitting in the kitchen, drinking coffee.

"Why did you dress up just to cook dinner?" Sophie asked.

"Because I felt like it," Toots shot back.

"I cannot believe you're actually cooking. The only thing I've ever seen you make is a bowl of Froot Loops and coffee, and I think, though I am not positive about it, that you're good at toast," Bernice said dryly.

"There's a first time for everything. If I'm going to be operating a bakery, I need to learn my way around the kitchen. So tonight I'm making grilled cheese sandwiches for dinner."

"Grilled cheese sandwiches! Hot damn! You'll have your own show on the Food

124

Network before it's all over with. Emeril Lagasse, look out." Sophie slurped her coffee.

"I have to start somewhere. I remember making grilled cheese sandwiches for Abby when she was little. She loved them. If you don't like them, you don't have to eat them."

Toots made quick work of putting together a stack of sandwiches. She removed the bread from the bread box, placing the slices assembly-line style along the counter. She topped each slice of bread with a big slice of cheddar cheese and topped that off with another slice of bread. She placed them all on a baking sheet, threw the baking sheet in the oven, and poured herself a cup of coffee before joining Sophie and Bernice at the kitchen table.

Again, Bernice's and Sophie's mouths hung open. "You don't bake grilled cheese sandwiches, you dummy," Sophie said.

"Says who?" Toots asked.

"Anyone over the age of six," Sophie added. "You *grill* them, in a skillet, on top of the stove. That's why they're called *grilled* cheese sandwiches."

"She is right, Toots," Bernice stated. "And I'll eat one, if they're not burnt."

"I appreciate your support. Both of you. I'm trying, okay? I have other talents besides cooking, just so you know."

The words were no more out of Toots's mouth when the scent of burnt cheese wafted toward them. Smoke billowed from the sides of the oven like a thick fog. She raced over to the stove, grabbed a kitchen towel, and yanked the bubbling cheese from the oven. She looked over her shoulder to see Sophie and Bernice laughing so hard, tears were rolling down their faces.

With her one free hand, Toots gave them the finger.

Between laughing and spitting, Sophie spoke up. "Looks to me like those other talents might be something you want to pull out of your apron," Sophie cackled. "Get it? Apron?"

"Yes, yes, yes, I do, Sophie. I can't cook, but I'm trying, okay? And whatever you do, don't you dare tell Mavis and Ida about this incident. Bernice, you neither, or I will fire you."

Bernice's bright blue eyes twinkled with amusement. "Yeah, yeah, yeah, whatever. You've been saying that for thirty years."

"You know, someday I might just do it, too," Toots said as she dumped the pile of burnt cheese sandwiches into the sink.

The girls were probably onto something. Maybe it was her forte in life just to be the money person, not the actual baker in this case. Obviously, her talents lay elsewhere, such as in decorating. Now, that was something she knew how to do.

"Okay, I can't cook. I'm having a bowl of Froot Loops for dinner. Anyone care to join me?"

CHAPTER 12

Ida careened around the curve, sliding off the shoulder, and yanked the steering wheel sharply to the left, almost hitting a vehicle in the oncoming lane.

"Oh, my goodness! Slow down! You're scaring the life out of me! When was the last time you were behind the wheel of a car?" Mavis asked as she dug holes in the dashboard with her nails.

"When I was fifteen. Why? Am I scaring you?" Ida shouted.

Mavis's pretty features crumpled into a look of horror. "Fifteen? Are you telling me you don't have a driver's license?"

The sleek Lincoln Town Car lurched around a second curve, only to fly through a four-way stop. They just missed being hit by a dump truck.

"Ida, I want you to stop this vehicle right now!"

"Hush! Let me do the driving," Ida stated

as she concentrated on keeping the car between the ditches.

"Ida, if you don't pull over, I'm going to . . . tell Toots that you don't have a license, and you had your thingamajig waxed today."

Ida glanced over at Mavis as though she had lost her mind. "How do you know that?"

"I picked you up from the salon, remember? I heard them say that when they tallied up your bill," Mavis said smartly. "Now pull over, please, before you kill us or someone else!"

Knowing this was a battle she wasn't going to win, Ida pulled over onto the side of the road, barely missing a yield sign as she did so. Mavis got out from the passenger side, walked in front of the car, then slid into the driver's seat as Ida slipped across the smooth leather seat to the passenger's side, where she should have been all along.

"I can't believe you would risk our lives like this!" Mavis said as she shifted into drive, carefully easing the Town Car back onto the narrow two-lane road.

"You didn't offer to drive after you picked me up. And I like being behind the wheel of her car," Ida said. "As a matter of fact, this is my new goal. I'm going to get my driver's license and buy the fanciest car on the market."

"I'm not so sure that's a good idea, Ida. Maybe you should consider driving lessons first."

Mavis didn't want to hurt Ida's feelings, but her being on the road would be like skydiving without a parachute or flying a plane without a pilot's license. The first opportunity she had, she would explain this to Toots, telling her that not only was Ida risking her own life when she got behind the wheel of a car, but she was also risking other lives. Mavis hated the thought of being a tattletale, especially after all the humiliation Ida had suffered the past several months, but she didn't have a choice. As Sophie would say, Ida would get over it.

As Mavis carefully made her way through the winding roads leading to Toots's home, she admired the giant oak trees dripping with Spanish moss. The camellias were in full bloom along the side of the road, and the sweet smell of magnolias scented the late afternoon breeze flowing in from the crack in the window.

While Ida had been at the salon getting spiffed up, Mavis had found the local FedEx without any trouble, had shipped nine boxes, then had spoken with the clerk about arranging a daily pickup from Toots's home. This would save her having to make a daily trip into town. Plus she needed every free moment she could muster in order to produce her clothing for Good Mourning. She had checked her Web site one more time before they left and had seen she had another twenty-three orders. Lucky for her, they were all size tens and twelves. Still, that would leave her barely twenty-four hours to sew, iron, and pack tomorrow's orders. On a whim, she had told Catherine what she was doing. Catherine had offered to sell Mavis's designs in her shop, but Mavis had refused, telling her she wanted exclusive rights to her designs. Being a business-woman herself, Catherine not only under-stood but agreed this was a good plan. Mavis told her about the factory she'd made contact with in California and also that she might have a supplier for a higher quality material than she was using now. Catherine agreed that soon Mavis would not be able to keep up with the demand.

If orders continued to come in through the Web site, Mavis would have no other choice. She would have to tell the girls what she was doing simply because she could not hide something that big, especially from Sophie, who already suspected she was up to something. It had been hard not to share her excitement with her friends, but until she proved to be successful or overwhelmed, whichever came first, Mavis decided it was best to keep her new venture a secret for as long as possible.

Mavis pulled through the wrought-iron gates leading up the winding drive to Toots's beautiful house. Ida hadn't uttered a single word since Mavis took the wheel.

Carefully, Mavis parked the car inside the garage, cramming the keys inside her purse so that she could return them to Bernice for safekeeping. It would do none of them any good at all if Ida were to get hold of the keys and decide to practice her driving skills.

Mavis and Ida entered the house through the back door that led to the kitchen. Greeted by the scent of something burning, each took a deep breath.

Toots, Sophie, and Bernice were running around the kitchen like three chickens with their heads cut off. Bernice had a broom in her hand, waving it back and forth in the air; Sophie had two kitchen towels, swinging them around as though they were a lasso; and poor Toots was filling the dishwasher with cereal bowls.

"What in the world happened?" Mavis asked as she ran over to the sink to assist

Toots. She dropped her purse on the counter and raised the window above the sink to allow the smoke to filter outside.

"Toots made dinner." Sophie smirked. "She owns a bakery now, and somehow that convinced her she knew her way around a kitchen."

"Are you talking about *our* Toots?" Mavis asked.

"The one and only," Bernice added.

In the prim and proper voice usually reserved for a man she was trying to impress, Ida said, "I don't believe I heard you correctly. Did I hear you say Toots now owns a bakery? Please tell me it isn't so."

"Unfortunately, if I did, that would make me a liar, and my nose would probably grow," Sophie said as she continued to twirl the kitchen cloths in the air. Ida thought she resembled a majorette in a marching band, minus the baton.

Hands immersed in soapy dishwater, Toots called over her shoulder, "I don't see why everyone is making such a fuss. I tried to make grilled cheese sandwiches. I burnt them. Big deal. It's not like the house caught on fire. This stink will be out of here in no time."

"Yeah, it's a shame we don't have any of those charcoal underpants you invested in.

We sure could use those right now. Filter out some of the smoke," Sophie muttered as she continued to march around the kitchen, waving at the smoke with the kitchen towels.

Mavis and Toots worked together at the sink while Bernice and Sophie continued to wave the smoke away. Ida sat down at the kitchen table, watching.

"Is it true what Sophie said? Did you really buy a bakery?" Ida asked.

"She bought that haunted bakery downtown," Bernice informed her as she swung the broom back and forth.

"Careful with that! You might hit me in the head," Ida shouted.

"Might do you some good," Bernice muttered to herself.

"I heard what you said," Ida replied.

"I was only teasing."

Ida rolled her eyes.

For the next fifteen minutes, the five women — rather the four women, since Ida refused to offer any help — finished cleaning the kitchen. The scent of smoke lingered in the air, but that was the only remaining evidence of Toots's attempt to make grilled cheese sandwiches in the oven.

Once the mess was cleaned up, Mavis stepped into her usual role as caregiver, cook, and general Goody Two-shoes. She made a fresh pot of coffee while Bernice put together sandwiches of cold chicken left over from a rotisserie chicken she'd purchased yesterday. Sophie and Toots declined, saying they were both full. Between the two of them, they'd emptied an entire box of Froot Loops.

"So while I was trying to make dinner, what were you two up to?" Toots asked.

"I spent the day at the salon, getting pampered. I haven't a clue how Mavis spent hers," Ida said as she admired the pale pink polish on her nails.

"Mavis? Bernice said Coco cried all day while you were gone. It's not like you to leave her for such a long period of time," Toots said.

"Oh my gosh, I can't believe I forgot poor Coco. Sophie said she would watch her. Where is she?" Mavis looked in the corner of the kitchen where she'd placed her bed that morning, before she left.

Sophie couldn't help herself when she said, "We're eating her."

The look of horror on Mavis's face was worth a million bucks. The little Chihuahua must have heard her mistress's voice, because she came running down the stairs, her tiny nails click-clacking against the hardwood floor.

"Sophie, that was a horrible thing to say," Mavis complained as she stooped down to pick up Coco. The tiny dog slathered Mavis's face with kisses. "Poor baby."

"I agree with Mavis. That's a terrible thing to say. I thought I told you to put that old bag in the drawer and leave her there. You are one crude woman," Toots observed.

As was the norm, Sophie gave Toots and the others the single-digit salute.

"I'm sorry. That was out of line. Mavis, you should know better by now. I would never, ever harm Coco. I know how much you love her. Now, is anyone game for a séance tonight? I've learned something new, and I would like to practice tonight. Before we left California, I went to this New Age bookstore and ran across an old book that describes the best way to channel the spirit of someone in particular. You think you girls are up for this tonight?

"I wouldn't want to force any of you. I think we have a much better chance of channeling whomever we call if we follow the instructions in this book to the letter, or that's what the lady in the bookstore told me."

"So we're back to séances and ghosts again," Toots said. "I still don't know what

Mavis did all day. I guess she can tell me later. You will, won't you?"

"Of course. Let me feed Coco and get changed. Maybe we can make contact with Herbert tonight." Mavis, with Coco clutched to her chest like a life preserver, raced out of the kitchen and upstairs to her room.

"So, is everyone game?" Sophie asked. "Give me a few minutes to prepare the dining room. Then we'll get started."

Bernice and Toots gave Sophie a high five. Ida, still frightened by her last experience, was reluctant to participate in another séance. She said so to Sophie.

"You can sit next to me, and I'll hold your hand. And I promise not to let anyone, and I mean anyone" — Toots gave Sophie the evil eye — "hurt, harm, or intentionally frighten you in any way, shape, or form. If anyone does, they'll have to deal with me."

"Oh, all right," Ida said, "but I can promise you one thing. If I feel the least bit uncomfortable, I'm out of there. Is that a deal?"

"I say we shake on it," Toots said.

As three of them had done for more than fifty years, each placed one hand on top of the others'. When the four women, minus Mavis but plus Bernice, who'd known about their secret handshake for years, had stacked their hands as they always did, they threw their hands into the air and shouted, "When you're good, you're good!"

CHAPTER 13

Once they gathered in the dining room, Sophie explained her new and hopefully improved version of a séance. It was quite a procedure, and she wanted to make sure the girls knew what they were getting into before they started. This new means of channeling required the participants to . . . participate, by dressing the part. It was sort of like an off-Broadway play.

"The book says that by following the required steps, we have a much better chance to attract a specific person. In any case, we won't have to rely on that damn water glass to see who is actually coming through when we can get straight down to business. I mean, shoot, do you really think someone wants to come from the other side just to tell us who they are? I'm sure they have more important things to do. So if any of you have any reservations, let's hold them back for now and give this a try."

"Sounds good to me. I want to say something like this was on TV. Except for the fact that the person performing it was a fraud, I think we might have a better chance of calling someone in particular. I think it'll be fun," Toots said.

Mavis, who normally appeared excited and more than willing to participate in the séances, seemed unusually frightened.

"Are you okay with this, Mavis? I've gone through a lot of preparation, and setting this up is very much an ordeal. If you're uncomfortable, let me know now," Sophie instructed.

"I'm fine, really. What exactly do we have to do different this time around?" Mavis asked, her voice exuding false cheer.

"First of all, we must show respect to the ones whom we want to channel. Now, I know I'm not supposed to know about this, but I do, and let's leave it at that. In the book it says we should wear whatever we would normally wear when attending a funeral."

Sophie let that bit of information hang in the air. She was looking directly at Mavis as she said this. Mavis's eyes widened, and she looked from left to right. "What are you referring to?"

"All those dark clothes you have? I think

140

if we all were to wear those mourning colors you're so fond of and have so many of, well, let's just say this. Dressing appropriately will show the person we are attempting to contact that we are truly in mourning over losing them."

"You want to wear *my* clothes?" Mavis asked.

"I want all of us to wear those dark, depressing outfits. Just out of respect for the dead," Sophie explained succinctly.

Flustered, Mavis wasn't quite sure what to say. "I'm not sure about this. Why can't we each wear our own clothes?"

"Look, Mavis, it's not like we are going to be dripping hot candle wax on them. We just need them for a few hours. Give us a break. We need the freaking dresses, and you are the dressmaker, so why don't you trot your little ass upstairs and see what you have? I know that in the last year you've been several sizes. Surely you have something that will fit each of us."

"Sophie, I can't believe you! You actually expect us to dress like we're going to a funeral? And even worse, you want us to wear Mavis's clothes?" Toots stated in total amazement.

"It's like I said in the beginning, this is different. Either you're in or you're not.

Your call. I'm not going to force anyone to do something she's not comfortable with. I just think if we follow the rules in the book exactly as they are stated, who knows? Maybe we can contact Elvis. Or better yet, Michael Jackson. They're still not sure how he died. Maybe his ghost, spirit, or whatever you want to call it, can clarify a few things. So, Mavis, are you willing to lend us some outfits?"

"Okay. But if anything happens to them, I'm going to hold you down and pour hot candle wax on your head. Then I'm going to yank out all that beautiful dark hair you're so proud of. That will ruin any chance you have of finding a new husband. Get the picture?"

This tirade was so unlike Mavis that the others could not prevent themselves from bursting out laughing. Again, it seemed that with every pound Mavis had lost, she had gained ten pounds of intestinal fortitude.

"Mavis, dear, you're beginning to sound just like the rest of us," Toots chided.

"Just for the record, I am *not* in the market for a new husband," Sophie insisted. "No way, José."

Mavis stood up, shifted her shoulders back, and lifted her chin a notch. "I'm going upstairs to sort out the clothes. Is there anything else?"

"We'll meet you in your room in five minutes," Sophie said.

Once Mavis had gone upstairs, the others looked at one another in astonishment.

"Who woulda thunk it?" Sophie said. "The mouse has turned into a lion."

Ida, Toots, Bernice, and Sophie retreated upstairs to don their mourning attire. As they walked down the hall to leave what they had on in their bedrooms, each felt a bit of trepidation, not knowing what to expect as they were all entering uncharted territory. Even though they'd made contact before this, they had never called forth a specific person.

Five minutes later, in Mavis's bedroom, they acted like giddy schoolgirls at a slumber party as they giggled and put on the dark gray dresses. Though jovial on the outside, Sophie, being extremely intuitive, could feel the fear emanating from her dearest friends like water from a spigot.

To lighten up the mood, she said, "You know, girls, if we're able to do this, it could open up a whole new business opportunity for us. Just think how many women there are out there who would like one last chance to tell their late husbands what pieces of crap they were. I think we might be onto something here."

"That would be the perfect job for you, Sophie, since you never have a kind word to say about anyone. Badmouthing dead men, seems like that's right up your alley," Ida observed.

"Better than what you would do to them," Sophie said.

"Exactly what is that supposed to mean?" Ida snarled.

"Stop it, you two! Arguing over dead men? Give us all a break. Quit sniping at each other. Sophie, let's go downstairs and prepare for tonight's séance. And not another word about anyone!" Toots commanded.

"You're no fun," Sophie said as she made her way down the hall. "You realize we haven't had a cigarette in the last half hour?"

"I've been chewing your nicotine gum. Now that you mention it, let's go have a smoke before we get started. It could be our last," Toots said dryly.

The two women grabbed their packs of cigarettes from the kitchen table, went outside, and sat down on the steps, where they each lit up. After two cigarettes apiece, they went inside, where Bernice, Mavis, and Ida looked like matching pigeons in the slate gray outfits.

Toots had a brief thought. If Abby or Chris saw them now, they would have them committed for sure. Five old women dressed like doves as they prepared to speak to the dead. But, the bottom line was this: They were having the time of their lives. And for now, that was enough.

Sophie retrieved the candles and wineglasses from the hutch in the kitchen. Holding her book in one hand, she read the instructions on how to properly place the glasses on the table. She followed the instructions to the letter.

"Is there anything I can do to help?" Ida asked.

"Put the tablecloth on first. Once the glasses are rimmed with salt, you know, kind of like a margarita, we'll place them on the corners of the table." Sophie poured table salt on top of a dinner plate. "Supposedly, this salt is to ward off any evil spirits we don't want to come through."

Once the table was properly set, the candles lit, the salted wineglasses placed in their proper position, Sophie, Toots, Mavis, and Ida proceeded to take their places around the table, each one of them sitting at a corner representing a cardinal point of the compass. Bernice sat between Toots and Sophie.

Sophie opened her book and began to read out loud. "Spirits of the dead, hear us in our hour of mourning. We're looking for the spirit of Walter Manchester. Bastard and drunk that he was. Walter, if you are here, please give us a sign of your presence. We are in grief over your loss." Sophie rolled her eyes. "We wish you to come through tonight. North, south, east, or west. Walter, wherever you may be, find your way toward us and grace us with your presence."

The room remained silent. Other than the ticking of a grandfather clock, nothing could be heard.

They remained in total silence, waiting for Walter to make his presence known. After several minutes, when nothing happened, Ida spoke up. "What do we do now?"

"The book says we should offer something meaningful, something this spirit might have cherished in life."

"Well, you gave him your virginity, so that's out of the question. Not that it was ever anything of value," Toots added with a smile.

In a harsh whisper, Sophie said, "You think so?"

"I know so," Toots remarked.

"If this is going to be nothing more than a pissing contest, I have better things to do,"

Bernice groused.

The dining room radiated a warm golden color from the flames of the many candles. If one were inclined to believe in such things, this was the perfect setting to receive spirits, ghosts, or an entity of any kind.

"Let's join hands. We'll give it a few more minutes and try to channel our energy. The book says this makes us a stronger unit."

"Oh, Lordy, Lordy. I don't believe we're doing this," Toots said.

Sophie kicked her beneath the table. "Hush!"

Suddenly, the room chilled. It was so cold that each of the women shivered.

"Did you feel that? I think something is happening." Sophie scanned the room.

"I felt it. It was a cold breeze, and I heard it, too. It was the air conditioner kicking on. I honestly doubt we've accomplished anything tonight. I suggest we end this foolishness and try it the way we did before. At least we made contact then," Toots suggested.

"I agree with Toots. Let's just start over tomorrow night. This doesn't seem to be working. Maybe the spirits don't like this house," Ida suggested.

"You may be right, but let's not leave just yet. If that skunk of a husband of mine doesn't want to make his presence known, I say we make him an offer he can't refuse. Toots, do you remember the wedding gift you gave me when Walter and I married?"

"No, not really," Toots replied.

"Well, I do. One of the gifts was a bottle of wine. You told me it came from Christie's, you know, the auction house in New York City?"

"Surely you're not talking about that bottle of *Château* Mouton Rothschild Jeroboam? Please, don't tell me Walter got his hands on that."

"No, he didn't. I've carried it with me all these years. I've been saving it for a special occasion. You don't know how hard it is to hide alcohol when you're living with a drunk. I knew it was a very expensive bottle of wine, something Walter would have given his eyeteeth for. He might've been a drunk, but a cheap one he wasn't. He only drank the best. I told him one of the girls at the office purchased it at Woolworth's, and the dumb ass was too snookered most of the time to realize that Woolworth's didn't even sell wine."

"If Walter is going to make his presence known, he better do it real quick. I'm ready to call it a day," Ida said.

"Let's give it one more serious try, and if

148

nothing happens, we'll call it a night," Sophie suggested.

Suddenly a foul scent blew gently throughout the room, followed by a loud banging noise that startled them.

"What was that?" Mavis said, her voice filled with fright.

"I hate to say it, but I think it's the shutter. It's banging rapidly, and it sure as hell isn't from the wind," Toots said, all traces of humor gone. "There isn't the slightest breeze out tonight."

Sophie looked from left to right. "Walter? If that was you, let us see or hear a sign of your presence. A sign that we cannot mistake for anything or anyone else. If you're here, make yourself known. Now!"

Just as the words left Sophie's mouth, she felt a force near her, then a silence that was deafening. Out of nowhere, all five glasses suddenly toppled over and started rolling on the table. Then, as fast as they started, they stopped.

"Bernice, go in the kitchen and bring back a corkscrew and an extra wineglass. We're going to open this now," Sophie said calmly.

"Sophie Manchester, you realize that bottle of wine is worth more than one hundred thousand dollars?" Toots said in utter amazement. "I hope . . . Never mind, it was a gift. You can do with it as you please."

Bernice raced back into the dining room, corkscrew in one hand, a wineglass in the other. Sophie took the opener and proceeded to open the bottle of sixty-year-old wine. She reseated all five wineglasses, wiped the salt off the rims, then filled them with the exquisite wine.

"I would like to propose a toast," Sophie said.

Each of the five women held her wineglass high in the air.

"To my late husband, Walter. He didn't come through tonight, so I must assume he's rotting in hell as we speak. I don't think there is anything I would enjoy toasting more than his ass roasting on hot coals for eternity."

All five clinked their glasses together. "To Walter."

After their first sip, they placed the glasses in front of them. A wine so old, so expensive, must be sipped. While they waited for the wine to warm their insides and tickle their tongues, a foul gush of air blasted through the room, once again causing the glasses of wine to tip over, emptying every last drop on the clothes Mavis had loaned them.

"My dresses! What just happened?" Mavis

cried out.

Toots, Ida, Bernice, and Sophie looked down at their borrowed attire. The wine had left deep, blood-colored stains.

"Walter, you asshole! No one else but you would pull a stunt like this. I wouldn't have thought you, of all people, would ever let one drop go to waste. You sicken me! You're a prick in death just like you were in life," Sophie yelled, her voice laced with anger.

Wind blew across the room, extinguishing the candles and leaving the room in total darkness.

Sophie looked down at her ruined dress. "These clothes look like maxi pads. I think I've proven that I can summon any specific person at will. We're going to have to do this more often. We have the power to solve some of life's greatest mysteries."

CHAPTER 14

"And that's my big secret," Mavis explained. Over breakfast, Mavis revealed what she had been up to for the past several months. She wanted to help lay those to rest who couldn't afford it, but in a dignified manner. When she told the story about Pearl Mae Atkins, the women all cried like babies. Even Sophie's eyes misted over.

"Why didn't you just ask me for the money?" Toots asked. "I would've helped you."

Mavis blotted at her eyes with a tissue. "I know you would, and I appreciate your offer. But this was something I had to do on my own. I checked my Web site this morning. I have thirty-seven more orders on top of the twenty-three from yesterday. After last night's . . . event, I'm five short. What is even worse, I've run out of material."

"So can't you just order another bolt of it? I'm pretty handy with a sewing machine, and so is Toots. If these patterns are as easy as you say they are, between the three of us we should be able to fill your orders ASAP," Ida said.

Mavis shook her head. "That's the problem. Not any old material will do. Because I want my customers to wear these clothes more than once, I invested in the best fabric I could afford. Not to be boastful or anything, but Oscar de la Renta sometimes uses the same supplier."

"That's pretty darn impressive," Toots said. "So what are your long-term plans? Do you want to stay Internet only, or have you thought of opening stores?"

"Right now the Internet is my best option. In the future, I wouldn't rule out a small catalog or something of that nature. I want to stay unique, not something that can be found at Sears or JCPenney. Yesterday, when I was visiting Catherine, she offered to sell my designs in her shop, but I told her no. She agrees with me. Good Mourning is a one-of-a-kind idea."

"Yeah, until someone else picks up on the idea," Sophie added. "Then you'll find your designs in Wal-Mart, Target, and, if you're really lucky, Walgreens."

Bernice piped up. "Hey, there is nothing wrong with buying your clothes at Walgreens. See these shoes I'm wearing?" Bernice lifted her foot up in the air. She wore a pair of knockoff Crocs in hot pink. "I paid four ninety-nine for these perfectly good shoes."

"It's perfectly acceptable to buy a pair of knock-around shoes at Walgreens. I don't think the average grief-stricken consumer looks for a mourning outfit in a drugstore, that's all," Ida informed them.

"I found a supplier yesterday in North Charleston. It's a warehouse on Meeting Street Road. They're called Jay C. King's. From what I could gather, that area is similar to the fashion district in New York City," Mavis explained.

"Then what's the problem? We go there, pick up however much fabric, come back here, and sew our asses off. And yes, I do know how to sew," Sophie informed them.

"I wish it were that easy. I learned from Catherine that there is no way they would sell to me because I only need a few bolts of fabric. This warehouse only sells orders in bulk, and even if they did sell small orders, you have to have an account with them to even think about buying from them. They're top of the line," Mavis said.

"You're positive they wouldn't sell anything to you?" Toots asked.

"Absolutely. Catherine told me they actually have guards, and a security system to rival that of Fort Knox."

Toots appeared deep in thought. "What if we didn't actually buy the material from them? What's stopping us from going into the place at night and taking it? I honestly doubt they would miss a few bolts of fabric." As soon as the words came out of her mouth, she realized how insane, how totally off the wall she sounded.

"You've got to be kidding. You're talking about *stealing?* Catherine said they have a steel door with a lock that not even a bulldozer could push. The lock itself, according to Catherine, is six inches of hardened steel. I don't think our fragile hands have the ability to bend that kind of steel even if we did eat our spinach," Mavis said laughingly.

"Apparently you and Catherine had quite a conversation," Toots said.

Bernice poured a fresh round of coffee, and Sophie removed a coffee cake from the oven. Once their necessities were replenished, the two women sat back down to resume their conversation with the others.

"Seriously, stealing is out of the question. I may have bitten off more than I can chew. I just love what I'm doing, but I have to be realistic. The supply-and-demand issue . . . Well, everything is happening faster than I anticipated, which I suppose is a good thing if I were better prepared."

"Success is always unexpected, Mavis. Let me call Henry Whitmore at the bank. If this warehouse is as exclusive as you're saying, I would bet my last dollar Henry knows who they are. I'll see if I can pull a few strings, if you want me to," Toots offered.

In a sweet voice, Mavis said, "I hate to ask. You already have enough to do."

"And that's what keeps me going. That's what makes me happy," Toots said.

Mavis was right. Toots did have enough to do, but doing was what kept her alive. Sitting around twiddling her thumbs was not in her nature. Staying busy, enjoying her life, her daughter, and her dearest friends, now that was embedded deep in her DNA. And when she could, helping those in need made her happy. She would be the first to admit that she liked the finer things in life, but she would also tell you that material things could be replaced, people couldn't.

"I'll go upstairs and make that call," Toots said, getting up from the table.

"And don't forget to call Dr. Pauley. Remember, he wants to check Mavis," Bernice added as Toots headed upstairs.

Toots gave Bernice the thumbs-up.

Upstairs in the privacy of her room, she looked up Henry Whitmore's home phone number, then Dr. Pauley's. Deciding Mavis's fabric issue was the more important one, she located Henry's number first.

Toots glanced at her watch before making the call. She wanted to make sure it wasn't too early for a business call. They'd all had a late night last night finishing off Sophie's sixty-year-old bottle of wine. It was fifteen minutes after nine. Late in the business world, but she knew for a fact that Henry seldom arrived at the bank before ten. She punched in his number, anyway, and he answered on the third ring.

"Don't tell me you decided to back out of the bakery deal. I was just about to call your new friend, Jamie," Henry said.

"Good morning to you, too, and no, I'm not backing out of the bakery deal. I need a favor," Toots explained.

"What now? Don't tell me you have invested in another business venture. I know you have millions in this bank. But if your spending continues, your accounts are going to shift into the six-digit mode."

If Henry weren't such a good friend, Toots wouldn't have allowed him to speak to her in such a manner. But he was, and it was okay.

"No, I'm not investing in another business, but I need a favor, and it's a very important one. And if you can help me out, I'll keep my millions in your bank until they throw dirt on my face," Toots said.

"Tell me what you need, and I'll see what I can do, though I can't make any promises," Henry said.

"There's a factory, rather a warehouse, in North Charleston, on Meeting Street Road. I need to set up a business account ASAP. Mavis needs several bolts of material for a new line of clothing she's working on, and they're the only place in town that has what she needs." Toots paused.

"You're talking about Jay C. King's? Am I right?"

"You guessed right. Now, what I need from you is this." Toots gave him all the details Mavis had given her. As luck would have it, Henry was golfing buddies with Mr. King. He'd call him immediately; he told her that King owed him a favor. And he didn't fail to remind her that she would owe him one more favor after this.

Dr. Joseph Pauley had been Toots's personal physician for over twenty years. He was in his midseventies but passed for sixty.

With a full head of white hair, clear blue eyes, at least six feet tall, and without an ounce of body fat on him, he was extremely handsome, and he was also kind and decent. Joe was "good people."

When Mavis had come to Charleston last year, it was Dr. Pauley who gave her the clean bill of health and the warning about her weight that had set her on the road she now walked. Toots couldn't wait for him to see Mavis. She seriously doubted he would recognize her. Joe was single; he might even want to date Mavis. She had a quick flash of the pair as a couple. It didn't seem plausible, but one never knew.

His receptionist answered the phone, and Toots chatted with her for a few minutes before scheduling an appointment for Mavis for the following afternoon. She knew this was simply a formality. Once Joe knew she'd called, he would return the call and more than likely come to her house, as he had before, to examine Mavis.

She replaced the phone and mentally checked these items off her shit-to-do list.

Toots raced downstairs, where the girls were still seated around the table in their pajamas, drinking coffee and laughing.

"Mavis, Dr. Pauley will probably be here this evening to examine you. I scheduled an

159

appointment for Wednesday morning, but as soon as Joe learns it's you, I'm sure he'll just stop by the house for a brief examination. I can't wait for him to see how far you've come in the last year. And Henry from the bank just so happens to be golfing buddies with your Mr. King. He said he would do his best to set up an account for you so that you can purchase the material you need."

Toots felt like a fairy godmother when she delivered the good news.

Mavis's eyes sparkled with excitement. "I don't know how I can thank you. You've already changed my life so much as it is." Mavis stood up, walked to the other side of the table, and gave her dear friend a hug.

"Don't thank me just yet. He said he would try his best," Toots claimed, then looked at her watch. "I've got several business-related matters on my agenda today. What about the rest of you? Any plans?"

Toots made a quick mental note to ask Pete to get her three sewing machines out of storage and fix whatever needed fixing so Mavis's orders could be filled without too much of a delay. It was times like this that Toots wished for the old days, when people didn't expect things to arrive in the mail a

160

day after they'd ordered them.

Ida spoke up. "I'm going to see about taking a driving test so I can get my driver's license. I really enjoyed getting behind the wheel of your car yesterday."

Toots looked as though she had been slapped in the face. "Are you telling me you don't have a driver's license?"

"I never had to drive in New York City. Thomas always had a limousine at my disposal, and of course, there were always those nasty taxicabs. So to answer your question, no, I've never had a driver's license, but I plan to change that, starting today."

Sophie pounced on that like a cat on a fish. "You're joking, right? Are you telling us that at sixty-odd years of age, you've never had a driver's license? Remember, I lived in New York City, too, though I never had a limousine at my disposal. I did take a few taxi rides, and I practically lived on the subway. Hell, I didn't even own a vehicle, yet I had a driver's license. I bet they won't even issue a license to someone your age, especially a first timer. And you actually drove yesterday?"

Sophie shook her head, bewildered that Ida had the balls to get behind the wheel of a car without a license. Yet in another sense she was kind of proud of her for taking the initiative to try something new, something she'd never dared before.

"Mavis wouldn't let me drive all of the way home," Ida stated.

"That's because I still value my life," Mavis informed the rest of them.

"Maybe she wants to hurry up and join Thomas, find out who killed him," Sophie added.

"I'm sure your face must be next to the word *tactless* in the dictionary," Toots responded to Sophie's barb.

Almost absentmindedly, Sophie flipped her the bird yet continued to get her digs in. "She could've killed someone, right, Mavis?"

Ida remained silent while Sophie verbally reprimanded her.

Coco, the queen of all dogs, yapped from her palace in the corner. Mavis hurried to the pooch's side, where she picked her up and brought her back to the table. "I think it might be wise to invest in some driving lessons before you even attempt to get your license. She did give me quite a scare yesterday as we were coming back from town. Just look at it as an adventure, right, Toots? Though I guess you should ask how long we're going to remain here in Charleston before you attempt to arrange for lessons," Mavis said to Ida.

They all focused their attention on Toots, their unofficial leader. "As I said before, there is no time limit or any immediate plan to race back to LA. As long as Abby is safe, and the paper is running smoothly, we can stay here in Charleston for as long as we want," Toots assured them. "Anyway, I'm sure Bernice loves our company."

"You know I do. It's just the extra work that I hate," Bernice joked.

"Bull. If I remember correctly, I'm the one that makes your coffee, makes your toast, and what is even worse, I serve it to you," Toots said as she refilled her mug of coffee. "I'm going outside to smoke. Sophie, you ready to huff and puff?"

Sophie grabbed her pack of cigarettes from the table. "I've already smoked six cigarettes today, but my lungs are craving another shot of nicotine."

Together, they escaped through the back door, where they sat down on the steps. Toots lit up, inhaled heartily, and Sophie followed suit.

"You really think you can get that fabric for Mavis?"

"I'm not sure. Henry can only try. If he isn't able, we'll just use plan B," Toots said between puffs.

"And what exactly is plan B?" Sophie asked.

"Damned if I know. I haven't dreamed one up yet," Toots shot back.

"Let me know as soon as you do. This means a lot to Mavis. I can't believe the change in her. And Ida, of course. Hell, I can't believe I'm chasing ghosts, talking to dead people."

Mimicking the voice of the little boy who starred in the movie *The Sixth Sense* with Bruce Willis, Toots said, " 'I see dead people.' "

Sophie gave her a playful punch on the arm, then crushed her cigarette out in the ashtray on the bottom step. "You think it's funny? You're the one that got all this ghost business started in the first place. If you hadn't bought that million-dollar dump in Malibu, we wouldn't be sitting here right now."

"I'll have you know, I paid three point eight million for that dump and tens of thousands more to spiff the place up. That tacky purple and pink was scary. I'll bet Lucy and Desi were spinning in their graves when that Pop-Tart bought their mansion and turned it into a hooker haven."

A former pop star had lived in Toots's

Malibu beach house, with purple and hot pink as the color scheme, mirrors on the ceilings, and a guitar-shaped mirror in one of the bathrooms. The word *hideous* didn't do the place justice. It had taken a few weeks to clear out the house and make it halfway livable, and in doing so, they'd stirred up the spirits, or this was what Sophie had explained to her.

After the first night in her room, when she'd seen those four clouds clustered around her bed, Toots instantly became a believer. She didn't need anything more to convince her there was another dimension. She had been smart enough not to share this newfound discovery, as some would think she'd lost her marbles. It was a good thing she had Sophie, Mavis, and Ida to corroborate this newfound wisdom. Who would've guessed a year ago she and her best friends would be where they were today? Talk about unpredictable.

"We better get inside. I promised Mavis I would help her stitch a few dresses, and I intend to do just that," Sophie said. "You do have an extra sewing machine around here, I hope."

"Actually, I have three, and don't ask me why or where they came from. I'll have Pete get them, oil them, whatever they need, but remember, Mavis is about out of material. We can't make clothes without the cloth," Toots said as she followed Sophie back inside to the kitchen.

Bernice was busy at the sink, washing dishes. "Before you ask, Mavis took that yapping dog out front, and Ida said she was going to search for a driving instructor on the Internet," Bernice said matter-of-factly.

"Good job, Bernice," Toots said, dragging out the words. "You're becoming a true mind reader."

Toots's cell phone rang as she headed upstairs to shower and dress. She had to meet Jamie at the bank before lunchtime to finalize their agreement. Toots couldn't wait to call Abby to tell her she was now partners in a bakery. Abby would like that, she knew.

But what would she say when Toots finally told her she'd also bought *The Informer* a year ago, when Abby was in fear of losing her job? She didn't think her daughter would be pleased one little bit. Abby was exactly like her father in that respect. Independent and a go-getter.

"Henry," she said when she saw his name appear on her cell phone's caller ID. "I didn't expect you to get back to me this quick. Is something wrong?" Toots entered her bedroom, tossing her shoes off as she

166

crossed the large room to get to the bathroom. With the phone stuck to her ear, she listened as she stripped down to her birthday suit.

"Tell me this isn't true!" Toots practically shouted into the phone. This was not good news at all. "Of course, Henry. Yes, I understand. No, she won't try to harm herself. We have a plan B," she said, then clicked off. Toots just didn't have a clue what plan B actually was.

Yet.

CHAPTER 15

At the end of what had been a very long day, Toots had accomplished much more than she'd anticipated, way more than she'd had on her shit-to-do list. She met Jamie at the bank, finalizing their deal, promising her that as long as she tried her hardest, Toots would stand behind her, and that she alone would be responsible for running the bakery. Not only had Toots gained a new business, but she'd gained a new friend, as well. She went with her gut instinct, trusting she'd made the right decision. However, with all her connections and her money, she wasn't able to perform the miracle that Mavis needed. She dreaded giving her the bad news. As a last resort, she decided to call Catherine at home. Maybe she knew a way around the normal purchasing procedures. Toots scanned through her address book, searching for her number.

She picked up on the first ring.

"Catherine, it's Toots. I hate to bother you at home, but I'm desperate." Toots went into great detail about Mavis and her dilemma, even though Catherine was pretty much in the know since Mavis had been in her shop yesterday.

"Is there a way around this? Do you have any connections at all?" Toots said, practically begging.

The silence from the other end caused her nerves to twang like an out-of-tune piano.

"There might be a way, though I'm not sure if it's worth the effort," Catherine said.

"Something is better than nothing," Toots replied.

"Hear me out first," Catherine said. "I can't believe I'm about to say this, but I am. You never heard this from me. Is that going to present a problem?"

"Absolutely not. Shoot," Toots said.

"I can't believe I'm doing this, but I like your friend Mavis. I used to date a man by the name of Frank Dunhurst. We broke it off a year ago. Frank wanted to date other women at the same time, and I was not comfortable with that. To make a long story short, Frank was a major womanizer."

"Okayyy," Toots said, curious where this was leading.

"Frank is the head of security for Jay C.

King's," Catherine continued.

"I see." She didn't, but it was worth hearing her out. "How can this help Mavis?"

Toots heard Catherine's deep sigh over the phone. "Frank is easily distracted. If Mavis wanted to make the moves on him, she might distract him long enough for one of your friends to get in his pants. . . . No, I mean in his pants pockets to search for the keys. He works the night shift."

Toots couldn't believe what she was hearing. It wasn't out of the question yet. "So you're telling me we might have a chance to get our hands on the keys to this warehouse if we find someone who is willing to seduce Frank?"

An image of Ida flashed before her eyes. This might not be a bad idea, after all. It was risky, yes. She didn't have a clue as to how Mavis would get in and out of the warehouse with a few bolts of material, but that was just a minor detail. She now had a half-assed plan B. Sort of.

"That's exactly what I'm saying," Catherine said.

"Any clue how to do this?"

Catherine's laughter made her smile. "If you don't know by now, Toots, something's been missing in your life."

"I don't mean *that*. I meant how do we

170

get inside the warehouse to get to Frank? Mavis said you told her the security there was equivalent to that of Fort Knox. What do you propose we do? Blow the place up?"

More laughter. "Not exactly. I wouldn't want to see you and your friends spend the remainder of your lives in prison. Like I said, you will have to distract Frank. Do something to bring him to the front gate."

Toots had a vision of Ida driving the Town Car through the gates naked. Impossibility certainly wasn't out of the question anymore. Hell, they conversed with ghosts. A simple man should be a cinch.

"I'll think of something. Thanks, Catherine. You've helped, big-time. I owe you one," Toots said.

"Just don't help anyone else lose weight, or I'll be out of business. Remember, I cater to plus-size women," Catherine said.

"It's a deal. I've just sunk a ton of money into a new bakery. I'll see that my skinny friends visit often." Toots ended the call with a grin on her face as wide as Mavis's ass used to be. This was almost as thrilling as owning a tabloid newspaper. Maybe a bit more, if she were completely honest with herself.

A tabloid newspaper, a fashion designer, and a bakery. And she couldn't forget

Sophie. A medium. After all, she did speak to dead people. Never in a zillion years had she imagined her golden years would be quite this exciting. She realized now why they were called the golden years.

Downstairs, in the formal living room, Pete had set up four square tables. Where they came from she hadn't a clue and didn't care. He'd oiled and primed her three barely used sewing machines, placing each one on a table. He'd moved Mavis's machine downstairs so she could sew with the rest of them. It resembled a mini-factory, minus the sweaty, overworked, and underpaid laborers, although they might be sweaty and overworked before things were done, and three of them weren't getting paid anything at all.

Mavis and Sophie leaned over their machines, each with several colored straight pins hanging from her mouth. Coco's palace had been relocated next to the fireplace. Bernice went home for the night, explaining she was expecting a call from her one and only son. Toots knew the call would never come. That was another story, one that would only break poor Bernice's heart. One could always hope, Toots thought.

"Aren't we a bunch of busy little worker bees," Toots said as she observed Sophie

172

and Mavis at their machines.

Mavis removed the pins from her mouth. "Not for long. I only have enough material left to make one more complete outfit. Then I'm done. That will leave me about thirty more orders left to fill, unless a miracle happens. I'm going to have to refund these poor people their money. FedEx will pick up the orders I've filled first thing in the morning. After that, I guess I'll have to hang up my CLOSED sign," Mavis said.

"Not so fast. I just got off the phone with Catherine. She has an idea, and I think it might work, even if it's a long shot. Still, we have nothing to lose. You want to hear what it is?" Toots asked.

"Of course I want to hear it. If there's even the slightest chance that I can save my business, I want to hear it. What's the plan?" Mavis asked.

Toots seemed almost hesitant to tell her what Catherine had suggested. "This is way far off the mark, but I think it's doable. Sort of."

Sophie spit the pins out of her mouth and into her hand. "Then spit it out," Sophie said, laughing at her own play on words. "Don't keep us in suspense any longer."

"Where is Ida?"

"She's in her room, downloading the

South Carolina driver's manual from the Internet. She said she was going to start studying before she took driving lessons because she didn't want to appear stupid. Personally, I think it will take much more than a driving lesson to wipe the stupid off Ida's face." Sophie grinned.

"That's a mean thing to say," Mavis quipped.

"And you're looking at a very mean and evil woman," Toots said, sending daggers Sophie's way.

"Damn straight," Sophie said, still grinning.

"I know you're talking about me," Ida said as she marched into the formal living room. She held a stack of printed papers as thick as a phone book against her chest.

"You didn't say you were going to get *War and Peace.* I thought you were simply going to download a driving manual," Sophie said.

Ida plunked the stack of papers down on the end of the sofa. "This *is* the driving manual."

Now that three of the most important people in her life were gathered in her living room, Toots figured it was now or never. "I was just going to ask you to come downstairs. I have something I want to discuss with all of you."

"You bought another business?" Sophie teased.

Toots rolled her eyes. "No, I haven't bought another business, you silly ass. What do you think I am? Crazy?"

Sophie stopped the sewing machine long enough to look her directly in the face. "I didn't say that."

"You didn't have to. It's written all over your face. Besides, you're not a very good liar."

"The hell you say. I kept Walter's abuse hidden from you for most of my life. I did a lot of lying, scheming, and sneaking in my day, so do not tell me I'm not a good liar."

That immediately sobered Toots.

Poor Sophie. No wonder she was as hard as a coconut shell. She'd had a rough time for most of her married life, putting up her defenses, trying to get through each day without a slap on the face or a broken arm. Toots needed to remember that, and so did Ida and Mavis.

"Okay, you're an excellent liar. Are you satisfied?"

"Say what you have to say," Sophie said.

"Before I was so rudely interrupted, I was telling Mavis and Sophie I spoke with Catherine on the phone. Seems she used to date a guy named Frank Dunhurst, who's head of security at that warehouse that's holding Mavis's material hostage." Toots let her words sink in before she continued. "Apparently, Frank is a man whore."

All eyes focused on Ida.

"How dare you? I'm not a whore! I just happen to like men."

Sophie snickered. Mavis cupped a hand over her mouth. Toots simply rolled her eyes, praying they wouldn't get stuck in an east-west position.

"The truth hurts," Sophie teased.

"Enough already!" Toots shouted, her frustration level way too high. It was a good thing she didn't have a weapon close by, or she would've conked Sophie on the head or smacked her in her mouth.

Toots placed both hands on her hips. "If you all want to help Mavis, you better listen up!"

CHAPTER 16

"Let's not argue. Tell me what Catherine suggested," Mavis said.

"As I was explaining before I was so rudely interrupted by Sophie, Catherine used to date this Frank, who just so happens to be head of security for Mr. King. Ida, this might be where you come in handy, so please don't take it personally. Apparently Frank is something of a ladies' man. Catherine says he's an easy mark. Now, you all know I swore off men the day I buried Leland, that cheapskate. I don't know if any man would get near Sophie with a ten-foot pole given that mean, crude mouth of hers. And, Mavis, I'm not sure you're skilled enough to pull off what we need to do in order to get Frank to open the doors to that warehouse."

Toots looked at all the women gathered in her living room. Never had she seen a more shocked group of women, minus Sophie, than she did at this exact moment.

Ida was the first to speak up. "I know what you're thinking, and yes, I'll do whatever it is, within reason, of course, to help Mavis. Just for the record, I want you all to know that I have sworn off men since that ordeal with that . . . pervert."

Toots knew how to butter Ida's bread. She was about to add a layer of very sweet honey on top, with an extra pat of butter. "I'm sure you have." Again, it took all of Toots's willpower not to roll her eyes at Ida's words.

Toots went on to say, "Out of the four of us, you're the prettiest, the best dressed, the most sophisticated. You know your way around a man. I mean . . . men are putty in your hands. Catherine is a very beautiful woman herself, and I've known her for years. She wouldn't go out with a slob, or a man who is what we might deem unattractive. If you're willing to take a chance, then we need to formalize plan B."

"Just tell me what I need to do," Ida said.

Toots held her palm out in front of her. "Don't even go there, Sophie."

Sophie crammed the gray material underneath the sewing machine needle. With her right foot, she pushed the pedal as fast as it would go. When she'd ripped about a foot of material through the sewing machine's sharp needle, she pulled the cloth out, bit the thread off, then tossed a finished skirt onto the sofa. "I haven't said a word."

Mavis spoke up. "Just tell us the plan. If there is the slightest hope that I can get these orders finished within, say, a week max, then I will be okay. I have a disclaimer on my Web site that says, 'Allow ten to fourteen days for delivery.' I haven't had the need to make use of the allotted time, but as I said, if there's the slightest chance I can get that material, I'll take it."

Toots had the glimmerings of a plan in her mind. "Let's go into the kitchen. I'll make a pot of coffee. Mavis, run upstairs and get my laptop. Sophie, open a fresh pack of cigarettes. Ida, find the sexiest outfit you own. This is going to be a long night."

Ten minutes later, they were gathered around the kitchen table, which seemed to be the center of all their gatherings — sort of like a command center. Toots booted up her laptop and downloaded the latest version of Google Earth.

"To get started, I'll need an address. Mavis?"

Mavis held out a slip of paper with the address for the warehouse written in capital letters. Toots clicked away at the computer keyboard and within seconds had a satellite view of the building. She moved the mouse around, clicked several times, bringing the warehouse into full view. Having used Google Earth in the past, Toots was quite familiar with its contents. She wiggled the mouse around again, and this time a date appeared on the bottom corner of the computer's monitor. It revealed the satellite image was only three weeks old, which was as good as could reasonably be expected. Better, even.

"See this?" Toots positioned her laptop so the others could see what she was looking at. A perfectly clear image of the locked gate filled the computer screen. "We have to get this close in order to make this work." Toots allowed the women time to absorb what they were looking at. "This is where I'm supposed to say I'm open for suggestions."

"Why not just have Ida throw herself at the man? She's an expert at that," Sophie said. "All you have to do is stand outside the gate, shake your ass, act like you're lost. Men love it when you ask them for directions. You'll have Frank eating out of your hand in a minute flat."

Ida raised a sculpted brow in Sophie's direction. "You seem to know all the answers. Why don't you try to seduce this Frank?"

"I'm too ugly, remember? Besides, I hate men," Sophie remembered to add. "Not that I'm a lesbian or anything."

"Who said you were ugly?" Toots asked as she homed in on the image. She clicked a few more keys, then saved the image in a .jpg file. "There!"

"Walter used to tell me that all the time. Why? Does it matter?"

Toots looked away from the computer. "It must matter to you if it's coming out of your mouth, Sophie. And just for the record, you aren't the least bit ugly. Walter was an ugly, mean man. He was miserable in his own skin and wanted to take it out on you. He isn't even a decent ghost."

Sophie smiled, and this time it reached her dark brown eyes. "That's why you're my best friend, Toots. You sure know how to make a gal feel good about herself. Even though I don't believe one freaking word of what you just said."

"How is it we always get distracted from the matter at hand?" Toots asked no one in particular. "We're supposed to be working on plan B."

"Yes, and we don't have all night, either," Mavis added. "I mean . . . we're going to do this tonight, aren't we?"

Toots hadn't thought that far ahead, but

Mavis was right. If they were going to plan a seduction, what better time than late on a Friday night?

"Ida, what about it?" Toots asked. She looked at her watch. "In an hour, can you be ready to . . . lay it on thick?"

"I'll make sure I'm ready in an hour," Ida said smugly. Without another word, Ida walked out of the kitchen, her head held as high as the queen of England held hers. Reminded Toots of Coco, too. Queen of all canines, or at least she thought she was.

After Ida left the room, Sophie spoke up. "It really doesn't make any sense. We can't just drop Ida off like some Forty-second Street prostitute and expect her to know exactly what bolts of material Mavis will need, how much, where it's located, yada yada yada." Sophie lifted her hands up in the air and made quote signs with her index fingers.

"Like I said, I haven't gotten that far. I'm open for suggestions." Toots clicked the computer keyboard, closing the Google Earth program.

"I don't know where the fabric is, either," Mavis said.

"What you're saying is, we're going to have to get inside that warehouse, and you're going to have to have what? Fifteen minutes, possibly thirty minutes to search for this particular material?" Toots asked.

Suddenly, Mavis seemed unsure of herself, as if she'd really bitten off more than she could chew. "I didn't think that far ahead. Is there any way we could ask this Frank where that particular material is located?" Mavis asked skeptically.

Mavis was extremely naive, Toots thought. "I don't know. I think this is going to be one of those play-it-by-ear deals. Between me and Sophie and you, we should be able to locate this precious fabric in what? Fifteen minutes?"

"You're willing to go to all this trouble just for me? Good God Almighty! You know we could get caught. What if we get caught and go to jail?"

"Then I will simply call Chris and have him bail our asses out," Toots replied. "I do have mucho millions . . . scattered about. It's a shame I can't just walk up and purchase some bolts of material."

"I wonder if Calvin Klein had to go to such lengths to buy denim for those jeans that Brooke Shields posed in all those years ago. Remember that?" Mavis asked.

"Yes, I do. Wasn't there something about she didn't let anything come between her and her Calvin Klein jeans? Wasn't she supposed to be going without her underwear or some silly thing?" Toots said.

"Yes, it was something to that effect. I could never go without my undergarments," Mavis added as an afterthought. "Then again, I'm not Brooke Shields."

"I don't think you'll have to worry about that, Mavis," Toots said. "Right now we need to get our asses prepared and get to that warehouse, or you're going to totally lose what ass you have left."

An hour later, they were cruising down Meeting Street Road in North Charleston. Just to avoid any slipups, Toots had programmed her handheld GPS with the address. So far so good.

Ida had truly dressed for the part. She wore a slinky black dress that hugged her curves in all the right places and a pair of spiked black heels that made her almost as tall as Toots. There weren't many women at sixty-five who could come close to pulling this off. But Ida could; she was a well-preserved sixty-five. They circled the block three times before locating a man walking the perimeter of the large warehouse. They assumed it was Frank. Sophie had brought her portable digital recorder along just in case they needed it.

"Set that recorder so I can get a close-up

view of Frank. I just want to make sure he's not ugly and has his own teeth," Ida said excitedly.

Sophie fiddled with the small recorder, then gave it to Ida. "You promised Mavis you would go through with this. If he's ugly, then you just have to deal with it. Close your eyes and pretend he's . . . Jerry!" Sophie cajoled.

Ida held the small recorder up to her eye and focused on the man in the distance. "Not bad, or at least not that I can tell from this distance." Ida angled the recorder lower, then refocused. "His ass doesn't look too bad, either."

"Once a slut always a slut," Sophie said.

Ida lowered the recorder and placed it on the seat beside her. "If I hadn't promised Mavis I would do this, I would knock you right upside your head with this stupid recorder. I'm not a slut. I can't help it if men fall all over me. I think you're just jealous. You've only been with that old drunk Walter. You wouldn't know a real man if he slapped you in the face," Ida said.

As soon as the words came out of her mouth, Ida wished she could recall them. Walter had spent most of their married life doing just that, and he was anything but a man. Ida would take whatever Sophie slung

185

back at her. She truly deserved it this time around, but Sophie didn't take the bait.

It was after midnight; the sun had long set. Toots parked the sleek car under a grove of trees across the street from the warehouse. Birdsong, cricket chirps, and the occasional croak of a frog harmonized in the background. The slight scent of horse dung permeated the night air. Apparently Charleston's famous carriage rides had a stable nearby.

"You two cannot be in close confines for more than a minute without arguing," Toots commented. "You're worse than two kids in the backseat on a long road trip."

Pouting, Ida said, "She called me a slut."

"I know. You should be used to it by now. Sophie has the class of a horse's ass. At times," Toots added hastily.

"Speaking of horses, what is that smell?" Sophie asked, her nose crinkling up in distaste.

"It's probably your upper lip," Ida informed her.

As was becoming the norm, they all burst out laughing.

"Maybe those tourist companies should consider a new hybrid bus. That smell of horse manure is taking the 'Go Green' thing a bit far," Toots said.

They remained in the car for thirty minutes, paying close attention to Frank and his movements. The next time he circled the warehouse and stopped by the gate, Ida would make her move. Because she wore a sexy black dress, they'd decided she needed a plausible, yet sympathetic story to feed Frank. Ida could do this; Toots just knew it.

They all stared ahead, waiting for Frank. When they saw him round the corner, Toots whispered, "It's showtime."

CHAPTER 17

Anticipation and a sense of excitement invaded the vehicle. Quietly, so as not to reveal them, Toots opened the driver's side door, then instructed Ida to open her door. Mavis and Sophie crawled out of the backseat like two teenagers sneaking out of the window on a Saturday night. Spurts of laughter could be heard by anyone close enough.

"Okay, there he is!" Toots whispered, pointing toward the man they were assuming was Frank. If Abby ever got wind of this, she would disown her as a mother; Toots was sure of it. "Are you sure you want to do this?"

"Of course. I wouldn't be here otherwise." Ida sashayed away from the car, stopping when she reached the edge of the street.

Toots, Sophie, and Mavis followed close behind.

"This is the worst plan B I've ever heard

of," Sophie whispered. "If we get caught, that means we're no better than common thieves. I can't believe I'm actually a part of this."

"Be quiet, or we will get caught. I brought ten thousand dollars in cash. It's right here." Toots patted the fanny pack strapped around her waist like armor. "Mavis, you said this was three times what your cost would be if you were to purchase the amount of material you need, right?"

Softly, Mavis said, "Yes, and I promise to pay you back."

Toots waved her hand in the air. "Forget it. Look." She pointed to Ida across the street. She was leaning against the fence, pretending to cry. They could hear her caterwauling from their position behind a large oak tree.

"She's good. I'll give her that," Sophie said in admiration. "Just don't tell her I said that, or I'll have to kill you."

"Shh, let's watch." Toots nodded toward the fence, where a man, the man they were all assuming was Frank and were counting on to be horny enough to drop his pants for Ida, stood on the opposite side of the fence.

Ida's crying turned into hiccups.

They watched.

Ida shook her head left to right, then up

and down. The man, Frank, passed what appeared to be a piece of tissue through the holes in the fence. He had manners. Chalk up one point in his favor. Ida took the tissue, then blew her nose so loudly, Toots was sure she'd blown her adenoids straight into outer space, crashing into the satellite used by Google Earth. She smiled at the visual.

Frank removed a large ring of keys clipped onto the side of his belt. He inserted a key in the lock and pulled the large gate inward toward the building. As instructed, Ida placed herself in the position where if the gate were to close, she would be squashed. Frank's head bobbed up and down like a toy dunking bird's. Her dress was so low cut, it was a miracle her boobs hadn't slapped against Frank's chest. Ida inched closer to Frank, her boobs mere inches from him. Toots was hoping he would look down, but he didn't. Ida shifted herself so she was almost touching Frank. She started crying again, only this time she wrapped her arms around Frank's neck, as though all strength had been sucked away from her. Then, the second Frank's arms encircled her waist, she instantly went limp.

"She *is* good," Toots whispered. "Watch for the signal."

The words were no sooner out of Toots's

mouth when they spotted Ida's right hand waving behind Frank.

"Let's go," Toots said. "Sophie, keep your mouth quiet."

Sophie nodded.

They trotted across the street, darting behind trees and shrubbery. When they had a clear run for the open fence, they stopped. This was only phase one of plan B. Ida had yet to get the keys.

They waited while Ida continued to bawl like a baby. At least five minutes passed before they heard the rattle of keys as they slapped against the dirt near where they were standing. With a Mini Maglite, Toots searched the ground in front of her. Spying the keys, she scooped them up, put them in her pocket, and motioned for the girls to follow her.

Ida had Frank plastered against the fence, her face covering his. Toots couldn't tell where Ida started and Frank ended. This was a good thing.

"Okay, ladies, it's now or never," Toots said.

Running like a one-legged man being chased by the bulls in Pamplona, Toots, Sophie, and thank-god-she-was-slender-now Mavis hoofed it across the street and inside the fenced area.

Not knowing how long Ida could keep Frank smashed against the fence, they skirted the edge of the warehouse until they found the door from which Frank had exited. Toots jostled the keys, inserting one after the other until she finally located the key that turned the lock.

Once inside, she removed her fanny pack, preparing to leave it in place of the material they were taking. Stealing. Toots hadn't ever stooped this low. She had to keep reminding herself it was for Mavis, who was the doer of good deeds personified. And not really stealing — maybe. More like an unconventional form of bartering, except that in this case it was greenbacks for cloth rather than tomatoes for tonsillectomies. Toots was sure that those Republican congressmen who had been all over the cable news shows would be very proud of them.

Inside, they were surrounded by bolt after bolt of brightly colored material. A man-made rainbow.

With their lights held out in front of them, Toots, Sophie, and Mavis scanned row after row of cloth.

"Two minutes more, and we're outta here," Toots whispered.

When she heard Mavis shout *"Yes!"* she knew she'd located what they had come for.

Toots and Sophie raced through the warehouse, searching for Mavis.

"Over here!" Mavis called out. "Hurry!"

With fear as their motivator, they each grabbed two bolts of the gray material, stuffing one under each arm. Toots dropped the fanny pack with the ten thousand dollars in their place. This might not be the most conventional thing to do, but sometimes you had to do what was right and convention be damned. At least that was what she told herself as she raced outside into the chilly night air with two bolts of fabric tucked under her arms. With Sophie and Mavis following closely on her heels, Toots made it across the street to the Lincoln in record time.

Huffing and puffing, she tossed the bolts of cloth in the backseat. Three seconds later, Mavis and Sophie followed suit. Once they managed to catch their breath, they piled inside the car. Dear, sweet little Mavis had had the foresight to pack a cooler filled with bottled water.

"Here." Mavis handed Toots two icy cold bottles of water. Toots gave one to Sophie.

Other than the sound of three women chugging water, the night was eerily silent. This was the part of plan B that required total improvisation. Given Ida's past history, she might spend the entire night sucking face with Frank.

Toots couldn't visualize Ida with a blue-collar worker — no way, nohow. Spending most of her life as a New York socialite clinging to Thomas's side whenever she could as his career as a medical supply magnate took him all over the world, Ida had always been clingy and needy, hence her constant desire for a man. Toots had never really cared for Thomas that much, thought him arrogant and self-righteous. But in reality, he was a perfect match for Ida, but Toots always suspected he had a woman in every port, like Alec Guinness in *The Captain's Paradise*.

The gate remained open while Toots, Sophie, and Mavis waited patiently for Ida to either finish her seduction or suddenly discover that she was "not that kind of girl."

The thought was so fleeting that it had no sooner come to mind than Ida plumped herself down in the passenger's seat. "Oh my gosh! That man has the worst breath I've ever smelled. I don't think I'll ever kiss a man again. Mavis, I just want you to know that your obsession with good deeds has ruined any future I might've had with a man."

Toots started the engine and eased the

large vehicle away from the grove of trees, hopefully undetected. "I want to hear all about it. How in the world did you manage to keep him smashed against that fence for so long?" Toots pushed the washer-fluid button, squirting window cleaner on the windshield. Hundreds of tiny bugs were clinging to the glass. She hit the wiper button and sent the bug carcasses to bug heaven.

"Yeah, I'd like to hear this, too. Maybe an old one-man woman like me could learn a few tricks. It's not like I'm dead. Who knows? I may hook up with a ghost," Sophie quipped.

They all laughed.

"Ida, I will do whatever you need to make this up to you. I feel simply terrible. I imagine dear Herbert is flipping over in his grave now." Mavis pretended to genuflect.

"I'll think of something, I'm sure," Ida said. "He was exactly as your friend Catherine said. A dirty old man. Never in my life have I smelled such horrid breath."

"You already told us that. Okay, his breath stank. Now tell us how far you let him go," Sophie said. "This reminds me of our high-school days. Remember how we always asked Ida how far she let 'that boy' go?" Sophie cackled.

"At least I had dates. That's more than I can say for you," Ida shot back.

"Unlike you, I had to work. Quit stalling and tell us the details."

"All right. I told him my fiancé tossed me out of the car because I wouldn't have sex with him in the cab of his truck. He said I didn't look like the type of lady that would ride in a truck, let alone have sex in one. Of course, he knew right then that I was a sophisticated woman with class, or at least that's what he said. You might want to take note of that, Sophie. With your vulgar mouth, you'll never catch a decent man. You remind me of a neighbor I had in New York City. Her name was Marsha. She dressed like a dime-store hooker and had the mouth of a truck driver."

"I'll go with the trucker. I have a foul mouth, but the hooker, you might want to rethink that. And who knows? Maybe I'd like a sleazy security guard with bad breath," Sophie singsonged.

"That is your type," Ida replied.

"Knock it off, you two," Toots called out. "I'm trying to concentrate on my driving."

"Frank was like putty in my hands. After I fed him that silly sob story, he wrapped his arms around my neck. I started kissing him, and he obviously kissed me back, bad breath

196

and all. He tried to put his hands down my dress. I told him it was too soon, that I wasn't that kind of girl. Over the next twenty minutes I did nothing but kiss and gag, making sure to keep my hands running through his hair, very close to his ears. When I heard you guys running, I suddenly feigned an attack of conscience. I told him I had to get back to my fiancé. He was reluctant to let me go. So I gave him Sophie's cell phone number."

Again, the four women giggled until their sides hurt.

"I don't believe that," Sophie said.

Ida laughed, hearty and loud, something she rarely did. "Oh yes, I did. What's that saying about revenge? Getting even is only half the fun."

Thirty minutes later, Toots drove down the winding road leading to her home. They'd left the lights on and the windows open. She pulled in front of the house, not bothering to park the car in the garage. As they got out of the car, they could hear Coco barking like an attack dog.

"Maybe that pooch is smarter than I thought," Sophie said. "She senses danger."

Mavis raced ahead to the front door. "That's not a danger bark. That's an I-need-to-go-outside bark."

CHAPTER 18

Bernice arrived at 4:00 AM, only to discover Sophie, Mavis, and Toots gathered in the formal living room, their sewing machines humming away. Coffee lingered in the air, and someone had made toast. Bernice could smell it.

"What in the world are you doing up early, sewing? You keep straining your eyes like that, and you'll all be blind before you reach the ripe old age of seventy."

Toots looked up from her sewing. "We just started an hour ago. We all woke up early and decided to get started. The post office closes at noon, and these packages have to go out this morning. We figured the more we had ready to ship, the happier Mavis's customers will be. Plus, I promised Jamie I would bring you all down to the bakery for a treat. She's been dying to meet you."

Bernice shook her head from side to side. "No way, José. I saw what happened to that fat man. I'll stay here and have a bowl of Froot Loops, thank you very much."

Toots rolled her eyes. "If that old building is haunted, which I seriously doubt, it isn't her doing. The building was left to her by her grandmother. She's simply a young woman trying to make a living. And she certainly doesn't look like a witch. She's a blond-haired, blue-eyed pixie. You will all adore her. She kind of reminds me of Abby."

"Then I can't wait to meet her," Mavis said. "I might even try one of those pralines you're so fond of."

"Have you talked to your daughter since you purchased this . . . sweet shop?" Bernice asked. "She might want to know what her mother is up to."

Toots hadn't, but she would. "Abby is busy running a newspaper right now. I'll call her this afternoon, after I take Mavis in to see Joe." Something told her Abby and Chris would be just fine without her right now. Call it a mother's intuition. Toots would know if Abby needed her; plus she would call. She was a smart girl. *Just like her mother,* Toots thought and laughed out loud just as Ida came downstairs and joined the others.

"Mind telling us what you're laughing at?"

Ida said, a slight tilt to her perfectly shaped mouth.

"I was thinking about Abby and Chris. There's a spark between those two, just like there was between John and me."

"I sensed that, too," Mavis said. "Chris is such a sweet boy. I think he would make a suitable mate for Abby, don't you?"

Sophie sputtered and sputtered, coffee flying all over the piece of material she had on her lap. "Earth to Mavis. This is the twenty-first century. You sound like someone from the eighteen hundreds. 'A suitable mate.' "

Mavis mopped up the spill with a baby wipe, a trick she had learned from George. Said it was an old secret in the dry cleaning business. And all this time they'd been spending a small fortune on dry cleaning, Sophie thought, when a three-dollar box of baby wipes would do the trick.

"You know what I mean," Mavis said sweetly.

"I've always hoped they would get together," Toots said.

"Something tells me you might just get your wish," Ida added. "I've seen the way they look at each other."

"Stay in touch with your daughter," Bernice said, then scurried out of the living room and into the kitchen.

Immediately, Toots knew why Bernice was so abrupt. As usual, her son had never called. She found her in the kitchen, scrubbing countertops that were already spotless.

"He didn't call, did he?"

"Does he ever?" Bernice continued to scrub the counters with a vengeance. "I never thought he would act this way, turn on his very own mother. Well, maybe that's the wrong way of saying it. He just plain forgot about me. Running all over the country, trying to find himself? I wonder how many trips it's gonna take before he learns that he is who he is no matter where he goes."

Toots grabbed a pack of cigarettes off the table. She opened the back door, then lit up in the kitchen, something she rarely did. Bernice needed to talk, and she needed to smoke. Concessions must always be made for whatever the circumstance.

Toots inhaled, loving every ounce of nicotine that ruined her lungs. "It's his generation. They're strange. Family and home don't mean as much to them as it did to our generation. Even Abby couldn't wait to escape to the big city after she graduated from college. I guess what I'm trying to say is, take what you can get, when you can get it, because I don't see future generations making a change."

Bernice nodded. "You're right. I'll be okay. I just need a while to pout, bitch, moan, and groan. I'm at the I-feel-sorry-for-myself stage now. I'll be fine. Go on and help Mavis finish those clothes. I'll bring in fresh coffee when it's ready."

Toots knew she'd been dismissed from her own kitchen, but that was okay. It was Bernice's way. They'd been friends since Abby was five. They were more than friends, Toots thought as she went back to the formal living room. They were family.

The next five hours they stitched, pressed, and packed. They had more than enough material to fill Mavis's orders, but not enough womanpower. Toots suggested Mavis contact a manufacturing company, because something told her Good Mourning was going to be big, very big. Mavis said she had a few contacts in California. After seeing forty-seven more orders on the Web site that morning, Toots figured she'd better start making phone calls. As much as she wanted to jump in, this was Mavis's gig. She'd fronted her the ten thousand dollars, but Toots knew as soon as Mavis had the cold, hard cash in hand, she would return the money. For Mavis, it was a matter of pride, so Toots would accept the money, albeit reluctantly.

Now, if they got away with stealing the material, they would be good to go. Toots was afraid to listen to the local news for fear their theft would show up on it. Telling herself to forget about it, she put last night's wild, crazy event behind her. She had places to go and things to do.

At ten, they had the boxes packed and ready to be taken to the post office. That left them all an hour to shower and change and get ready for the ride into Charleston. Toots couldn't wait for Jamie to meet her dearest friends, and she couldn't wait for those dearest friends to meet her new business partner.

With a stop to deliver the packages to the post office, it was past lunchtime by the time they arrived at The Sweetest Things. Unlike her last visit, Toots viewed the bakery with the eye of a partner instead of the consumer. Half a dozen customers lingered around the display case. Melted butter, sugar, and rising dough gave off a pleasing scent. When Jamie saw her and her friends, she came flying out of the kitchen, flour dusting the bridge of her nose and cheeks. Her hair stuck up in tufts like tiny bird feathers. Her blue eyes sparkled like sapphires.

"These must be the godmothers. I've heard so much about all of you."

Toots made quick work of introducing her friends to Jamie. Once they'd all gotten past the introduction and formalities, Jamie sat them down and served them her most delectable pastries, petits fours, and pralines. Sticking to her die-hard rules, Mavis had only one praline. Toots had three pralines, two chocolate-chip cookies, one slice of red velvet cake, and a large glass of milk. This place would ruin her figure if she stuck around. Being a silent partner was a very wise decision on her part. As much as she loved sweets, she would be like the blueberry girl in *Willy Wonka & the Chocolate Factory.*

After they finished gorging themselves on Jamie's pastries, she showed them the kitchen, then showed Toots the books, the dollars coming in, and what was going out, plus what her future expectations were. She was pleased with the figures so far, even though it had been only a day since word started circulating via the grapevine that the fat man had had clogged arteries and had acted against doctor's orders by even being in line at the bakery while awaiting surgery to open those same arteries up. All things considered, Toots was very satisfied with her decision to buy into the bakery. Her gut told her she was straight on.

"Jamie, you're the best baker in the world, but don't be offended if I don't show up too often. Another day like this, and I'll turn into a diabetic."

Jamie gave Toots a hug, thanked her several times for her trust and support, and gave Sophie, Mavis, and Ida hugs as well before they left. Knowing they wouldn't have an opportunity to do this anytime in the near future, Toots decided to take her friends on a tour of Charleston. She drove through the Battery, down Rainbow Row, and ended at the slave market. She parked the car, and for the next three hours they roamed through the stalls, buying all sorts of silly things. Mavis bought three bottles of hot sauce, telling them hot sauce acted as an appetite suppressant. Sophie bought a deck of tarot cards, and Ida purchased a sleep shirt, a tacky purse, and a silver necklace she knew would turn her neck green within an hour of putting it on. Toots bought nothing. *Been there, done that,* she thought.

On the ride home, they were all quiet, each lost in her own thoughts. Sophie had another séance planned for that night. She promised that this time they wouldn't be disappointed.

Chapter 19

As Sophie, Toots, Ida, and Mavis prepared for the evening's séance, a hint of trepidation filled the air.

"I'm not sure if we should go through with this. If we're able to contact spirits, and they have the ability to manipulate the objects around us, I'm afraid something might go horribly wrong," Ida said as they placed the candles around the table.

"You're the one who wanted to make contact with Thomas. This was your idea. I'm just the medium, that's all," Sophie said.

"But what if what he said was true? What if he was really poisoned by something other than tainted meat? Then what?" Ida asked.

"Then I will call Chris. He won't laugh at us. He's seen what's gone on at the beach house. It's too bad all that expensive equipment Sophie invested a small fortune in didn't reveal anything. If it had, we'd have our own TV reality show by now," Toots said.

"Are you sure this is safe? I wouldn't want to open any of those . . . portals you two are always discussing," Ida said.

"You read my mind, Ida," Sophie said. "I called the woman in California who I bought the book from, and I told her our situation. She gave me some advice. In the book it says we have the ability to contact a specific spirit. We need to eliminate the chance that it could harm us. Even if the person was family in life, he or she could be malicious in death. The book has specific instructions on how to make sure that if any spirits come through, they will not be able to harm us."

"How do we do that?" Ida asked.

"In the book, there is a chant we can say to assure that no spirits harm us and only come forth with good intent," Sophie explained.

"What is it? Something like 'Dear dead people, please don't choke us to death'?" Toots said, laughing.

"No, it's nothing like that. It's whatever we want it to be. Just consider it something like a prayer that protects us from evil and evil actions," Sophie explained again. She was so serious that the others blinked. This

209

was a different Sophie.

Ida lit the candle in front of her and placed it in the center of the table. "I'm hesitant to believe that, but the book did work last time, so I'm willing to give it a shot. Maybe this will set my mind at ease."

"Sophie, do you think you could add something to the effect of 'Please don't mess with my clothing, since I don't want to ruin any more mourning clothes,'" Mavis pleaded.

"We don't need to wear mourning clothes this time around," Sophie told her. "Just remember, this is something I've never tried before. Again, you all have to be willing to have the bejesus scared out of you."

"You're so eloquent," Toots said. "Are you sure you know what you're doing?"

"Yes, I'm sure, or at least as sure as one can be given the circumstances. You don't have to sit here and participate. I'm not going to force you. If you're chicken, then just leave. Frankly, I think we should expect just about anything. Remember, we are here to contact Thomas. We want to find out who and why and if he was murdered. We might not like what we hear. He could've been murdered by someone we know, possibly someone in this room." Sophie cast an evil eye in Ida's direction.

"Don't even say that!" Ida exclaimed. "As far as I'm concerned, Thomas died of food poisoning. If anything other than that happened, I certainly had no involvement. I can't believe you would even think such a thing, let alone say it."

"I know you didn't kill Thomas. I just think we need to get ahold of our emotions until we're finished. No matter how upsetting it can get, we need to hold ourselves together so we can find out the truth," Sophie said seriously.

Mavis walked around the room, checking the candles, closing the drapes, and making sure the air conditioner vents were directed away from the table. "Okay, Sophie, it's set up the same way as before. Are you ready to do this?"

They each took their usual seats around the table, all traces of their earlier silliness locked away. Though this had started out as fun and games, it had turned into something very serious and possibly very scary.

"This is something new I'm going to try, so don't laugh," Sophie said. "In order to communicate with Thomas in a way we can understand him, the book says we should use a method known as psychic writing."

"What the hell is psychic writing?" Toots asked.

"Well, it's where a loved one of the deceased concentrates and thinks of the person she wishes to communicate with while holding a pencil and scribbling in circles on a piece of paper. The book says that if the spirit comes through, it has the ability to manipulate the writing and get its message across. Ida, that means you're going to have to do this. Are you up for this?"

"Yes I'm up for it, but I'm hesitant to think that it will work. What am I supposed to write so that the spirit will guide my hand and deliver a message?" Ida asked.

"*You* don't write anything at all. *You* just need to concentrate and scribble in circles. *The spirit* will channel his or her energy into you, and it's supposed to trigger your subconscious into writing the message. We just need a pad of paper and a pencil. The book says that the graphite in the pencil helps energy flow through you and allows the spirit to communicate in words rather than moving water glasses."

"This might sound crazy, but it just might work. I have a leather binder that belonged to Thomas. He took it everywhere with him on his business trips. I even think there's some old paper left in there. If he's going to come through, that definitely would be the object he would write on. He used to sit in bed at night dictating notes for his secretary to type."

"That's not a bad idea. Why don't you run upstairs and find that? Then we'll get started," Sophie suggested, displaying none of the goofiness and sarcasm involved in her normal way of communicating. This was becoming more important to her. If she could help those on the other side, then she was going to do everything in her power to do just that. Maybe this was her true calling in life. And hadn't Madame Butterfly told her she had a gift?

Sophie flipped through her guidebook while waiting for Ida to locate Thomas's binder. Mavis ran to the kitchen to check on Coco. Toots reclined in her chair, looking as relaxed as a cat sunning herself in the window on a warm day.

"Here it is." Worn, aged from years of use, the leather-bound binder still held several sheets of legal paper. Once yellow, these had whitened with age, the paper now brittle and delicate.

"Is everyone ready to get started?" Sophie looked at Ida, then at Mavis, and lastly at Toots as they returned to the séance room. All three nodded in the affirmative.

"We need to hold hands. Ida, you just hold Mavis's hand and keep the pencil in your right hand. When we are finished with our protection prayer, start scribbling in circles and don't look at the pad no matter what happens," Sophie instructed.

Ida reached for Mavis with her left hand while holding the pencil in her right hand. Sophie reached for Toots's left hand, while Toots linked her right hand with Mavis's left hand. Once they were in position, Sophie began her prayer.

"To our highest power, we ask for your protection from benevolent spirits, and ask St. Michael the Archangel to watch over us and protect us from malevolent spirits who might want to inflict harm upon us. We are here to summon the spirit of Thomas McGullicutty." Sophie bowed her head as she spoke.

"Thomas, we received your message, and we know your death is suspicious. We are here tonight to find out what caused your early exit from this earthly realm and sent you into the afterlife before your time." Sophie began to chant in a whisper, "Please help us help you. Please help us help you."

The others caught on quickly and began to chant. "Please help us help you." They repeated this several times. Ida's hand poised on the paper, she began to scribble, her eyes closed.

"Thomas, if you have a message for us, please come forward," Sophie said in a soft voice. So out of character was her behavior that Toots opened her eyes just to make sure it was really Sophie speaking in such soft, melodic tones. It was.

Sophie continued to request that Thomas make an appearance. "You've appeared to us before. You must have a reason now. You can reveal the cause of your death. Tell us now so we may be able to find justice for you and you can have peace."

Toots peeked at Sophie again. She was into this. Big-time. And it was scary. Big-time.

"Oh my gosh!" Ida cried, scaring them all. "I feel like . . . like someone has plugged me into an electrical outlet!"

In a low, almost seductive tone, Sophie said, "Focus, Ida. Focus on Thomas. Keep your mind open."

Ida nodded. "I feel some type of supernatural energy rushing through me." Continuing to keep her eyes closed, she scribbled in circles.

"Continue to think about Thomas," Sophie encouraged.

Ida's hand went wild across the paper. She was writing so fast, Sophie was afraid she might be pretending just for show. Then she saw the terror on her friend's face and realized that not only was Ida afraid, but she no longer had control of her hand. That was beyond anything she'd expected.

Suddenly, the temperature in the room dropped at least twenty degrees. Someone not of this world was definitely in the room with them. Sophie opened her eyes and scanned the room. Though she couldn't actually see anything, she could feel a spirit. It was an unhappy spirit.

Ida suddenly began to write in a precise motion. Left to right. Left to right. Sophie peered at the paper. The words *It's Thomas* were slashed across the page at least a dozen times, if not more. She took a deep breath. *This is truly serious,* she thought. *Okay, I can do this.*

"Thomas, thank you for making yourself known. We know your death was unexpected. Is there something you want to tell Ida?" Sophie paused, waiting for a response.

Ida's writing slowed; then suddenly she began to write so fast, the sharp edge of the pencil tore the page. Not wanting to lose a word, Sophie quickly slipped a fresh sheet of paper in place of the tattered one.

In a quick fluid motion Ida started writing again. *My Daughter. My Daughter. My Daughter.* Over and over, Ida continued to write these words.

"Thomas, do you know who poisoned you?" Sophie asked. She peered at the sheet of paper. Ida was still writing the words *My Daughter. My Daughter. My Daughter.*

Quietly, so low they could barely hear her, Ida said, "I can feel the energy leaving my body. Ask. Him. Who. Killed. Him." Ida spoke each word as though it were painful, as if she were struggling to speak.

Sophie caught Toots's attention. She mouthed, "We need to stop."

Toots nodded in agreement.

"Thomas, you may leave now. We have your message. We will speak to you again." She almost said, "We come in peace," but decided this was too serious for her offbeat humor.

Ida's hand went limp, as though the bone had simply liquefied. The pencil fell out of her grasp, rolling to the floor.

Mavis gasped, jumping out of her chair and knocking over the candle in front of her. Ida went completely limp, falling back into the chair's cushions. Toots ran around the table, hoping to catch Ida in case she started to fall. Sophie grabbed the papers Ida had written on before they were destroyed.

Tonight they'd opened a doorway.

Exactly where it would lead them, they had no clue.

CHAPTER 20

Bernice picked the perfect day to stay home. After Saturday night's creep show, Toots didn't want her there. She didn't want to be responsible for causing her to have a heart attack.

They'd actually had to use smelling salts to bring Ida out of whatever sort of trance she'd been in. She swore she had no memory of writing, no memory of passing out. Toots wasn't sure if she believed her or not. What she was sure of was that there was nothing funny about it anymore. It was all too real.

Toots finished making the first pot of coffee, then stepped outside for a smoke. She and Sophie hadn't been smoking nearly as much as they normally did, which was probably a good thing. Even though she liked to smoke, she knew it wasn't healthy. At sixty-five, almost sixty-six, Toots figured quitting at this stage of the game would be nothing more than slow torture.

"What are you doing up so early?" Sophie asked.

Toots almost jumped out of her skin. "Damn you! Don't you ever sneak up on me like that again. And for your information, I get up at five every day, sometimes earlier. I'm smoking."

"Well don't be stingy," Sophie said.

Toots removed a cigarette from the package and lit it with the tip of her own. She passed the cigarette to Sophie.

For once, they were quiet, each lost in her own thoughts. The previous night still lingered in the early morning air. It was as if Thomas were still lurking around, just waiting for their next move.

They sat that way for a few minutes longer; then Toots stood and stretched. "I'm going inside. The coffee is ready."

Sophie followed her back to the kitchen. "Pour me a cup, too. Add extra sugar. I need a spurt of energy."

Toots dumped the contents of the sugar bowl into Sophie's cup, thinking it would serve her right for sneaking up on her. She carried both cups to the table. "You think Ida will be okay?" Toots asked. "She really gave me a scare last night."

"Me too. I think that physically, she's fine.

I don't know if this will have a residual effect on her mental status. I sure as hell wouldn't want to send her back into the land of germs."

"I really believe Ida is truly over that now. What do you make of the writing?" There. She'd said what had been bothering her all night. It wasn't the fact that a spirit had entered her house; she could live with that. It was the fact that Thomas's ghost, or whatever the heck it was, had said, "My daughter. My daughter. My daughter."

Sophie took a deep breath. "I think Thomas went to the grave with a lot of secrets. I feel sorry for Ida, but don't you dare tell her I said that, or I will kick your saggy butt."

"You won't have to keep that promise," Ida said as she entered the kitchen. Normally, she wasn't an early riser, so both Sophie and Toots were surprised to see her up already. "I don't want you to feel sorry for me, either. So there." Ida poured herself a cup of coffee and joined them at the table. "Mavis says she'll be down later. She's making arrangements for a small factory to produce her mourning clothes. She's really cornered the market. I bet Mavis is going to end up being a rich old woman just like we are."

"I can't believe you actually referred to yourself as an old woman," Sophie said.

"If it's any consolation, I don't think like an old woman."

"None of us do," Toots said.

"You need to quit avoiding the subject. I think we need to talk about what happened last night," Sophie said.

"I don't like you when you're serious," Ida said.

"Me either, but I really want to discuss what happened last night. This isn't some silly prank, Ida. This is for real. You want to see those papers you scribbled? I have them right here." Sophie got up and walked over to the counter, where she'd left them before joining Toots for a smoke out on the porch. She placed them on the table, in front of Ida.

Hesitantly, Ida reached for the papers. She scanned them, then shoved them across the table. "It doesn't make sense. We never had a daughter."

Sunlight filtered through the kitchen windows, casting a golden glow on the polished wood floors. The scattered red and green throw rugs were faded, their color dull from too many washings. The red cabinets needed a new coat of varnish, too.

Toots got up to refill their cups. "Anyone

want a bowl of Froot Loops?"

Ida and Sophie declined her offer.

Toots removed a large box from the pantry, took the milk out of the refrigerator, then grabbed a bowl and spoon, bringing them to the table. "Don't watch me eat. It makes me nervous."

"Whatever," Sophie remarked before directing her attention back to Ida. "I really think this is something we need to look into. You said Thomas died from eating tainted meat. Did the authorities ever check the source where the meat came from?"

"Of course they did. It was that nasty butcher shop where they washed old chicken and repacked ground meat."

"Who did your grocery shopping?" Toots asked.

"What is this? The Spanish Inquisition? I bought groceries. Sometimes. I had a housekeeper, Lucy. She would go to the market now and then. We dined out most of the time. With Thomas's work, it was a requirement. The police asked me all these questions. They were satisfied with the answers. As horrid as it sounds, I had an autopsy done on Thomas. His intestines were full of that E. coli bacteria. He'd been sick for about a week. He'd just returned from a business trip. I can't remember where, but at first he thought he had the flu. Then he remembered he'd eaten that steak right before going away on his last business trip. Why would anyone want to do away with Thomas? He was a bit dull, but he was a very good husband and an excellent provider. Thomas didn't have a lot of friends, at least none that I know of, but he was very well respected in the medical community. You're making too much of this."

Sophie shook her head. "Remember, you're the one that wanted to do this. You're the one who about jumped out of her skin when you saw those words dripping on your bathroom mirror. You're the one who asked me if I would try and make contact with Thomas. I did, and now you act like it's nothing. Well, it is something, and you need to acknowledge that."

"In fifty years of friendship, I don't think I've ever heard you talk that long without cussing or making fun of someone. I am sure this is a new side of you. And, like Ida, I'm not sure I like you this way," Toots said.

"I second that."

"Joke around all you want. What if something really did happen to Thomas? Do you want that on your conscience? I know if it were my husband, I would want to know."

"And what if it did? What are we supposed

to do about it now? I don't know if I can stand an investigation of this sort."

Toots wasn't going to say it, so Sophie figured it was up to her. "What do you think those words *my daughter, my daughter, my daughter* meant? Do you think Thomas was giving you a message? Is it possible he has a daughter?" There. It was out in the open. Sophie wouldn't be the least surprised if Thomas had left a daughter somewhere along the way. Many times, she and Toots had had their doubts about Thomas's fidelity.

Ida looked as though she had been slapped in the face. "Don't you think that if Thomas had a daughter, I would know? I certainly don't remember giving birth to a child. Don't you think that is something I would remember?"

Sophie wanted to shake some sense into Ida. "I know that *you* never gave birth to a child, Ida. I'm not that stupid. Is it possible that Thomas could've had a child with another woman? Maybe when he was younger, before you met? Didn't you have a whirlwind romance right out of college?"

"I was working as a photographer when I met Thomas. His company actually hired me to do freelance shots for some brochures they were printing. We hit it off right from the beginning and married a few months later. What's the big deal? We were married for nearly forty years. Not many can say that these days." Ida tossed her hands up in the air. "What is it you want me to say?"

"I don't want you to say anything. I just want you to acknowledge what happened last night. I want you to accept there may be a possibility that Thomas does have a daughter out there somewhere."

"Okay, for the sake of argument, let's say Thomas does have a daughter. What am I supposed to do about it? Welcome her into my home with open arms? Sing her a lullaby?"

"Don't think I'm nosy by asking this question, but it needs to be asked. Just how many millions did Thomas leave you when he died?" Sophie asked.

Flustered, Ida answered, "I really don't know. I would have to ask my banker. Certainly there is enough to live on for the rest of my life without worrying about my next meal. Why do you ask?"

"Because if Thomas does have a daughter out there somewhere, she might want to get her hands on Daddy's pocketbook. Are you getting the picture now?"

The stricken look on Ida's face was pitiful. It was clear that she'd never given any thought to the possibility of Thomas having been unfaithful.

CHAPTER 21

Toots placed a call to Abby as soon as Ida and Sophie went upstairs. Even though it was three in the morning in California, Abby picked up on the first ring.

"Hi, Mom. What are you doing calling me at this obscene hour? Did you and Sophie get into a fight?" Abby asked.

"I've been up for hours and knew you would be, too. Like mother like daughter. I just wanted to hear your voice. I miss you. How is man's best friend?"

"Chester is heartbroken. Ever since you whisked his woman away, he's done nothing but pout."

"I didn't realize dogs pouted. I learn something new every day. Poor Chester. He and Coco were quite the couple. Have you been to the beach house to see Chris yet?"

"I was there the other night. He invited me for dinner. I brought Chester. We had a great run on the beach. I met his college buddy, Steve. Nice guy."

Toots could hear the happiness in her daughter's voice, and her heart swelled with pride. Abby was the best daughter a mother could ask for. She'd been easy from the beginning. Three hours in labor, she came into the world with a little cry. At two months, she slept through the night, and at nine months, she took her first step. Toots remembered every single milestone of her daughter's life. Mothers were supposed to take note of that stuff.

"It sounds like you're getting along just fine without me, which is a good thing because I may be here longer than I thought."

"You *live* in Charleston, Mother. Of course you're going to be there for a while. Los Angeles is just your . . . hangout." Abby laughed.

"How are things at *The Informer?*" Toots knew already, of course, as she checked her e-mail daily. As the power behind LAT Enterprise, it wouldn't do for her to miss an e-mail. Who knew when something super-duper important might happen that would require her attention?

"Great. We're ranked at number two now, just below *The Enquirer.* Not a bad place to be in this business. Though I have to admit,

I'm running out of stories for my column 'Ghostly Encounters.' I doubt I'll ever top the Marilyn Monroe thing, anyway. Vampires are all the rage in Hollywood now. I need to search for a Dracula look-alike."

Toots smiled. "It's all those crazy movies, and I absolutely refuse to watch them. When I was a young girl, I was terrified of vampires and werewolves. Bela Lugosi, I'll never forget him. He starred in the first Dracula movie."

"Mom, is there something you wanted to tell me? It's late, and I'm tired."

"Oh, Abby, I'm sorry. You should hang up on me when I ramble. No, there isn't anything I wanted to tell you. Just wanted to hear your voice. Night, night."

"Good night, Mom," Abby said, then clicked off.

She'd rambled on so much, she'd forgotten to tell her about the bakery. It would keep until later. Before she could change her mind, Toots placed another call. This one to Chris. Just in case there was something to this Thomas poison theory, she wanted to make sure Ida was out of harm's way.

Five rings, then his voice mail picked up. "This is Toots. I have a favor. I always say that, don't I? And I love you." She hung up the phone, slightly annoyed at herself. It seemed the only time she called Chris was when she needed a favor, a bit of legal advice. She made a note on her ever-present mental shit-to-do list to stop asking Chris for favors all the time. He really would think of her as his wicked stepmother if this continued.

After seven, Toots hurried upstairs to shower and dress. She hated wasting one minute of her day. She wasn't sure what the girls had planned, but whatever they had, it was bound to be something out of the norm.

She dressed in a faded pair of Levi's she'd owned forever. A dark green blouse complemented her auburn hair. She pulled her hair up, securing it with a dark green hair clip. More blush than normal, as she looked washed-out, tired. Who wouldn't, she thought, after last night? A swipe of coral lipstick, and she was good to go.

Downstairs, she was greeted by Mavis, who was about to take Coco out for a stroll.

"Want to come with us?" Mavis asked.

"I'd love to."

Again, Mother Nature had worked her magic, Toots thought as she and Mavis dragged Coco to the back lawn. The azaleas and camellias painted the landscape with an array of brilliant colors. Magnolia and oak trees provided just enough shade from the sun. Toots couldn't imagine a more serene place. It was spring, a time of renewal, and new beginnings. She inhaled the misty morning air, catching a whiff of her favorite night-blooming jasmine. Mother Nature's perfume.

Content to sniff and inspect the variety of shrubbery, Coco led them along a stone pathway Toots and Abby had constructed when she was in high school. Each stone had its own story, a memory. Toots wouldn't have traded the old rocks for solid gold.

"I don't know when I've seen you this happy," Toots commented.

"I don't think I've ever been this happy!" Mavis exclaimed. Her sparkly blue eyes shimmered with excitement. "I'm really a totally different person than that potato-chip-eating, soap-opera-watching, obese woman that I was a year ago. I don't even have the same thoughts anymore. I suppose that's a good thing." Mavis chattered away, and Toots simply listened. A quiet moment with a dear friend on a day exploding with possibilities was one to treasure forever.

Coco spied a squirrel in an oak tree, stopping to growl, revealing tiny white teeth and pink gums. Toots was sure that Coco was more frightened than the squirrel.

"No, Coco," Mavis said. "Mind your manners."

The back door slamming jolted Toots and Mavis to attention. Sophie came running down the path, portable phone in her hand. Huffing and puffing, she held the phone out for Toots. "It's Jamie. She says it's an emergency."

Toots took the phone from Sophie. "Hi, Jamie. What's up?"

"It's a disaster, a total and complete disaster! The place was ransacked, with flour dumped everywhere! My baking sheets are ruined! The display case was shattered! I don't know what to do! I called the police. They came and wrote a report. They said no businesses in the area had been vandalized except ours. I guess I just need a shoulder to cry on. I really don't know what to do."

"Oh no. Are you at the bakery?" Toots asked.

Sobbing, Jamie answered, "Yes. I had to let my apartment go. I wanted to tell you, but it didn't seem appropriate after all you've done. I've been camping out in the kitchen at night, scrubbing up in the ladies' room. It's not that bad, really. Or at least it wasn't until this . . . this catastrophe!"

Toots remembered thinking right after

Leland died how boring her life was, that she needed some excitement. It seemed she was getting her wish and then some. "Stay there. I'm on my way. And, Jamie, don't worry. I'm very good at fixing things." She gave the phone back to Sophie. "I'm going to the bakery. It's been vandalized. If you want to come along, meet me out front in ten minutes."

Toots raced back up the stone path as though her life depended on it. Inside, she grabbed her purse and cell phone, found Ida pouring coffee in the kitchen. "I'm going into town. The bakery's been trashed. If you want to go, meet me out front in ten minutes." Toots said this as she raced through the house, searching for her car keys. Finding them on the counter, next to the creepy scribbled papers from the previous night, she scooped them up and raced to her Lincoln. She looked at her watch. She'd give the girls the allotted ten minutes; then she was leaving. She slid behind the wheel, waiting, thinking again that it was a good day for Bernice to stay at home. If she got wind of the bakery incident, the whole haunted-witch-ghost theory would be rehashed again and again. Toots didn't even want to go there.

Mavis, Ida, and Sophie, along with Coco

in her carrier, came out the front door with one minute to spare. Toots hit the automatic unlock button. Sophie rode up front, with Ida and Mavis in the backseat. Mavis placed Coco's carrier between them.

Toots broke the speed limit, crossing her fingers that a patrol officer wasn't hiding in a copse of trees, as they were known to do. They all remained quiet on the ride to the bakery, each content with her own thoughts.

Half an hour later, Toots lurched the giant vehicle in between a compact car and a Harley. She practically sprang out of the car. The girls trailed behind.

The door was locked, and Toots tapped on the glass. She cupped her hands against the glass, trying to look inside to access the damage. What she saw made her cringe.

Jamie hurried to unlock the door. Toots was amazed that it hadn't been shattered. Poor Jamie looked deflated. Her perky blond hair was dull, flattened against her head. Azure eyes were shadowed. She was covered in flour. Had the situation not been so disastrous, Toots would've laughed. Not giving it a second thought, she wrapped her arms around Jamie, just as she would if it were Abby.

"Thanks for coming so quickly." Jamie raked a dusty white hand through her hair.

"I've cleared a path, but be careful. There's broken glass everywhere."

Toots assessed the damage as she followed Jamie through the bakery. Hundreds of pounds of flour looked like volcanic ash. Cookie sheets were crunched in half; giant wooden spoons, which Toots knew were used for making pralines, were shattered like Pick-Up Sticks. The large display case was completely destroyed.

"This is the worst." Jamie pointed to a giant mixer in the corner of the kitchen. "This is the best money can buy. I paid twelve thousand dollars for this piece of machinery. How an eight-quart commercial mixer with a high-torque direct-drive transmission, steel gears and shafts could be so easily destroyed is beyond me. Whoever did this must've had an ax or something." Jamie shook her head as she showed Toots what was left of a Vollrath commercial mixer. Though she didn't know that much about commercial kitchen products, Toots knew quality when she saw it, and this fit the bill.

"There's more," Jamie said. "Here." She stopped in front of two giant ovens. Each held at least a dozen baking sheets. "This is another major expense. The two of them cost more than I'll earn in the next two years."

Tears brimmed in the young woman's eyes, streaking down her face and leaving silvery ribbons from the light dusting of flour still on her face. Jamie blew her nose on an apron, tossed her hands in the air. "We're totally ruined. Totally ruined." Jamie plopped down on a wooden chair and bawled like a two-year-old.

Toots stooped down to Jamie's eye level. She brushed a strand of sticky blond hair from her cheek. "Jamie, I've always said things can be replaced, but people can't. This is fixable, trust me. I'm very good at fixing things, and people, too, sometimes." Toots looked to Sophie, Ida, and Mavis, who remained in the front of the bakery, out of harm's way.

"She is. She's helped every one of us. This will be a breeze for our dear Toots," Mavis added. "And we're going to do whatever we can to help, too. Right, girls?"

"You're damn straight," Sophie said, sounding more like the old crude Sophie they all knew and loved.

"I'll do whatever I can to help, too," Ida chimed in, though she didn't sound as if her heart was in it, but she had other things to worry about. Like a dead husband who might've met his maker too soon.

"Now dry up your tears. We're in this

together. Remember, I'm your partner, too. First, I want to know how you managed to sleep through this if you've been living here," Toots said, not out of nosiness, but out of curiosity.

"I spent the night at the YMCA. I'm so ashamed, but I needed a real shower, and they're free. I guess I should be thankful, but if I'd been here, maybe I would've been able to stop whoever did this." Jamie started crying again. "Now not only am I out of business, but I'm gonna have to find a place to stay while I take care of this mess."

"What about your insurance?" Ida asked.

"It will cover some of the damage but not enough to make a difference, certainly not enough to get the place back in operating condition. I can get my old job back at Publix. Thank God I left on good terms."

Toots was thinking. She needed a plan. She'd helped Mavis out of her dilemma, and so far she remained free. She hadn't heard anything on the news and hoped that this Mr. Jay C. King would accept the ten grand she'd left behind and forget about it. That material Mavis used was a bit on the ugly side as it was. Toots felt sure there wasn't a massive demand right now but knew that there would be soon because Mavis's Good Mourning line was on its way.

She felt it in her bones.

Okay, she had a plan. "Did you get a copy of the police report? We'll need that to file the insurance claim."

What she didn't voice was that she was glad she hadn't been here when the police arrived. Who knew? She could be on their local most wanted list. She made a mental note for her shit-to-do list. Call Henry at the bank. If anyone would know if an arrest were imminent in the warehouse break-in, he would. He might also be suspicious if she was too inquisitive. She'd play that by ear. Later.

"Yes, I have it here, somewhere." Jamie shuffled through a stack of papers on one of the large stainless-steel tables that had survived the destruction. "Here it is." Jamie gave Toots the report.

Toots scanned the report, saw the list of damaged items. Then where it said, "Remarks," Toots saw where the responding officer wrote, *No signs of forced entry.* She looked at Jamie. "Did you read this? It says there are no signs of a forced entry. How can they possibly think that?"

Jamie motioned her over to the front and only door. "See. The lock is intact, and there are no markings. The police think whoever did this had a key. Besides you, no one else has a key. I can't see you breaking into a bakery," Jamie said, a little bit of her spunkiness returning.

If she only knew, Toots thought.

"Unless I destroyed this myself, it looks like the police are writing this one off. I doubt they'll spend more than an hour investigating. This is a tourist area. You would think that would be some kind of incentive, but apparently they don't consider a bakery break-in top priority."

"I agree. Now I have a plan. Let's go down to that little coffee shop around the corner, The Daily Grind. They have the best cappuccino in town. We can walk. I need to smoke."

"Me too," Sophie added.

Jamie laughed a real, genuine laugh. "You all smoke? OMG, this is hysterical. Let me grab my backpack." Jamie ran to the kitchen, where she retrieved a lavender Jan-Sport backpack stuffed so full, the zippers looked as though they were about to pop. She grabbed a ring of keys from the outside pocket. "Let me lock up. I don't know if it will do any good, but old habits are hard to break," Jamie said.

The five women walked slowly down the street. Carriages full of tourists being led by a team of horses clip-clopped down the street. Tour guides with groups of people wearing bright-colored shirts, cameras hanging around their necks, milled about the many historical landmarks. The occasional cry from an infant reminded all that not everyone wanted to spend the afternoon discussing history.

The Daily Grind was buzzing with customers. "Sophie, find us a table outside, and I'll get the drinks. Jamie, what are you having?" Toots asked.

"I'll have a green tea frappuccino, light soy, two Splenda, no whip."

Toots laughed. "I see you've been here before."

"Yes. Late nights, when we were getting the bakery ready, I ran over for a few double shots of espresso."

Toots placed their order. The barista gave her a metal sign with the number thirteen, telling her to place it on her table and they would bring their drinks when they were finished. She did not like that number. "Miss, may I have another number? I haven't had much luck with thirteen."

The barista laughed and replaced it with a nice, safe number seven.

"Thank you."

Sophie, Ida, and Mavis were seated at a round iron table. A red-and-white-striped umbrella shaded them from the sun. Coco sat in Mavis's lap, taking in all the different sounds and smells.

Once their drinks were served, Toots leaned in close so the other patrons wouldn't hear her.

"Okay, here's the plan."

CHAPTER 22

"First and foremost, you will not be staying at the YMCA. I have a perfectly nice guesthouse that's sitting empty right now. You can stay there as long as you wish. It's fully stocked with all the essentials. You can shower whenever you like. There's even a Jacuzzi tub if you're one of those soakers. I am myself. There's nothing I like more than a good soak with a stack of tabloids and a nice bottle of wine."

Jamie shook her head. "I can't accept your offer, Toots. You've already done more than anyone ever has. It'll take me years to repay you."

"You better take her up on her offer. She can be ruthless when she wants to be," Sophie informed her.

Jamie just laughed.

"Second, I'll have Pete make arrangements to have the bakery cleaned. Jamie, order all the new equipment you need and send me the bills. We'll work the financial details out later. Also, we'll want to install a top-notch security system, one that's monitored. I'm going to buy a full-page ad in the paper. Sort of like a new grand opening or something. We'll do a buy-one-get-one-free sale. Jamie, how good are your cupcakes?"

"I've been told they beat those at Magnolia Bakery in New York City."

"I've sampled those myself. They're dry," Ida said. "I never saw what all the fuss was about. It was that show *Sex and the City* that brought them so much fame, not the quality of the cupcakes."

"That's good to know. Then we'll use that in our ad, in a subliminal way, of course. Jamie, how quickly can you order and replace the ovens and that giant mixer?"

"I can't let you do this! You hardly know me!"

"I always go with my gut instinct, and I'm rarely wrong," Toots said. "And my gut instinct is telling me that you're good people. You need a break, and I intend to give it to you. I have a daughter your age. She lives in LA, runs *The Informer*."

"The gossip paper? OMG, I *love* that paper! I buy it every week." Jamie was ecstatic.

"Me too." Toots almost told her she was

244

the owner, but that wouldn't be fair to Abby, since she still assumed she was working for a big corporation, LAT Enterprise.

"It would be wonderful to have a youngster in the house," Mavis said.

Sophie and Toots both rolled their eyes.

"I'm thirty-one. I don't know if that qualifies as a youngster," Jamie said.

They finished their drinks, and Toots went inside to order a second round. At this rate, with this much caffeine, they'd be up for the next three days.

When she returned, Toots asked, "Did I give you enough time to accept my offer?"

Jamie grinned, showing a movie-star smile. "Okay, I accept, but I want to draw up some sort of agreement where it says you'll take your investment back before I'm allowed to take any of the profits."

"You'll want to pay yourself a salary. You can't live on sugar alone," Toots said.

Ida, Mavis, and Sophie all turned to stare at Toots. Then they burst out laughing.

"Toots lives on sugar and nicotine. Talk about a true case of the pot calling the kettle black. Toots lives on Froot Loops, coffee, and nicotine," Ida informed Jamie. "She hates healthy food. Mavis lost more than one hundred pounds in a year."

Ida turned to Mavis. "I thought she should

know that since you only had one praline the other day. I didn't want Jamie to think you didn't like baked goods. I indulge on occasion, but not as much as Toots and Sophie. They're slowly killing themselves with all the garbage they put in their bodies."

"Ida, that's enough. Do you want me to tell Jamie about your former illness?" Toots interjected.

"Please, don't fuss over me. I'm overwhelmed by all of you. I hope when I'm your age, I'm as gutsy as you are."

"Then let's take Jamie back to the house, and we'll get the ball rolling. I bet we can have the bakery up and running in a week," Toots said, standing up to indicate it was time to get their butts to work.

"Jamie, do you want to follow us in your car?" Toots asked on their walk back to the bakery.

"This shouldn't come as a surprise, but I don't own a car, either. I have my bike. I could follow you if you'll drive within the speed limit."

At the bakery Jamie unlocked the door, grabbed the insurance papers, stuffed them in her backpack, scanned the mess, and shook her head. "I don't see how it's going to be humanly possible to have this place up and running within a week, but if you ladies think it can be done, then I believe you. It's like I've found my very own band of fairy godmothers," Jamie said, then embraced the four women in a group hug. Coco, not wanting to be left out, barked. Mavis picked her up. Jamie scratched the pooch between the ears and for that received a rewarding dog lick.

"You can ride with us. I have another vehicle that just sits in the garage, collecting dust," Toots said. "It's yours to use for as long as you need to. It's a Land Rover, so you'll be able to haul stuff to and from the bakery."

Jamie broke down. It was simply too much. She'd had no one in her life, except her grandmother, and now she'd been graced with four fairy godmothers who epitomized the true meaning of helping their fellow man. She wiped the tears from her face with the back of her hand. "What can I say?"

"Say yes so we can get this show on the road," Sophie said.

"Yes!" Jamie said and piled into the back-seat with Ida and Mavis. They put Coco's carrier in the trunk, and Coco stayed on Jamie's lap for the entire ride.

When they pulled through the handmade

wrought-iron gates, it almost took Jamie's breath away. The azaleas and camellias were in full, brilliant bloom; the giant trees reminded her of courtly gentlemen bowing in welcome. A sweet floral fragrance teased her olfactory senses. She wasn't sure what it was, but it was now her new favorite scent.

"The smell. What is it?" Jamie asked in awe.

"Night-blooming jasmine. It's my favorite," Toots said as she pulled up in front of her house.

Jamie leaped out of the car, running across the gardens like a child. She held her arms up in the air as if she were trying to embrace the beauty.

Toots grinned from ear to ear. There was nothing she enjoyed more than making someone happy. And, from the looks of it, Jamie was overjoyed.

"I take it you approve," Toots said as she followed Jamie into the gardens. "It's like nature's wonderland. Pete, he takes care of the lawn. He's one of the best. I thank him every time I see this. In the spring, when I see all these gorgeous flowers and the shrubbery, I remember to give him a great big bonus check."

"Well, he does a wonderful job. I could sleep out here."

"You can if you want. Sometimes in the summer I take one of the lounge chairs into the gardens and just sit back and soak it all up. I'm very blessed," Toots added.

"Deservingly so, I should add. I've never met anyone quite like you."

"Thanks, dear, but there are nicer people than me. I can be a hellion when I want. Just ask the girls."

"If you don't mind, how did you all come to be such good friends? You're each so different from the other, yet I can feel the closeness you share. I've never had a friend like that. Is it wonderful?"

"It's the best. We grew up together in New Jersey. Went to Catholic school together, and we've never been apart for long. Mavis lives in Maine. She's a retired teacher. Sophie was a pediatric nurse in New York City. Her husband, Walter, just passed away a few months ago."

"I'm sorry," Jamie said sincerely.

"Don't be. He was an ass," Toots said. "Ida was a New York City social butterfly. Her husband was extremely wealthy. He died about two years ago. Ida went through a terrible bout with OCD, but she's over that now, thank goodness. She drove us all crazy, but the past is prologue. She's almost back to her normal stuck-up self. We're all widows," Toots said as she took Jamie's hand. "Come with me. I want you to see the guesthouse."

Toots led Jamie to the edge of her property, where, clustered among angel oaks and four giant magnolia trees, a small stone cottage appeared to be tucked under the trees' protective branches. A variety of blooms sprouted from the dirt like bright strings of confetti. A small pond trickled beneath a stone bridge.

"This is your guesthouse?" Jamie asked.

Toots located the door key under a large pot of ivy. "It's going to be your home for as long as you want. Now, let me show you the inside."

Toots pushed the wooden door inward, stepping aside to allow Jamie entry. As she watched Jamie take in the quaint little home, she was again reminded of how blessed she really was.

"This is like something out of a storybook." Again, Jamie whirled around like a child. "I've never seen a place like this."

Toots led her to the small living area, where the walls were painted a soft celery green. The floors were hard rock maple and sparkled like diamonds. An earth-colored love seat and ottoman sat next to a rock fireplace. A small table and lamp had been placed strategically so that one might sit by the fireplace with a cup of tea and a favorite book. The kitchen was separated from the living area by an arch. More pale green walls and maple cabinets, with a butcher-block island in the center. Dark green granite countertops continued the outdoorsy feel of the cottage.

The master bedroom overlooked the gardens. One wall was nothing but glass. In the master bath, the Jacuzzi sat in front of a floor-to-ceiling window.

"This is so . . . incredible. I can't believe someone doesn't live here," Jamie said.

"You do, my dear. Now, let me show you a few things. For starters, these windows can be covered in a flash." Toots picked up a remote, pushed a button, and pale green cloth rolled down in folds, covering the windows. "Just in case you decide to spend some time soaking. Though I've never seen anyone here, except for Pete, but you would be safe to leave them open if you wanted to soak up the scenery. Bath towels are in here." She opened a small closet. "Soaps, shampoos, bath salts, whatever you need. Razors. I think Abby left a box of tampons here somewhere." Toots rummaged through the closet. "Yes, right here. The bedding is as soft as down. The bed is firm without being too hard."

"This is a dream. I think I might have to pinch myself. I feel like . . . Goldilocks. I don't know how I'll ever repay you. Well, I do in terms of money, but in terms of . . . generosity, wow! This is more than . . . Well, I've gushed enough. I love this place. It's perfect."

Toots flicked the lights on, then returned to the kitchen, where she opened the refrigerator. "I always keep the basics here just in case Abby comes home. There are eggs, butter, cheese." Toots poked through the cabinets. "Plenty of stuff here. Of course, you're welcome to share whatever we eat, but I have to warn you, none of us cook except Mavis. And all she eats is healthy stuff. We're getting by on Froot Loops and toast, so if you're in the mood, you're always welcome. Now, I'm going to call Pete and get the ball rolling so we can have our bakery up and running. Since it's Sunday, he can start with the cleanup first thing tomorrow morning or Tuesday at the latest. You'll need to start arranging for replacement equipment to be purchased and delivered."

Toots turned for the door, then remembered that she had forgotten to show Jamie where the telephone was. "There's a phone book in the bedside table. Oh, and we have wireless Internet, too. You can order as much as you can online and not have to wait until tomorrow, but I suppose the heavy-duty stuff will have to wait. Have the bills sent to me. I'm going to leave now so you can soak up your new digs."

Jamie followed Toots to the door, gave her another hug.

She'd truly found a quartet of fairy god-mothers.

CHAPTER 23

Toots returned to the house and found the girls in the kitchen, clustered around the table like three old hens. Bernice was busy making Long Island iced teas.

"I thought you were sick," Toots said.

"I got better," Bernice said. "I figured you girls needed something to drink and eat besides cereal and toast. I stopped at Publix and picked up fried chicken, with all the extras."

"I am a bit hungry, but I don't want coffee. We had so many of those specialty coffee drinks this afternoon, I need something to take the edge off. Maybe we'll just get drunk," Sophie told Bernice.

"I've got a few phone calls to make. Then I'll join you," Toots said.

Upstairs in her bedroom, Toots made fast work of calling Pete so that he could arrange for the bakery to be cleaned. After she gave him all the details, she told him he could pick up the key to the bakery first thing Monday morning. Once those arrangements were finalized, she made the dreaded call to Henry.

She quickly dialed his home number. He answered on the third ring. "Henry, it's Toots. I know it's Sunday, and I'm sorry to disturb you. Having said that, how are you?"

"I'm fine, but something tells me you didn't call me to find out the state of my mind. What's going on?"

"Henry, you're a rotten old man. Actually, I called to tell you that the bakery was broken into, so I'm going to need to transfer some money into the bakery's checking account. We're going to have to replace most of the equipment, and it isn't cheap."

"That's all?" Henry asked.

"Why? Is there something more you think I should be asking you?" Toots inquired.

Henry chuckled. "No, I just wanted to let you know about a conversation I had with Mr. King yesterday."

Toots's heart rate quadrupled. Oh no. The dark stuff was about to hit the proverbial fan. Toots had visions of wearing prison stripes and eating bologna sandwiches with Kool-Aid for the rest of her life.

Toots's voice cracked, "Oh, really? What does that have to do with me?"

"Yesterday afternoon I received a call from Mr. King. He was quite jubilant about an incident that happened at his warehouse the other night. Seems someone sneaked inside while the security guard was helping a woman in distress. It seems she had an accomplice who *removed* a bunch of ugly gray material and left ten grand in its place."

Shit! Shit! And double shit! Those prison stripes and bologna sandwiches were about to become her new reality!

"And you're telling me this, why?" Toots asked.

"It seems all that material was outdated and was about to be shipped to his outlet warehouse in Charlotte. He said something about the net value being a hundred bucks. This gave me a good laugh. I thought you, of all people, would want to know that."

Good-bye, bologna!

Toots took a deep, refreshing breath. "I'm glad you shared that with me, Henry. It's made my day."

"I'm sure it has. That break-in at your bakery you just mentioned, they didn't happen to leave ten grand, did they? Seems Charleston may have some moral-minded thieving going on."

"Kiss my rear end, Henry. Just transfer the money. I'm hanging up now."

Toots raced downstairs, relieved. The girls were gathered around the table, getting looped on Long Island iced teas. She was about to join them. "I just got off the phone with Henry from the bank. You're never going to believe what he told me. Apparently someone broke into Mr. King's warehouse and stole a hundred dollars' worth of fabric that was about to be shipped to his outlet store. The culprits left ten grand in its place. Why would someone be that silly?" Toots asked, grinning from ear to ear.

Her statement was greeted with a round of applause. Bernice looked at them all as if they were one slice short of a loaf.

For the next half hour, the women dined on fried chicken and potato salad and chugged Long Island iced teas. Toots explained to Bernice that Jamie would be staying in the guesthouse, but there was no need for her to worry about keeping it clean. Jamie said she would take care of that.

"You're always taking care of someone, aren't you?" Bernice stated.

"It's what I do best," Toots slurred. "And before you ask, no, I am not drunk. Maybe a little tipsy."

"Whatever you say. I'm going to be upstairs the rest of the night cleaning the bathrooms and changing sheets. If anyone needs me, that's where I'll be, so you're gonna have to do the dishes yourself," Bernice announced.

"What else is new?" Toots said to no one in particular.

As soon as Bernice left the room, Ida, a little tipsy herself, spoke up. "Sophie, Mavis, Toots, you guys up for a little séance tonight? Something tells me I need to try to contact Thomas one more time. I need to try to top Toots in the good-deed department."

"Why do you want to? I thought you were too creeped out to want to try again," Sophie said.

"I have been thinking about it. The *my daughter* stuff has got me wondering. Maybe Thomas really did leave behind a potential person of interest we should know about."

"I'm game if you are," Sophie said. "What about the rest of you?"

"I suppose I could since I've made arrangements with that factory in California to start working on my clothing line. I won't have to spend every waking moment in front of the sewing machine. I'm so excited about my new business venture," Mavis chortled.

"We are, too," Toots added.

"What about your new friend Jamie in the guesthouse? She's not gonna come in and interrupt us or anything, is she?" Sophie asked.

"No. Something tells me Jamie's gonna spend the rest of the night soaking in the Jacuzzi," Toots stated.

"Then let's get this show on the road," Sophie declared.

Once again, the four women prepared to contact Thomas. Maybe this time the mystery surrounding his death would be solved.

CHAPTER 24

The women set up the table just as they had the night before. This time, however, rather than trepidation, all they felt was desire, the desire to get to the bottom of the mystery of Thomas's life, not just his death. If they were lucky, maybe this time Thomas would come through with enough information for them to get a better understanding of his previous message.

"Then it's settled. Tonight we will attempt to contact Thomas again. We'll use the psychic writing technique so we can get more detailed information. Ida, you'll have to be in a complete state of relaxation and just allow his energy to flow through you," Sophie informed her.

Ida smoothed a hand over her already smooth pageboy. "If he is willing to come through again, I'm up for it. If it means he has to channel his energy through me, then I will do my best to handle it, no matter how frightened I become."

Sophie nodded. "I agree with Ida. No matter how scary it may get, we need to give this our best shot. I'll admit I was a bit leery before about using our bodies to channel the spirit, but under the circumstances, I do not see any real alternative if we hope to achieve the result we want."

Toots and Mavis remained solemn during this interchange between Sophie and Ida. However, it was hard to miss the skeptical expressions on their faces.

Each sat in her place around the table in the same fashion as before. They began the séance with the protection prayer, the same one they had used last time. "For good luck," Sophie said.

"We're going to need more information. You must concentrate deeply and put aside all other thoughts and focus on channeling Thomas's energy," Sophie reminded Ida.

In her calm, melodic voice, Sophie began her call to the spirits from beyond; only this time, as in the previous, the spirit had a name. Thomas. "We are here tonight to once again call on the spirit of Thomas. If you can hear me, once again, lend us your thoughts. We need to know more about the daughter you revealed to us."

As before, the room's energy began to

change. An immediate chill was felt. By now the women recognized this as the sign someone was attempting to come through.

"Thomas, are you here with us tonight?" Sophie intoned.

The nervousness Ida was feeling was evident by the sweat on her hand, which was causing her pencil to slip. She quickly wiped it away and started to focus her thoughts on Thomas. She grasped the pencil in her hand with a death grip. Ida began to scribble circles. Then the circles turned into letters and the word *Yes* became visible on the notepad.

In little more than a whisper, Ida spoke. "He is with us. I can feel his energy once again. Ask the questions, Sophie."

"Thomas, the daughter you mentioned. Is she connected to your death in any way?"

All three women watched as Ida's hand scribbled furiously across the paper. Ida wrote the words *Murderer, Murderer, Murder.*

Deep intakes of their breath could be heard throughout the room.

"Is she the one who poisoned you?"

The word *Yes* was written on the notepad, then circled violently, perhaps to indicate that was the reason Thomas had been trying to make contact with the women the entire time.

For once, Sophie was glad they'd all imbibed a bit too much. Her hands shook as she continued. "Thomas, this daughter. Do you know her name? Can you tell us when you first found out about her? Do you know how and why she poisoned you? Why she wanted to murder you? Please, Thomas, answer these questions so that we may bring closure and allow you to leave this world peacefully to go to the other side."

The chill in the room turned icy cold.

"I can feel his energy leaving my body. It's not like the last time. I feel a warmth overcoming my entire body. It is as if Thomas has finally said what he wanted us to know. I think he's finished his business in this world and moved on to the next, knowing that we —"

Before Ida could finish her sentence, Mavis let out a scream. "Oh my God! Look what she has written down!"

The paper was filled with scribbles, and between the squiggly lines was a sentence written very clearly.

"What does it say?" Sophie asked Ida.

In a weakened voice, Ida replied, "Nancy. Nancy. Nancy. Never knew her. Never knew her. Never knew her. Chicago. Chicago. Chicago. Money. Money. Money. Hate. Hate. Hate. Murder. Murder. Murder.

Beware. Beware. Beware." That was what the paper said.

"What's the significance of three words rather than only one?" Toots whispered.

Sophie held up a hand, shaking her head. "I'm not sure. Possibly this woman knew who her father was all along. She could've killed him for money, the oldest reason in the book."

As fast as it came, the chill left the room. "He is gone," Ida announced in a shaky voice.

The candles flickered, and the room temperature returned to normal. The women were silent, each in a semi-catatonic state.

Sophie took the paper from beneath Ida's hand and read the words again. "And I thought Walter was a bastard. Ida, it sounds like this woman knew who her father was all along and quite possibly killed him, thinking she would inherit his money."

"I need a cigarette badly. Let's go to the kitchen," Toots said.

Mavis snuffed out the candles and pushed the chairs beneath the table. They trailed out of the room, into the kitchen. Toots and Sophie went out on the back porch to smoke.

"I'll make coffee," Mavis said.

"I don't want any coffee. I think I need a stiff drink," Ida said flatly. She found a bottle of scotch. She liberally poured a dose into a coffee cup, then added a splash of water. Maybe she would turn into an alcoholic like Sophie's Walter. At that point, nothing would have surprised her. She took her drink and joined Mavis at the table. A few minutes later Toots and Sophie stepped back inside.

Mavis was the first to speak after they'd all gotten themselves a drink and made themselves comfortable around the kitchen table. "I'm certainly not a detective, but it sounds like this daughter knew who Thomas was all along. Maybe she thought she would inherit his money."

"That doesn't make sense. She wouldn't receive a dime. Ida would be the only person to inherit Thomas's money upon his death. She was either really stupid, or she didn't know he was married," Toots said.

"I believe that's what Thomas is trying to tell us. This daughter murdered him for the money. When she found out he was married, she knew she wouldn't inherit a red cent. Could be that's what he meant by the word *beware*. Maybe she does know about Ida. Maybe she's going to come after Ida. Who knows? Ida doesn't have any kids or next of kin. Maybe she wants to get Ida out of the picture, then come forward as Thomas's daughter and collect all his millions," Sophie said. "Of course, since she was ignorant enough not to know that Thomas was married, so his wife and not she would inherit, she might well be stupid enough to think that she can somehow get her grubby little hands on the money, even though now it is Ida's, and she and Ida are related to one another about as closely as Barack Obama is related to Sarah Palin."

"This sounds like something out of a cheap dime-store detective novel," Toots said.

"True. I believe this is why Thomas is coming through to us. He's trying to warn me that this woman could be coming after me. Remember, he only gave a first name. That makes me think he didn't spend enough time with her to get to know her last name. Maybe all they had was a chance encounter. He went to a medical convention in Chicago. When he got back, he got sick. And to think, the entire time we thought it was food poisoning. I never even suspected something like this could happen. Certainly not on a business trip," Ida said, her voice becoming clearer with each word. Even though she was sipping scotch, it wasn't affecting her thought processes or her ability to communicate.

Mavis contemplated Ida's words. "But if he was poisoned in Chicago by this Nancy, how is it possible that he died days after getting home? Aren't most fatal poisonings usually within hours?"

"I'm not an expert, but I did spend thirty years working as a nurse. There are many different types of poisons that can kill someone slowly with just one dose. If we can find out what he was poisoned with, we could go to the authorities. Then they would exhume his body and test for it. I've seen stuff like this on TV before. It's nearly impossible to test for every type of poison, but if we can figure out what kind it was, they can test just for that and determine whether or not it was what killed him," Sophie said, all traces of her hard, sarcastic self temporarily gone.

Ida lost it. "This is just too much for me to take in. First, I find out my late husband had an affair that might have led to a child. Then I learn that there's a strong possibility she murdered him." She began to cry, heart-wrenching sobs. "I can't believe this is happening to me."

"Don't you shed another tear. This bitch Nancy is going to get what's coming to her.

Rest assured of that. If you take on one of us alone, you might be able to claim victory, but united, there's nothing that will bring us down. We have a bond that won't be broken by some murdering, money-hungry skank. We're here to support you, Ida, and we're not going to let you out of our sight. As far as Thomas's indiscretions go, I'm sorry, but most men are dickweeds. Not all, but most. I think he paid the ultimate price for his infidelity, and now he's trying to make it up to you and prove that even in death he's willing to look after you. I think that's why he's coming through to you so easily. He wants to warn you. Look at it this way. Not too many women can say their husbands came back from the dead to make sure they were protected. He made a mistake, and now he's trying to make amends. You could think of him as a ghost in shining armor." Sophie reached across the table for Ida's hand. The others looked at her as though she were out of her mind.

"I didn't think you had it in you, Sophie," Toots said.

"Had what in me?"

"The ability to show compassion."

"Well, that just shows how much you don't know," Sophie smirked.

In response to which, Toots flipped her the bird.

CHAPTER 25

It was after midnight, and the women were still sitting around the kitchen table, discussing Thomas's death. Bernice had called it a day an hour earlier, telling Toots not to expect her before noon the next day. Little did Bernice know that Toots would pay her just for showing up. She didn't have to do a thing. She wasn't just her housekeeper; she was her dear, dear friend.

"We need a way to look into this further without throwing ourselves into the middle of it. If we start digging up reasons behind Thomas's death, they are most likely going to point the finger right back at me. After all, I'm the one who benefited the most from his death," Ida pointed out.

"I'm going to call Chris. He can put us in touch with someone who will be able to help us out. Plus, we can trust him. I'll call him right away," Toots suggested.

"Do you think it's a good idea to bring

someone else into this mess? Remember, our source is a ghost. We could all end up committed," Sophie said with a smile.

"Sophie, I could be committed already for 'bartering' ten thousand dollars in cash for a hundred dollars' worth of conservative gray fabric. Don't worry. If it'll make you feel any better, I'll send him a nickel so we can take advantage of attorney-client privilege. But trust me, that won't be necessary," Toots explained.

"Then go ahead. But if this shit goes sour, don't blame me. I'll be the one saying I told you so. It's not Chris I don't trust. Just make damn sure whoever he brings in is trustworthy."

"Let me run upstairs and get my address book. I'll be right back."

Two minutes later Toots was back at the table with the phone and her address book in hand. "Hopefully, Chris can recommend someone who doesn't mind bending the rules to get to the truth."

Toots slowly pressed the buttons on the phone one at a time, deliberately looking at each of the other women as she pressed the numbers. She cupped her hand over the receiver. "Ida, once I do this, there's no turning back. Are you sure you're okay with this?"

"I'm positive," Ida stated firmly.

Chris picked up on the first ring.

"Chris, it's Toots again. How are you?"

"Hey, Tootsie. What's up?"

"You know I hate being called Tootsie. But I'll let you get away with it. Just this once, though. You're looking after Abby, right?"

"And then some."

"I'm not going to ask what that means. Actually, I know. And I approve. Just so you know."

"Good. Tell me the real reason you called," Chris said.

"I won't waste time, so here it is. We believe that someone had Thomas murdered. Ida's husband. Officially, he died of food poisoning. But it's been brought to our attention that he may have been intentionally poisoned by someone who wanted him dead. We need to find out who and why."

"Wow! That's some bombshell for you to just lay on me. Why do you suspect this?" Chris asked.

"Promise not to laugh?"

"Scout's honor," Chris said.

"Thomas came through during one of our séances and told us he was murdered. He's been trying to communicate with us. We believe he'll never be at peace until justice is brought to the person or persons responsible for this. Sophie did something new. She used a form of communication called psychic writing. We made contact with Thomas, and he kept saying, 'My daughter, my daughter, my daughter.' "

"Holy cow! Okay, what can I do to help? I'm willing to do whatever you need. You want me to take the next flight out there and start looking into this for you?"

"No, I can't have you do that. We need an outsider. Someone who can't be connected to us. Someone who can snoop around and find out anything connected to a child Thomas might have fathered with another woman, and why Thomas would want us to have this information. People can't know we're digging up facts about his death, since it's likely to bring suspicion directly on Ida. It's only a matter of time. Someone out there knows he was poisoned. We're scared to death he or she might try to point the finger at Ida if there's the slightest inkling she knows the truth behind his death. We need someone who is willing to break a few rules in order to get to the truth. Someone who might be able to finesse a few laws in the name of justice." Toots thought she sounded just like Angela Lansbury on those old reruns of *Murder, She Wrote.* "And we're really afraid the daughter might come after Ida. It could happen, Chris."

If Chris felt any shock or disbelief at what the zany women were up to, he didn't show it in any way. "I think you're right to be concerned about contact that can be traced back to Ida. In fact, think of it this way. Suppose the daughter is able to get Ida convicted of Thomas's murder. Then, since she cannot legally benefit from her own crime, Ida cannot inherit Thomas's money, and voilà, the next of kin, namely, the daughter, inherits. My guess, however, is that the daughter must be pretty stupid not to have already tried this ploy.

"Anyway, I think I know just the person to help you. His name is Goebel. He was a New York City detective for over thirty years, known for getting his suspects to confess. He was forced into early retirement and started his own private detective agency called Goebel Global Investigations. He's willing to do whatever it takes for his clients. I'm not sure what his views are on the supernatural, but he does what he needs to do.

"Case in point. I called him to help me on a case where we were suspicious of an actor showing up to work high on cocaine every day. The producers were looking for a way to fire him without violating any union rules, so they had me look over his contract. There weren't any stipulations that would allow them to fire him for drug use, but there was a term in the contract that stated if he showed up late on the set three consecutive days he would be terminated. I called Goebel and he came out here and decided to 'babysit' the actor for a few days. Made sure he wasn't able to show up on the set, so the production company was able to terminate his contract and get him off the show entirely."

"He definitely sounds like the kind of guy we need for this type of investigation. Give me his information, and I'll call him and bring him up to speed on just what's going on. We need him to locate a possible child Thomas fathered out of wedlock, find out if she had anything to do with his death, or why she would even want him dead. If you can put us in touch with him, it will get us headed in the right direction."

"Consider it done. I'll inform him of the situation and make sure he's on your front porch steps in a few days. When you're finished chasing the bad guys, you can make me some oatmeal-raisin cookies. You know how much I love those."

"I'll overnight the cookies as soon as

they're out of the oven. I wish your father was still alive to see the man you've become. Any woman would be proud to call you her son. I love you, Chris."

Toots hung up the phone before she started to cry. She was truly blessed. A note on her mental shit-to-do list: Have Jamie make as many oatmeal cookies as she could tomorrow. Then she'd have Mavis's FedEx man pick them up for shipping.

"Okay, girls. Good news. Chris says he has a guy who can do what we need. He's retired from the New York Police Department and is out on his own. Chris says he doesn't mind breaking a few rules in the interest of justice. I don't know about the rest of you, but I'm exhausted. I'm going to call it a night," Toots announced, standing and stretching like a cat.

"Me too," Sophie said.

"I'm gonna take Coco out one more time. Then I'm ready to end this day, as well."

Ida remained seated at the table. "I think I'll have one more drink and toast Thomas's ghost while I try and convince myself I'm not going crazy."

"We're all a bit crazy, Ida. Just go with it," Sophie said.

"I think I will. Good night, girls," Ida said as she filled her cup with scotch.

CHAPTER 26

Toots was up at her usual five o'clock, preparing for the day. In the kitchen, she made a pot of coffee, took the Froot Loops out of the pantry, and removed a stack of bowls from the cabinet and several spoons from the silverware drawer. She would set everything out just in case the girls wanted breakfast. As Bernice wasn't planning on showing up until noon, she figured that if they wanted any more than this, they would have to figure something out since they all knew her culinary talents stretched only as far as a slice of toast. She checked her e-mail first thing — all was well with *The Informer*. Chris, true to his word, told her in an e-mail to expect Goebel on her doorstep sometime that evening. He worked fast; Toots would give him credit for that.

After breakfast she planned to drive to Wal-Mart to pick up the ingredients for Chris's oatmeal-raisin cookies. Last night, before she went to bed, she had seen that the lights were still on in the guesthouse, and placed a quick call to Jamie, asking her if she knew how to make oatmeal-raisin cookies. Jamie said she always used her grandmother's recipe and would bake them in the guesthouse since she had a fully equipped kitchen. An e-mail from Pete said the bakery would be cleaned and repainted, and the broken machinery removed, in forty-eight hours. Toots liked it when things flowed smoothly.

She sat out on the back porch, smoking a cigarette and enjoying her first cup of coffee of the morning. It was going to be another gorgeous day. The sounds of birds chirping, squirrels ruffling through the pine straw, and the occasional low croak from the frogs that dwelled in the pond by the guesthouse were very soothing. The screen door behind her opened, though this time it didn't scare the pants off of her. Sophie, wearing cutoff jeans that hit just below the knees, orange flip-flops, and an LA Raiders T-shirt, sat down next to her.

"I love your outfit," Toots said dryly. "I'm going to Wal-Mart in a few minutes. You want to go with me? You'll fit right in dressed like that."

"Excuse me. We all don't get up in the

morning looking like you. Not that it's any of your business, but I haven't had my shower yet," Sophie shot back. "When you're ready to go, I'll run upstairs and change. We're running low on séance candles."

"Jamie is going to make Chris those oatmeal-raisin cookies. Poor kid thinks I've been making them myself all these years, when they're nothing more than the Pillsbury kind that you slice and bake."

"If he likes them, that's all that matters," Sophie said.

Toots simply nodded, enjoying the peacefulness of the early morning. This had always been her favorite time of day since she was a little girl. New days were a chance to make each one better than the day before.

She smoked one last cigarette before heading inside. "Can you be ready to leave in fifteen minutes?"

"I'll meet you out front in ten." Sophie took off like a bat out of hell, racing up the staircase like she was a kid.

Toots loved it.

Just as she said she would be, Sophie was waiting outside in ten minutes. As she was walking out the door, Mavis and Ida appeared. Toots asked them if there was anything they needed from the store, and both said no. They were going to stay behind and relax.

A half hour later, they were back. They had the ingredients for homemade oatmeal-raisin cookies, séance candles, four cartons of cigarettes, two extra-large boxes of Froot Loops, two gallons of milk, a ten-pound bag of sugar, and a loaf of bread. Toots had also purchased four large Rubbermaid plastic containers for Jamie to pack the cookies in.

"I'm going to run this stuff over to Jamie, check on her to see what she's heard about the new equipment, and if humanly possible, I want to see if she can have these cookies ready in time for the FedEx pickup," Toots said.

"I think I'm going to take a nap. If that detective is going to arrive tonight, it could be a late one for all of us," Sophie suggested.

"When is it not?"

"Go deliver your stuff before the butter melts."

Toots hoisted three bags in her arms, trying to arrange them so she would have one free hand to flip Sophie the bird. In doing so, she spilled the contents of one bag out on the ground. Luckily, it was just the plastic containers.

Smiling and shaking her head, she trudged

down the stone path that led to the guest-house. Jamie was waiting for her at the door.

"Here, let me take those bags." Jamie took the groceries, then headed toward the kitchen, where she placed them all on top of the butcher-block island. She unpacked the ingredients and placed everything neatly in the order in which she would use them.

"Do you think you could have a box of these ready to ship before eleven o'clock? That's when FedEx makes its pickup."

"For you, absolutely. If you want, I can pack them up and watch for the FedEx truck myself, save you another trip."

"You're a doll. That would be great. I received an e-mail from Pete this morning, and he says they will have the bakery cleared out, repainted, and the old machines disposed of in a couple of days. Have you ordered the new equipment?"

"I just got off the phone with them. They said they can have it delivered within three to five working days. I can't believe how fast this is turning around. I loved the Jacuzzi last night. I don't remember ever being so relaxed. I love it here."

Toots smiled. "I knew you would. We didn't want to bother you anymore last night. We all needed a good night's rest and some downtime. Now, whatever you need, pot and pan wise, just order it. I had Henry transfer more money into the business account. Use it as if it were your own. I left the keys in the Land Rover, just in case you need to go into town when I'm not home. You've got my cell number if you need me, okay?"

Tears filled Jamie's eyes. "Okay." She walked Toots to the door, giving her a hug before she left.

Toots raced down the stone path through the back lawn to her spot on the back porch steps, where she sat, smoked two cigarettes, and considered what to do with the rest of her day.

She decided to take a nap. As Sophie had said, it could be a very long night.

CHAPTER 27

After a dinner of peanut butter and jelly sandwiches, the women gathered around the kitchen table to discuss Thomas and his probable affair or affairs — they weren't sure which. Certainly Ida had no clue.

Suddenly they heard the creak of wood, followed by a loud thumping noise, on the front porch.

"I think someone is here," Mavis said.

"I bet it's Goebel. Chris said he would be arriving sometime this evening," Toots reminded them as she headed for the front door. All three women followed her. Coco stayed in her palace in the corner.

Ida, Sophie, and Mavis peered out the window, watching as the man stood outside the front door. He was a large, portly, unshaven man wearing a fedora and gnawing on half an unlit cigar and looked like someone who had just rolled off a park bench. A homeless person, although given his bulk, it looked as though he hadn't missed a meal in quite a long time. The four women gathered around the front door to greet the man, who had taken the first flight available to come to their rescue. Or, to be more precise, *Ida*'s rescue.

A single knock on the door and, before he got a second chance to pound his fist again, Toots opened it. "You must be Goebel. Please come inside. We were just about to have a drink. We have lots to discuss."

"I thank you for the Southern hospitality, ma'am. I'm not used to such kindness from strangers back in New York. When people see someone like me approaching the door, I'm usually greeted with a single finger rather than a warm reception."

Toots burst out laughing. She liked this man immediately. He cut straight through the flesh and right to the bone.

Toots introduced Ida first, then Mavis and Sophie. "Let's go to the kitchen, where we can sit down. There's lots to talk about," Toots said.

Once the drinks were poured, a round of scotch for all, except Mavis, who sipped a glass of ice water, Toots took control of the conversation.

"Chris tells me you were a detective with the NYPD. How long have you been out on your own?"

"I've been freelancing for almost ten years now, but it sure doesn't seem that long. When I worked for the NYPD, I got so sick of all the red tape, thieves and convicts having more rights than me, so I decided to branch out and find a way to do things the best way. My way." Goebel tossed back his drink and slammed the glass down. "I allow myself one drink per day. That was damn good. So, Chris tells me you need to locate someone."

For the first time since Goebel arrived, Ida spoke up. "We need for you to locate a woman named Nancy. We have reason to believe she might have murdered my late husband in an attempt to gain his money. She could be coming after me next. You see, my husband . . . I don't know how to put this. . . . I just want you to know I'm not . . . we're not crazy, but he showed himself in a séance and told me he had a daughter and that she poisoned him. I know how that must sound to you, but we were all there . . . at the séance, and it most certainly did happen."

All four women watched for a negative reaction. When they saw none, they all breathed a sigh of relief. They all knew their story sounded a bit crazy. Hell, it wasn't just a bit crazy; it was a lot crazy.

Goebel held his hand out, shaking it from side to side. "You can save the explanation. Chris filled me in on the background information. I'm not saying that I believe in that sort of thing, but I can tell you that I'm good at what I do. If this woman exists, I'll find her. Ghost story or no ghost story."

"We don't have much to go on. If we're to believe Thomas's ghost, and yes, I know how silly that sounds, this woman was in Chicago the same time Thomas was. He died just a few days after he returned to New York City. I believe this Nancy confronted him and either demanded money or tried to blackmail him. When she didn't get what she wanted, I believe she poisoned him," Ida explained.

"That's a hell of an allegation," Goebel said. "In order for me to get started, I'm going to need the names of the hotels and the airlines that Thomas used on his last trip to Chicago."

"His secretary has all that information," Ida said. "She was responsible for arranging all of his travel. She's still there at the firm. I'll call her and arrange for her to fax the records as soon as possible. You do have a fax machine, right, Toots?" Ida asked as an afterthought.

Toots rolled her eyes. "Ten-year-olds have fax machines. Of course I have a fax machine."

"Certainly isn't any of my business, but how are you going to be able to find a person when you only know her first name?" Mavis inquired politely.

"If Thomas did father her, and she knew he was her father, there might be a good chance that his name is listed on her birth certificate. Pretty simple, huh? I have a friend who can look up any type of government-issued document I may need. That's where I'll start."

"Mr. Goebel, we think she might be coming after Ida next. If she murdered Thomas for his money, she must not have known he was married. And at our last séance, Thomas was trying to warn us about her," Sophie said.

Goebel stood up, adjusted his too-tight pants, then rubbed his large stomach like it was a magic lamp where an overfed genie resided. "You ladies don't need to worry. As long as I'm here, I can promise you that nothing is going to happen to any of you. I think it might be a good idea for you all to lie low for a little bit and let me get my hands dirty.

"If Thomas was murdered for his money,

Miz Ida will be the number-one suspect. Before we go to the police and tell them we think he was murdered, we need some evidence that will prove Ida wasn't involved and points to this Nancy person Thomas mentioned. I'll need to make a few phone calls and check a few things out first. I'll be at the Cozy Man Bed-and-Breakfast. If you need anything or have any further information, you can reach me on my cell phone." He removed his wallet, took out a business card, and gave it to Ida.

"I'm going to start working immediately. I'll be here tomorrow, say, around dinnertime. You ladies sure look like you can cook, and it's been a long time since I've had a good Southern meal," Goebel said. "Hint, hint."

"Uh, yes, of course. Mavis is a wonderful cook. How does seven sound?" Toots asked.

"Perfect. I'll see you ladies tomorrow night." Goebel spun around like a top. When he reached the front door, he actually bowed, one hand in front and the other behind his back. Then the would-be Rhett Butler said good night.

As soon as the door closed, the women looked at one another, not sure what to say.

Sophie broke the ice. "What do you girls think?"

"I think I'm going to have to learn how to prepare a Southern meal, and quickly," Mavis said, suddenly flustered. "I'm from Maine, for goodness' sake. Toots, do you have a cookbook I could study?"

"Calm down, Mavis. You don't need to cook a thing. Bernice is the best Southern cook this side of the Mason-Dixon Line. She'll get a kick out of this, trust me."

The relief on Mavis's face was palpable. "Thank goodness! That poor man. I bet he hasn't had a home-cooked meal in . . . a while."

"I wouldn't fret about it too much, Mavis. He certainly hasn't been starving. That much is obvious," Ida observed, a grin lighting up her face for the first time in days.

They all laughed as they made their way back to the kitchen. Toots put on a pot of coffee. "I don't know about the rest of you, but I think he's perfect. Not too many people can be told one minute they're looking for evidence of a murder that was reported by a ghost, then wonder what they'll have for dinner in the next. Yes, I think he may be a little unorthodox, but I think that's exactly what we need. Chris says he's a little out there but that he always gets the job done. I wouldn't be surprised if he walked through the door, dragging a bound and gagged Nancy by the hair."

The tension that had been building the past few days eased just a little bit. Though he appeared to be the complete opposite of the professional sleuth, they were all hopeful this Goebel character would lead them to Nancy.

CHAPTER 28

As soon as Goebel closed the door to his rental car, he whipped out his cell phone to call his former partner. Big Willie owed him a favor, and it was now time to cash in on it. He absolutely loved it when people owed him favors. Just loved, loved it.

"Hey, Big Willie. How's it hangin', you old Irish son of a bitch? It's been a long time."

"Goebel Global, how the hell are you? I'm assuming not too good, because if you're calling me on poker night, you must need something. Skip the small talk and tell me what I can do for you."

Goebel kept one eye on the GPS as he drove back to the Cozy Man Bed-and-Breakfast.

"You know, BW, that's why I always liked you. You never were one for bullshitting. I'll get straight to the point. I'm on a case, trying to locate someone. I don't have a lot of

291

information to go on, just a first name, the city, and the date. What I need from you is to look for any birth certificate for a female with the father's last name listed as McGullicutty. Probably about thirty years ago, born in or around Chicago. The kid's first name was listed as Nancy. You get all that?" Goebel asked his former partner.

"Birth certificate, father's last name McGullicutty, female, somewhere near Chicago, first name Nancy, about thirty years ago. That correct?" Big Willie asked.

"You're right on the money. I'm gonna need this as soon as possible. My clients believe that this person could have been responsible for murder, and they might be planning another."

"Damn women today! Nothing shocks me anymore. Give me a few hours, and I'll see what I can come up with."

"Okay. As soon as you find anything, call me on my cell. I'm going back to my B and B to boot up my laptop and do a little searching of my own. And with any luck, I can get some information to help me get this ball rolling." Goebel punched the END button, then tossed his cell on the seat.

Fifteen minutes later, the monotonous female voice from the GPS informed him he had arrived at his destination. Inside his room, he took a quick shower, squeezed into his favorite pair of old sweatpants and a holey white T-shirt and went to work.

For the next three hours, Goebel skimmed through dozens of newspapers published in and around the Chicago area, reading birth announcements. Nothing caught his eye. As a private investigator, he had a database of information that would rival some small police departments. Yet with all his resources, he knew that finding someone with such limited information was next to impossible. This was needle-in-a-haystack land. But he had never walked away from a challenge and wasn't about to start. He'd dedicated his entire life to making sure guilty parties paid for what they did. He wanted to help the women back at the house. Plus, that Southern home-cooked meal he was promised wasn't going to hurt, either. He was pinning all his hopes on Big Willie's coming through with just a shred of information that could lead him in the right direction. Once he had Thomas's itinerary, he could work from that angle. He closed down his computer for the night, turned the television set on, and surfed the channels, stopping when he saw that the History Channel had a special program on Nostradamus. Maybe there was something to this ghost stuff these ladies seemed so sure of. He finally fell asleep with the television set on, only waking a little after six, when the grumbling in his stomach got to him.

Never one to piddle around when there was work to do, he piled out of bed, showered and shaved, then went downstairs to partake of the breakfast part of the B and B. Two elderly couples were already seated in the large formal dining area. Goebel gave them a friendly nod and proceeded to the sideboard, where he poured himself a cup of coffee and placed an order with the host of the bed-and-breakfast for two eggs, sunny side up, and heavily buttered toast. He was sitting at a corner table, sipping his coffee, when he felt a vibration in his pocket. He pulled out his cell phone and saw the caller ID, which told him it was Willie. He swallowed another gulp of coffee and answered the phone. "Whaddaya got for me?"

"I looked in every database I had access to. I didn't find anything that you would consider solid evidence. There were four birth certificates with the names you mentioned. I checked them out, and none of them belonged to the Nancy you're looking for. It looks like this woman you're looking for was never born, or she doesn't want to be found.

"There was one odd thing I found out. When I came up with no information about the birth certificate, I called a former colleague who works as a private detective in Chicago. I told him what I was looking for, and he told me something very peculiar. I told him I was looking for a woman named Nancy who was born about thirty years ago and whose father had the last name McGullicutty. By the tone of his voice, I could tell something was off. He asked me if her father was named Thomas McGullicutty. I told him I wasn't sure. He then proceeded to tell me that not that long ago, a young woman by the name of Nancy had hired him to find her long-lost stepmother, the wife of her late father, Thomas McGullicutty. When he said this, I didn't want to lead him to the fact that we suspect her of murder, so I asked him to go on. He said she was trying to locate her stepmother to give her some personal items her late father had left for her. So I quickly made up a ruse and told him that her stepmother was looking for her, too, hoping that he would reveal the address. He bought the story, hook, line, and sinker."

"So you're telling me you actually have an address for this Nancy?" Goebel asked.

"That's what I'm trying to tell you, numb

nuts. Big Willie always comes through. Now you owe me one. How about letting me use that summerhouse of yours for my next vacation?"

"No problem, you blackmailing son of a bitch. How long do you want it for?"

"Well, it is a summerhouse, right? How about the whole damned summer?" Big Willie guffawed.

"If I wasn't in another state, I'd pimp smack you. Since you were able to find the information I couldn't, consider it done. Place is yours for the summer."

"Thanks, Goebel. I'll get back with you when I'm ready for the key."

Goebel clicked the END button on his cell phone. Big Willie finagled something from him every time. He'd been his partner for most of his career as a police officer. He figured he owed Big Willie a lot more than a place to stay for the summer. They'd kept one another alive, watched each other's back more times than he cared to remember. A stay at his summerhouse was cheap at twice the price.

CHAPTER 29

On Tuesday, Jamie backed the Land Rover out of the garage, still appalled by the entire episode at the bakery. She didn't have a clue who would want to do her any harm or destroy an old building left to her by her grandmother. Jamie knew that the value of the land where the building stood was priceless. It'd been passed down in her family from generation to generation for more than three hundred years. Selling it was totally out of the question.

Toots and her friends had been a true blessing. Her incredibly generous offer couldn't have been made at a better time. All the more reason to think of her as her very own personal fairy godmother.

What puzzled her more than anything, though, was who did this. She couldn't think of anyone who disliked her enough to resort to such tactics. She had a few people with whom she hung out on the rare occasion that she had a free evening, but they were really just acquaintances, not close friends. As far as she knew, they wouldn't even consider such an act. Like her, they would be totally stunned at what had happened, just as she had been when she'd returned to the bakery after her shower at the YMCA.

She didn't have a lot of hope that the police were going to pull out all stops for this investigation. Since there was no evidence of a break-in, at least according to the police officer who'd written up the report, she suspected they thought she was behind this act of destruction, though for what purpose she had no clue, since her insurance wouldn't even cover the cost of most of her equipment. She'd only been able to afford the skimpiest policy, telling herself that when she was established, she'd get a new policy with better coverage. Fortunately, what little cash she had had been in her backpack, so robbery for financial gain couldn't possibly be a motive. She crossed her fingers that the culprit of such mass destruction would be apprehended and punished according to the law.

Loving the feel of the Land Rover, Jamie smiled again. Her entire world was a brighter and much better place because of a kind and generous woman who liked her pralines. Who would've thought? Somehow, she knew her grandmother was looking down on her, giving her that silly little wink she'd been so well known for.

She was going to spend the day helping Pete and the crew he'd hired to clean the bakery. It was the least she could do, especially now that she had a partner who had virtually given her carte blanche to do as she pleased. Yesterday Jamie had ordered the new ovens and the mixer, along with a new display case that she'd gotten for half price because it was a return. She would cut corners in any way possible, except on the quality of her ingredients. She'd lost a couple of hundred pounds of flour, which was easily replaceable from her local supplier, but fortunately the vandals had left her large array of spices, flavorings, decorating tools and materials untouched. The fondant used for elaborate decorating remained in the large walk-in refrigerator. Jamie was grateful, as those ingredients, at least the top-of-the-line brands she insisted on, didn't come cheap.

When she arrived at the bakery, a team of professionals had already removed all the mess from the floor. The smashed mixer, along with the useless ovens, were piled in the back of a large truck.

She spied a man in his early fifties, wearing a cap that read GARDENERS DO IT ON THEIR KNEES. Smiling, knowing this had to be Pete, she went to introduce herself.

"I'm Jamie, owner . . . half owner of this catastrophe. You must be Pete," Jamie said, holding out her hand.

He took her hand, his grip firm enough without being painful. "You're the one staying in the guesthouse, aren't you?" Pete asked.

Worried that Pete might think she was taking advantage of Toots, she nodded. "Yes, and I really can't tell you how much she's done for me. That's why I came today. I want to pitch in wherever I'm needed."

Pete expressed his agreement with a quick nod, then pointed to what used to be her baking sheets piled high in a corner. "I was going to take those to be recycled. You know where the recycling center is?"

"No, but if you tell me, I'll find it. The Land Rover has a GPS."

"You driving Toots's car, too?" Pete asked.

Jamie felt uncomfortable under his scrutiny. It wasn't like she'd asked for any help. "Yes, I have her car, too. She insisted I use it since it's gathering dust in the garage. I always heard it was better to drive a car now and again. Letting one sit idle too long causes all sorts of problems."

"That'd be Toots. Has that Lincoln. Likes it better than the Rover. You need it gassed up, you just let me know. I keep the cars ready just in case."

She wanted to ask, "In case of what?" but refrained. Jamie supposed this was Pete's way of an apology of sorts. Not wanting to interfere in his relationship with Toots, Jamie spoke up. "I'll be sure to do that, though I won't be driving unless I have to pick up supplies. I have my bike. That's my personal preference in transportation as far as travel goes, and I like the exercise."

"Can't move heavy-duty stuff on a bike," Pete said. "Back that Rover up over there." He pointed to the alley behind the bakery. "I'll load this up, and you can be on your way."

Jamie returned to the car and made fast work of backing the Land Rover into the alley. Within minutes, Pete filled the back of the Land Rover with four dark green construction bags. Removing a stubby pencil from his shirt pocket, he scribbled the address for the recycling center on a business card. "You plan on coming back when you're finished?" Pete asked, handing her the card.

301

"Of course," Jamie said, shifting the gearshift into drive.

"There's really no need. The drywall guys are gonna patch the walls. They'll need to dry overnight. Ain't any reason for you to be here," Pete said, nodding in the bakery's direction.

Biting her tongue, Jamie said, "I suppose I could go back to Toots's and bake cookies all day. Maybe I'll make a strawberry short-cake." She tapped her finger against the steering wheel. "The possibilities are end-less. I don't suppose you or the guys" — she nodded just as he had — "would want an afternoon snack, maybe something to take home for dessert tonight?" Pressing down on the accelerator just enough to move the vehicle an inch, Jamie let off the gas when she saw the change that came over Pete.

"What kinda cookies are we talking about?" he asked.

Jamie smiled. It worked every time. *That old adage saying the way to a man's heart is through his stomach is so true,* she thought. "What's your favorite?"

Please not oatmeal-raisin. Not that she didn't like oatmeal-raisin cookies, but she had just baked six dozen for Toots's friend in California and really wanted to try a new

302

recipe she'd seen in a magazine.

"Anything, as long as it don't have raisins," Pete said.

Jamie wanted to kiss the man but knew that if she did, he'd think her more strange than he did already. "I'll surprise you. And I promise, no raisins." She pushed on the gas, inching down the alley until she reached the main street. At a traffic light, she quickly punched in the address on the back of the business card. The female drone told her she had 6.8 miles to her final destination. Jamie hated these impersonal voices. Why didn't someone come up with a GPS that you could program with your own voice rather than just the typical aggravating male voice or the stern female? The light changed, and Jamie pictured the woman, or rather the voice from the GPS, as a strict schoolmarm type. When you made a wrong turn, she definitely let you know.

Jamie arrived at the recycling center. A guy who was probably close to her age removed the dark green bags from the rear of the vehicle, gave her a slip of paper, and told her to go to the office if she wanted to collect her money.

"Money?" Jamie inquired.

"Money. You know, the green stuff? Scrap metal. You get money for it." The guy stared at her like she was from another planet.

"Actually I thought I was disposing of a bunch of broken pans." Should she take the money? Of course she should. It could be used to replace the baking sheets. "Point me in the direction of the office."

The guy told her to drive back the way she came in, but, instead of taking a right, to take a left. She would see the small brick building where the word *office* was spelled out in giant aluminum letters.

She thanked him, found the office, where she gave the slip of paper to an older woman engrossed in a soap opera on a small black-and-white portable television set. The woman, unhappy at the interruption, smacked two twenty-dollar bills, a five, and three pennies in the palm of her hand.

"Thanks," Jamie muttered. She left the office, leaving the woman to her afternoon addiction. Counting the money in her hand, she stuffed it in her pocket, realizing it would cover only half the cost of one good baking sheet. Back in the car, she thought she should've sprung for the better insurance coverage. It was too late now.

Heading back to the guesthouse, as she referred to it, she made a quick stop at Publix, where she purchased the makings for the recipe for the cookies she'd seen in a magazine, grabbing three pints of fresh strawberries to top the shortcake. She guessed Toots and the girls wouldn't mind a dessert. It was the least she could do. *No, it isn't,* she thought when she remembered that the reason she was here now was because Toots adored her pralines. She raced back through the store for ingredients to make pralines.

She arrived back at the guesthouse and unloaded her groceries. She removed three plastic mixing bowls from the kitchen cabinets, a handheld mixer, and got to work. Mixing butter, cream, and pecans with her grandmother's secret ingredient completed the prep for the pralines. Secondly, she mixed the new cookie concoction, and for the next two hours, with only two small baking sheets, she alternately used them for the cookies and the pralines. When she finished, she made shortcake for the strawberries for later.

Using one of the leftover Rubbermaid containers Toots had purchased, she packed up the cookies, tucked a few pralines in foil, then drove back to the bakery. By the time she arrived, Pete and two men, whom she assumed were the drywall guys, were cleaning trowels and mud buckets.

"I was about to think you'd run out on

me," Pete said.

"Never." Jamie gave him the container of cookies and the foil-wrapped package. "This should keep your sweet tooth satisfied for another day or two."

"Hmm, I suppose so. We're about finished for the night. Toots gave me her key, so I can lock up if you want me to."

"No, actually I wanted to stick around for a while. I need to go through what's left of my inventory. So go ahead. I'll close up. And, Pete, thanks for doing the cleanup so quickly. Toots said I would be back in business in a matter of days. And she was right."

"The lady is smart. If she says it's so, then it is," Pete said.

The two drywall workers had remained silent during their interchange. Packing up their tools, they called "See you later" to Pete; he gave them a quick wave, then turned to Jamie. "You sure you want to stay here after what's happened?" Pete said.

Jamie truly hadn't given much thought to her safety. Several other shops that flanked the bakery were still open, so she felt reasonably safe. And besides, it wasn't that late. "I'll be okay. It shouldn't take me too long to make a list of what I have and what I don't have. But thanks for asking," Jamie replied.

Pete gathered a clipboard piled high with papers, gave his usual nod, then left through the one and only exit. As soon as the door closed behind him, she clicked the dead bolt in place. Even though it wasn't quite completely dark outside, she ran through the front of the bakery, clicking on every light possible, just in case.

There was a small room in the kitchen, next to the giant refrigerator, that had, according to family history, always been used for refrigeration. Jamie knew from her grandmother that throughout the years, the place had been used for one line of business or another that required refrigeration. When it had come time for her to open her bakery, the refrigeration system was old and outdated but in working condition. Another item she had added to her list of updates as soon as she felt she was established financially. Giant refrigerators and walk-in freezers were not in her budget. Even though Toots had given her carte blanche, she wasn't about to ask her to tackle an extra expense when it wasn't needed. The small room where she kept all her baking supplies, or at least the intricate ones, might have been used as a butler's pantry at one time. Floor-to-ceiling shelves lined three walls. A single light-bulb barely provided enough light for her to see. She'd had a couple of tall lamps, but those had been destroyed in the break-in, as well. A legal pad and pen were always placed on the bottom shelf. When she ran out of supplies, it would be her habit to jot down whatever she needed on this list. However, she hadn't been in business long enough to need to do so. Tonight she wanted to inventory the stock, just in case there was something she had missed.

For the next thirty minutes, Jamie organized the shelves, taking each individual item and wiping it with a wet paper towel, since some of the spilled flour still clung to cans, jars, bottles, and plastic bags. Suddenly, out of nowhere, the small room, which was normally a bit on the hot side as there was no ventilation, turned cool. Chilled, she rubbed her hands up and down the length of her arms, shivering at the sudden change of temperature.

As she dusted the remaining flour off the shelves, an eerie feeling came over her. Alarmed, she stepped out of the pantry area and into the kitchen. That, too, felt extremely cold. *An unnatural cold,* she thought as she walked the length of the kitchen, searching for the source of the sudden gust of bone-chilling air. In front of the bakery, the area that was lit up like a lighthouse wasn't cold at all. *Weird,* she thought.

She peered through the glass on the door, thinking maybe her creepy feeling had been from someone looking in the door out of curiosity. Looking left and right, she saw nothing to indicate that anyone had been in front of her store. Maybe she should have listened to Pete.

Trying to shrug off the inexplicable feeling of dread she suddenly felt, she headed back to the kitchen, where she did a final once-over, looking in nooks and crannies, making sure she was alone. In doing so, she felt stupid, like a frightened child who needed Mommy and Daddy to check for monsters under the bed. But something wasn't right. And it wasn't her imagination. She felt as though eyes were following her as she quickly paced the length of the kitchen, searching for an area where one might hide. She saw nothing, just as she expected.

Out of nowhere she heard footsteps stomping, as though someone were running up and down the stairway. Her heart raced, and her mouth was so dry, her lips stuck together. Paralyzed with fear, Jamie stood in the center of the kitchen, too stunned to move.

Out of nowhere, a rush of air passed her. She whirled around, thinking that someone had just walked through the kitchen, because that was exactly what the gust of air felt like. Jamie did not like this feeling. Eyes, unseen eyes, following her, maybe waiting, for what she didn't know. Unlike the girls in the horror movies who always ran upstairs and hid in the bedroom, she wouldn't make their mistake. Without another thought, Jamie grabbed her bag and keys and raced to the front door, unlocked the dead bolt, and yanked the door open. Her hands were trembling so bad, she could barely insert the key in the lock. Finally, on the third try, she was successful.

Frightened, Jamie raced to the Land Rover and broke all the speed limits to get home. She parked the vehicle in the garage. Her hands were still shaking as she entered the guesthouse.

A memory from her childhood suddenly overwhelmed her.

The building where she had so lovingly placed her hopes and dreams had been used as a funeral parlor at one time.

CHAPTER 30

You would have thought Bernice was Julia Child, the way she pranced around the kitchen, preparing the evening's special Southern dinner. She had insisted that Toots and the others remain out of her kitchen, explaining that she didn't need any distractions. As was the norm, Toots flipped her the bird. Then she and the girls took up temporary residence in the formal living room. They were all half watching *Antiques Roadshow* when they heard a car pull up in the driveway.

"I bet that's Goebel. I hope to hell he found something. This waiting is making me nuts," Sophie said.

A loud *knock-knock-knock* could be heard from the foyer, and Toots raced to answer the door, with Sophie, Ida, and Mavis trailing her like three baby chicks.

Toots opened the door, revealing a spiffed-up, slicked-back, and shiny Goebel. His thinning brown hair was neatly combed. He wore a pair of beige Dockers, a white polo shirt that clearly outlined the shape of his stomach, topped off with a navy jacket. There was no trace of the stubby, smelly cigar.

"Come in. We've been expecting you," Toots said. "I hope you're hungry, because Bernice is cooking up a storm in honor of your visit and has forbidden any of us to enter her kitchen."

Goebel stepped inside, the aromatic odors from the kitchen bringing a grin to his chubby face.

"Are those biscuits I smell?" he asked.

Toots cupped his elbow and led him to the dining room. "I'm clueless. Like I said, Bernice wouldn't allow us in the kitchen. Before you ask, she's my dear friend and likes to call herself my housekeeper. For the record, none of us cook except Mavis. She doesn't do Southern food, however. Consider this meal a down payment on whatever information you've dug up."

"I'll consider it after I've eaten," Goebel responded smartly.

Bernice had decorated the formal dining room as though they were expecting royalty. She had set out the best china, the gold-plated silverware, and the cloth napkins

from Scabal, one of the world's top manu-
facturers of fine linen. From the looks of
things, Bernice had prepared a feast that
would make the editors of *Southern Living*
salivate.

Shrimp and grits, a South Carolina favorite, accompanied by fried chicken, served as
the main entrée. Fried green tomatoes, fried
okra, collard greens, black-eyed peas, and
mashed potatoes with sawmill gravy were
the side dishes. Hot buttered biscuits and
fresh corn muffins topped with pepper jelly
completed Bernice's Southern meal.

Now that the formal living room had been
cleared of the four square tables and sewing
machines, Bernice insisted they *retire* there
— Toots almost fainted when she heard her
use that word — where she would serve
them coffee with real cream and her special
dessert, which she made only when someone
died, a Lady Baltimore cake. Toots wondered if this was an omen of sorts.

After they were seated, and coffee and
dessert served, Toots asked Goebel, "Did
you just eat my down payment or not?"

Goebel laughed, his large stomach shaking like the proverbial bowlful of jelly.
"Another meal like that, and the rest is free."

"I'll keep that in mind," Toots said. "Did
you locate this woman, Nancy?"

"I searched everywhere possible, or at least within my database, and I came up with nothing. I cashed in a favor my former partner owed me, and he came across something quite interesting."

"And?" Toots prompted. "Did you find something that would connect Nancy to Thomas's death?"

Goebel held his hand out in front of him as if to ward off further talk. "You're not a patient woman, are you? My partner got a few leads that led nowhere. He called an old friend to assist him in finding any other possible information about this mysterious Nancy. As it turns out, the detective my friend called had recently been hired by a woman who went by the name Nancy. This is where it's a small world comes in. Not too long ago, probably within the last few months, this Nancy told him that her father, one Thomas McGullicutty, had passed away within the last two years. Nancy explained that she needed his assistance in locating her father's widow because she had only recently come across some of her late father's personal effects and wanted to return them to her father's widow."

Ida had remained silent throughout dinner and dessert, letting Toots take the lead, asking questions that needed to be asked, but when she heard this, she could no longer remain quiet. "What! Wait a minute. Are you telling me this . . . Nancy hired a private detective to locate *me?*"

"It appears that way. Big Willie never mentioned to his friend that Nancy is being investigated for murder. Apparently, the guy was bored. Willie said he talked like he'd been injected with a phonograph needle."

Sophie decided it was time to put her two cents in. "That has to explain why Thomas is coming through so easily! He wants you to find his killer, Ida."

Mavis, with Coco in her usual lapdog position, never moved an inch during the entire conversation. Maybe Coco was psychic, too. Dogs, she knew, sensed these oddities, though chances were slim that Coco would be the next Miss Cleo.

"That's what I'm trying to do, Miss Sophie," Goebel said. Then he winked at her.

Sophie jumped out of her chair like her rear end came equipped with springs. "Did you just wink at me?"

Goebel laughed so hard between chuckling and the force of his weight, the chair actually slid across the slick wooden floor. "Naw, I didn't wink at you, Miss Sophie. My eye was sweating, and I just needed to blink a few times."

They all laughed, providing a bit of comic relief from the topic of their conversation.

"This Nancy must have made contact with Thomas, possibly explaining who she was. Knowing Thomas, he would never turn his back on a pretty female, daughter or not. It makes sense for her to believe Thomas wasn't married because if he were, surely the woman would know Thomas's fortune would be left to his widow?" Ida said.

"She must have had close enough contact with him to administer whatever he was poisoned with. Maybe they shared dinner or a drink," Ida said dejectedly, the wind temporarily knocked out of her sails.

"It's just as I thought. Thomas is trying to warn us that Nancy is coming after you," Sophie said. "If Nancy can pin Thomas's death on Ida, then Ida inheriting Thomas's money is legally null. The money reverts to Thomas's estate, and as the last of Thomas's living heirs, Nancy claims her inheritance, despite not being mentioned in any will."

Mavis finally contributed to the conversation. "If this is true, she is one twisted person who will stop at nothing until she gets what she is after. We need some kind of evidence, something to take to the police." Coco growled to let them know that she, too, agreed with her mistress.

Toots refilled their coffee cups. "That's where you come in, Goebel. Is there anything you or your friend can do at this late date? It's been over two years since Thomas died. Where would you find evidence? At least something credible we can take to the authorities."

"I'm one step ahead of you. I was able to get her address. I plan to do a little 'investigating' of my own. If the woman is dumb enough to murder Thomas before she found out if he had any living relatives, she's probably dumb enough to leave some evidence lying around her house. After all, to the best of her knowledge, she still thinks no one knows she committed a crime. She assumes everyone believes her father died of food poisoning. So why would she need to get rid of any evidence that might link her to a murder that no one knows about?" Goebel explained. "Even more important, if she hoped to frame Ida for Thomas's death, she needed to keep some of the evidence of her own involvement around to plant on Ida. I rather suspect that you ladies all being together for the last year or so threw a monkey wrench into Nancy's plans. Once Ida sold her place and left New York City for undisclosed parts, Nancy was stuck.

That's why she finally decided to have a detective look for you. You ladies gettin' this?"

"Us ladies do," Sophie singsonged, grinning as she poked fun at Goebel. "We definitely have the upper hand since we know what she is going to try to do. She got away with murder. Now she has decided to get away with framing someone for the murder she committed. It would be logical for her to assume she'll get away with it. I wonder, though, why she's waited so long. Two years is a long time to . . . wait. All we need to do is catch her before she gets to Ida."

"I have to return to New York to testify in a trial tomorrow and Thursday. But I'm booked on an evening flight to Chicago on Thursday. I have her address. I'll pull a stakeout on Friday, and while she's at work, I'm in. If there is anything to be found, trust me, ladies, I'll find it. I'm willing to do whatever it takes to get the job done."

"Chris said as much when I called him," Toots added. "While you're searching her house, is there anything we can do to help?"

"She works for a company called Cryotech. After a quick Google search, I learned that Cryotech's annual charity gala is this Friday. It's a ten-thousand-dollar-a-plate deal, the funds going to AIDS research. This Nancy is a biological engineer. She's expected to make an appearance, according to what I read. I think we should attend. I'm not one hundred percent sure anything will come of it, but it could give us a better understanding of who we are dealing with. Maybe we can find a coworker who has some dirt on her."

"Are you saying you want all of us to go to Chicago to attend a charity event with you?" Sophie asked.

"No, that would be a waste of time and money. Though I don't think I should go alone. A guy like me sitting alone usually draws unwanted attention. What I need is an escort. Someone who is willing to pretend to be my lady friend for the evening. What about it, Miss Sophie?"

"Are you asking me on a date? If so, I hope you're footing the bill for the ten-grand-per-plate dinner," Sophie said, grinning like the Cheshire cat.

"I'll take care of all expenses," Ida said. "It's my liberty and fortune that's hanging in the balance. A twenty-thousand-dollar dinner is a small price to pay."

"Does this mean you'll go?" Goebel asked.

"I'm thinking, okay?" Sophie tossed back. "I'm a recent widow. I don't know how that would look."

Toots chimed in. "Since when have you cared how things looked? Two seconds ago? Stop playing hard to get and say yes."

Sophie flicked the single-digit salute to Toots, not caring that Goebel witnessed her ornery behavior. If she was going to fly to Chicago to meet up with the man, he might as well know what he was in for.

"Oh, all right. I'll go. This is just for pretense, nothing more. You got it?" Sophie said firmly. "This is for Ida," she added.

"Absolutely," Goebel said. "Look, if I'm going to make my flight back to New York early in the morning, I have to leave now. The meal was the best I've had in twenty years. Make sure and tell Bernice. Sophie, I'll meet you at the Fairmont at Millennium Park in Chicago, Friday night around seven. Let me know your flight info, and I'll pick you up."

Sophie actually blushed.

"And you'll want to bring something sexy . . . I mean something formal to wear. This is a black-tie event."

"What? You think I don't know how to dress? I lived in New York City. I have been to Fashion Week, I'll have you know!" Sophie squawked.

Goebel pulled his bulk out of the chair.

"Ladies, I will keep you posted. Sophie, I will see you Friday." Without further conversation, Goebel let himself out.

Toots, Mavis, Ida, and Sophie looked at one another and broke out in gut-splitting laughter.

"I think Sophie's got a boyfriend," Ida singsonged.

All but Sophie started chanting, "Sophie's got a boyfriend! Sophie's got a boyfriend! Sophie's got a boyfriend!"

CHAPTER 31

After giving his testimony on Wednesday afternoon and facing cross-examination on Thursday, Goebel had three hours to retrieve several items from his office and get to the airport for his direct flight to Chicago. He'd asked his taxi driver to wait, telling him he would make it worth his while.

Twenty minutes later, lugging two large suitcases, he piled into the taxicab and headed back to LaGuardia. The taxi driver dropped him in front of Delta Air Lines, where he tossed his two bags to the skycap, flashed his ID, and received his boarding pass. He threw a twenty-dollar bill the man's way and headed for security. Being a VIP flyer did have its perks, he thought as he saw the long lines waiting to get through security.

The flight took off as scheduled. When the plane reached ten thousand feet, a female voice gave them permission to use any approved electronic device. He booted up his laptop and brought up the Google Earth image he'd saved as a .jpg file. He zeroed in on the neighborhood where Nancy lived. He had an Enterprise rental car waiting rather than his usual Hertz because Hertz had screwed his eyes out one time too many. Paybacks were a bitch. The flight was close to three hours, so he leaned back against the headrest and closed his eyes, knowing this would be the only time he'd have to catch a few winks. When the plane touched down at Chicago's O'Hare International, he retrieved his luggage and whipped through the airport O. J. Simpson style. Only he struggled for breath. After locating his rental car, Goebel punched Nancy's address in the GPS and made a beeline for her house to do some reconnoitering before starting the stakeout the next day.

Satisfied that he could do what was needed tomorrow, Goebel checked into his hotel, turned on the TV, and spent the evening thinking about his "date" tomorrow night with Miz Sophie. He was betting that she cleaned up real nice.

The next morning, he cruised past the house and drove around the block to park the rental car one street over. Looking left and right before he got out, he popped open the trunk, making sure no one was watching him. He opened his luggage, where his stock of disguises was laid out like those in a theatrical dress rehearsal. He had a variety of work shirts, hats, wigs, and eyewear. He chose the yellow and red Speedy Delivery ensemble that included a fake package and a computerized signature pad, though if scrutinized, one would know they weren't the real thing. Goebel didn't plan on getting scrutinized. He always kept an evidence-collection kit handy, just in case. He stuffed this and a micro recorder in his pocket. A deliveryman in any neighborhood never raised suspicion.

Getting back in the car and driving around the block, he pulled up directly in front of Nancy's house. Making his way up the driveway, he scouted for the best way to enter the house undetected. He could pick the lock on the front door, but if he did that, he'd be unable to lock it on his way out. Deciding to go around back, he noticed a basement window halfway open. He chose this as his point of entry. Once again, he glanced over his shoulder to the left, then to the right. Seeing there were no curtains pulled aside or a set of blinds with a slat slightly opened, he assumed the coast was clear.

Goebel slid his portly figure through the narrow window, almost getting his arms caught as he slithered halfway down. Thinking to himself, he realized that another Southern meal like he'd had Tuesday night and he would never be able to make a repeat entry. He made a mental note to watch his intake of fried food.

After several twists and turns, he found himself in the basement. Looking around, he discovered it was unlike any basement he had ever seen, cluttered with all kinds of unique objects he didn't recognize. As he made his way across the room, he noticed that the far side of the room was immaculate and well lit. He observed something that looked like a high-school chemistry set. There were beakers, containers of chemicals, and paperwork, all neatly organized, all in sequential rows.

This has to be something important, he thought. But what? No one with a basement this cluttered would bother cleaning up only one side if there wasn't a purpose behind it. He started examining the objects on the counter. They looked like they'd been used for some type of project. Maybe Nancy was a chemist, too. Not knowing what he was dealing with, he grabbed one of the respirators hanging next to him and put it on. He bent his head to tighten the straps on the back of the mask, and a stack of papers in front of him caught his eye. He realized he was looking at Google search results. Reading them, he saw that someone had requested the results for *How long does it take ricin to kill someone?*

He picked up the articles and began to read more.

Ricin is a potent substance that is made from castor beans. The symptoms of ricin poisoning are similar to the flu, and it is often overlooked as either food poisoning or influenza.

Goebel recalled the information Ida had given him about Thomas's last days and realized that the evidence of his murder was staring him right in the face. It all made sense when you added it up. Nancy, working for a chemical engineering company, would have knowledge of and access to the materials needed to process castor beans into ricin. Looking at the Google searches, he saw a picture of what ricin looked like after it had been processed into a deadly poison. A brownish powder, similar to a finely ground sand. Glancing across the counter, he saw the beaker with a brownish residue on the inside.

"That must be what she used to make it in," he muttered to himself. Goebel pulled out a sterile cotton swab from the evidence-collection kit in his jacket pocket and began to swab the inside. "Now we have the bitch right where we want her," he mumbled under his breath. "At least I hope we do."

Realizing that he now had enough evidence to bring to the authorities, Goebel decided it was time to get the hell out as quickly as possible. He positioned the respirator, beaker, and papers back exactly where they were found. He quickly returned to the window he had used to enter the basement. Raising his arms, he attempted to pull himself up but quickly realized that coming down was the easy part. There was no way he was going to be able to climb out the way he had come in. He could use one of the objects on the floor to boost himself up, but he wouldn't be able to put it back once he was out. Besides, he didn't want to warn this Nancy that someone had scoped out her minilab.

Deciding to go out the front door, he headed up the basement stairs. When he reached the top, he slowly turned the doorknob. The door opened, but only an inch. He noticed a padlock dangling from the other side of the door. Because he was a first-rate detective, he deduced it was there to keep people from finding her lab downstairs. In a rare moment of anger, he took his fist and pounded on the wall next to him. "Dammit!" he said, striking it once, then again. The third time he hit the wall, he felt something different. Turning his head ever so slowly, he saw a secret panel, a door of sorts, that led to a small room, no bigger than a bathroom stall. Curious, he opened the door and pulled on the chain that dangled from the bare light-bulb above him. What he saw left him speechless.

A shrine.

Every inch of the wall he was staring at was covered with pictures of Thomas and Ida. Every newspaper article that had ever featured them as a New York society couple was tacked on the walls. Looking around, he noticed the head cut off in a picture of Thomas. The pictures were branded with profanities, all done with a thick black Magic Marker. The words *revenge* and *bitch is next* were marked on nearly every picture of Ida, only with a blood-red marker. Goebel shook his head and squeezed his eyes shut. When he opened them, nothing changed. He took one of the old newspaper articles concerning Ida's photography and put it in his jacket pocket. Realizing he still needed to find a way out, he froze in place when he heard footsteps above him.

"Shit!" he muttered under his breath. "She's home! Must have taken a half day off from work to get ready for the charity do tonight." It was something he hadn't planned for. Big mistake.

He quickly closed the door to the hidden room and searched for a place to hide. The piles of clutter were his only saving grace. He spied an old blow-up mattress, quietly made his way to the table where the mattress lay, slowly pulled the rubber bed over his ample body, and silently prayed she wouldn't come downstairs.

Knowing that if he was caught breaking into her house, he could lose his license and even end up in jail, he tried to control his breathing so as not to make the mattress move. As he tried to focus on his breathing, he heard the footsteps getting louder. When they reached the door to the basement, he heard the one sound that scared the crap out of him — the snap of the Master Lock being unlatched. The basement door swung open with a creak that he remembered from old horror movies, then a loud thump. When he didn't hear footsteps, he realized Nancy had gone into her secret shrine. Trying to hear everything he could, he listened, holding his breath as she started to talk to herself, her voice rising until the words were audible. He allowed his breathing to slow as he clicked on the micro recorder, hoping to pick up her words, which he could now hear quite clearly.

"Mother, my revenge is almost complete. I've got the plans in motion to take care of that backstabbing bastard's wife. I'll find a way to make sure she never spends those millions that should rightfully belong to me. As for my father, he got what he deserved. He drank the ricin like it was Kool-Aid. He even invited me to his room before I told him who I was. Leaving you alone to raise a child by yourself, broke and penniless, swearing he would take care of you. For his lies, I made sure to take care of him. No one suspects a thing. Just like they won't suspect anything when his widow dies. I can finally get the money that should have been left to me in the first place. Now you can rest in peace, Mother. I've taken care of all of our plans. I won't have to live in squalor and filthy places, like we were forced to when he got you pregnant and never laid eyes on you again. His money will be mine no matter what it takes. I will always love you. I hope you are proud of me for getting back at him. Good-bye for now, Mommy."

Shocked at what he'd just heard, Goebel stayed under the blow-up mattress until he heard her footsteps retreating. Several minutes later, he heard water running. Assuming that she was taking a shower and realizing that this might be his only chance to get out, he quickly dashed out from beneath the mattress and saw that the padlock was swinging from the door. He scurried for the front door like a fiddler crab making his way down his burrow.

Inside his rental car, he raced three blocks over, then parked in an alleyway, hoping no one saw him. He had to get the swab to someone immediately, needing to confirm if it was ricin or not. He had a buddy in New York he worked with on occasion, Ted Lawrence, a forensic toxicologist. He worked for a private lab that he could access anytime he was needed. Goebel trusted him as his credentials were impeccable. Not only was Ted a forensic toxicologist, but he was also an expert in forensic pathology. Goebel would messenger the swab to Ted. He'd tell him there was a bonus if he had the results sometime tomorrow morning. Cash was always a good incentive. Tonight, at the charity event, he would watch Nancy, see how she acted, watch for any outward signs of abnormal behavior.

While he sat there, he thought about what he had just heard. Nancy was not only insane but also grossly ignorant about the basic facts of the law. Or perhaps her thinking that she could murder Ida and inherit *Thomas's* money, which Ida had already inherited and which therefore would be left to *Ida's* heirs, if there were any, and under no conceivable circumstances to Nancy, was also a symptom of her insanity and not just ignorance. Could she possibly think that murdering Ida would magically set the clock back two years and result in Ida's money once again becoming Thomas's, which Nancy could inherit? That belief seemed so far beyond rational that anyone who held it probably qualified as belonging in a loony bin. Oh, sure, perhaps some total dimwit, homeless and strung out on drugs and booze, might not think the world worked like that and might not be insane. But this Nancy was a scientist, had advanced degrees. No way someone like that could believe what she did without being nuts.

One could feel sympathy for Nancy and her mother for what that philandering bastard Thomas had done to them. But that did not excuse what Nancy had done and was planning to do. Even if one thought that

Thomas deserved what *he* got, how in hell did that carry over to Ida, the innocent wife whom nasty old Thomas had cheated on? And for Nancy to think that somehow she would get Thomas's money . . . ? Goebel shook his head in amazement. *Takes all kinds,* he guessed.

After a while, he checked his watch. Toots had e-mailed him Sophie's arrival information. He had plenty of time to get to the hotel, then to the airport.

CHAPTER 32

On Wednesday morning, Jamie was pacing back and forth in the small kitchen when she decided that she didn't want to be alone after last night's *frightmare.* She'd spent the night dreaming of unseen eyes watching her. Giving up the fight, she'd gotten up at four and spent the morning hours scrubbing the oven, the floors, and cleaning out the refrigerator, even though all were virtually spotless. She looked at the clock above the stove. Seeing it was only a little after eight, she peered out the window above the sink. The French doors leading to the patio area were open.

Grabbing the shortcake and strawberries, she let herself out, then practically jogged down the stone path that led to the back door of the main house. The acrid smell of cigarette smoke clinging in the air suggested Toots and Sophie had recently been outside for a smoke.

Jamie tapped on the back door.

"We're in here," a voice called out.

She pushed the door open with one hand while holding the containers of strawberries and shortcake in the other. Toots, Mavis, and Ida sat at the table, cups of coffee in front of them.

"I . . . I thought you all might want some dessert. I made this shortcake yesterday, and I can't eat it all by myself," Jamie said.

"Come inside, dear. Have a cup of coffee," Mavis said. Coco ran to Jamie's side, spent a few seconds sniffing her leg. Apparently Jamie passed inspection, because the little brown ball of fur ran back to her palace in the corner without going into hysterics.

"I'd love some," Jamie said and sat down, placing the strawberries and shortcake on the table. "I wasn't sure you all would be up."

Toots laughed. "Honey, no one sleeps in around here. Mature ladies of our age don't sleep late. We were just getting ready to take Ida to her doctor's appointment with my old family physician. Why don't you come with us? We can stop at the bakery and see what progress they've made."

At the mention of the bakery, Jamie's pulse quickened. "I was there last night.

Everything was spotless, well, almost everything." She debated telling them about her strange supernatural experience last night. But she didn't want them to think she was crazy.

With a discerning eye, Toots watched her. "Are you all right? You seem distracted," Toots stated.

"This will probably sound silly, and I hesitate to mention it. However, either I'm going crazy or something else is happening at the bakery." Jamie went into great detail explaining what had happened last night. She told them about the chilling air, the eyes that she felt watched her, even though she was in the bakery completely alone.

Toots looked at Ida and Mavis. "Where is Sophie?"

"She's upstairs, trying to decide what to take with her to Chicago on Friday."

"She needs to hear this," Toots said. "I'll be right back. Don't move."

Jamie was sure she was about to be booted out in the cold. The women probably thought she was out of her mind.

When Sophie came downstairs, Ida said, "Jamie, tell your story to Sophie."

Jamie recounted last night's events. None of the four women seemed the least bit surprised. She was sure they would think she needed to be committed to the nearest insane asylum. Again, the women surprised her.

Without revealing too much of their experience with ghosts and séances, Sophie sat across from Jamie, took her hand in hers, then looked at Toots for direction. "Your grandmother ever tell you anything about the building's history?" Sophie asked.

Hesitant to voice what she was thinking, yet knowing she had to say the words, Jamie spoke quickly. "I had a memory last night. When I was a child, I couldn't have been more than eight or ten, I overheard a conversation I wasn't supposed to hear. My grandmother was in the kitchen of her little mobile home, that's where I lived until she died, and she said something about the building once being used as a funeral parlor." There. She'd said it. She waited for their reaction.

Clearly, her words hadn't affected them as she thought they would.

"It makes perfect sense," Sophie said. "Anytime there's a change in temperature, vibrations, drifting shadows, a feeling of being watched, as well as a variety of other movements and activity during plasterwork, or any type of renovation, it's known to wake the spirits of the past. Each restoration stirs a rising of sinuous activity left from the past and draws it into the present."

Jamie appeared confused. "What does that mean?"

All eyes focused on Sophie. "It simply means the bakery is haunted."

Jamie's bright blue eyes widened. "Are you serious?"

Toots spoke before Sophie had a chance to answer. "Sophie is a . . . medium."

The room was totally quiet.

Bewildered, Jamie asked, "You're saying the slight renovations we did caused a spirit to appear?"

"More or less. Look, if we leave now, we can stop at the bakery before Ida has to be at the doctor's. I'll be able to get a better sense of the place."

"That's a perfect idea. Jamie, toss your berries in the refrigerator. Bernice will be here this afternoon, and she'll think she's died and gone to heaven, as strawberries are her favorite fruit," Toots said.

"Uh, okay," Jamie said.

Ten minutes later, they piled in the Lincoln and Toots drove to the bakery. As usual, her foot and the gas pedal were at war with the speed limit signs posted. She drove ten miles over the legal limit, telling herself if she was pulled over, she would say one of them thought they were having a heart attack. Crummy excuse, but if needed, she'd use it.

As soon as they arrived at the bakery, Toots and the girls followed Jamie inside. Luckily, none of the workmen had arrived yet. Sophie walked through the front of the bakery, closing her eyes as if in deep thought. When she entered the kitchen, she stopped dead in her tracks. Even though it was a clear, sunny Wednesday morning, with the outside temperature in the midseventies, the inside of the bakery was ice cold, the kind of cold that hurt your skin.

"You don't have the air-conditioning on, do you?" Sophie asked.

"No."

Mavis and Ida trailed behind Toots as Sophie wandered through the small space. Again, she closed her eyes. "I feel an energy looming within this space. It's a female."

"How do you know that?" Jamie asked from her position across the room.

Sophie remained quiet, holding her index finger in the air, asking for silence. "This woman suffered greatly in life. A deep emotional hurt. Sometimes souls stay on earth when there are unsolved issues after death." As soon as the words left Sophie's mouth, an increase in air pressure was palpable in the small room. Sophie felt extremely uneasy, overwhelmed, unlike anything she had experienced so far. "There is more than one spirit. Toots, I need to do a cleansing on this place immediately. Are there any health-food stores or an herb shop close by? I need a bundle of dried sage."

"There's a metaphysical bookstore, Blue Moon, right down the street. I can be there and back in fifteen minutes and still get Ida to her doctor's appointment in time, provided this cleansing doesn't take all afternoon. How long, Sophie?" Toots asked.

"Five minutes if it works. If it doesn't, then you're going to have to keep this place empty. I've been studying this. Tarot cards, too. I'm teaching myself to read them. I'll read for all of you when I get back."

"Okay. Stay here. I'll be right back." Toots raced out the door as if their lives depended on it. And maybe they did.

Twenty minutes later, Toots returned with a bundle of dried white sage. "That place had everything, Sophie. Everything. They sell tarot cards, too."

"Okay, let's do this," Sophie urged.

"Before we get started, how will we know if this . . . cleansing worked?" Jamie asked.

"We'll just know," Sophie said. "That feeling you get when the hair on the back of

340

your neck rises will be gone. We may have to do a routine smudging, cleansing, whatever you want to call it. Let's get started."

Sophie lit the bundle of dried white sage. A pleasant-smelling scent arose from the bundle. Sophie lowered the bundle of white sage by her left foot, then fanned the smoke around her, working her way up and over her body, stopping at the top of her head. She repeated this procedure on Mavis, Ida, Toots, and, lastly, Jamie. "This is to remove any negative energy you yourselves may unknowingly have," Sophie explained.

With the bundle of dried white sage held out before her like a sword, Sophie began at the entrance to the bakery and fanned the smoke toward the walls and the corners. She walked the entire perimeter of the bakery, fanning the smoke. In the corners, up the walls, on the ceiling. In the kitchen, where Jamie had experienced her feeling of uneasiness and fear, Sophie waved the herbs back and forth as though she were waving a magic wand. She did the same in the room where Jamie stored her baking supplies. Next, she opened the ancient walk-in refrigerator and waved the smoky wand of herbs up and down and side to side, rising on her toes and waving it, lastly, by the ceiling. And then the smoke was gone. She placed the

341

ashes on a small plate she saw on the large aluminum table in the center of the kitchen. "I want each one of you to dip your finger in the ashes. Then close your eyes and blow. Visualize any negative energy being pushed away."

Everyone followed Sophie's careful instructions. Minutes passed, and the room became noticeably warmer. If there were any more spirits lingering in the old building, they were hiding.

"Okay, let's get out of here. Ida has to get to the doctor's office," Toots reminded everyone.

On Friday morning, Toots, Ida, and Mavis were sitting around downstairs, waiting for Sophie to come down for the trip to the airport. Jamie had just arrived and was telling them that there had been no further ghostly visitations at the bakery, and the new equipment was arriving day by day. She hoped to reopen sometime the following week.

When Sophie came downstairs, everyone gasped. She was dressed to kill in a sharp black pantsuit and reminded Jamie of a smaller version of Sophia Loren. Her dark hair hung loose around her shoulders, taking a good ten years off her age. Professionally applied makeup made her look like a totally different person, or rather a new and improved version of herself. Jamie wondered why all the hoopla. Maybe she had a date.

"You're beautiful," Mavis said. "I haven't seen you like this since we were in college. Your makeup looks phenomenal. Who taught you how to apply it that way?" Mavis asked, apparently in a state of shock. She'd taken such an interest in her appearance this last year, trying new hairstyles, and makeup no longer seemed out of character for the once frumpy woman.

"Ida," Sophie said. "Years ago."

"I didn't realize you were so talented, Ida," Mavis said.

"I'll teach you my tricks another time," Ida explained. "Now, Sophie has a plane to catch. Jamie, do you want to come with us to the airport?"

"I don't think so, Ida. There's still lots to do at the bakery. I'll see you guys later. Sophie, I hope you have a good time in Chicago."

"So do I, Jamie. So do I."

CHAPTER 33

The Fairmont Chicago, Millennium Park Hotel brimmed with Cryotech employees attending the charity benefit for AIDS. They were dressed in their finest, glittering like sparkling jewels in a treasure chest. Goebel, wearing his new tuxedo, observed the hubbub as waiters dressed in crisp white shirts and creased black slacks gracefully maneuvered through the crowd, holding high in the air trays overflowing with champagne flutes. Sophie said she would meet him at seven o'clock. It was ten after. *Figures she would be late,* he thought. He almost hadn't recognized her when he picked her up at O'Hare International that afternoon. She was dressed to kill in a black pantsuit and white blouse that displayed her fine figure. With her hair down, she looked ten years younger than when he had seen her on Tuesday night. She looked like a whole other person. She was gorgeous.

The thought had no sooner passed through his brain when he spotted her in the crowd. Wearing a dark green, sleek, thigh-hugging evening dress with little sparkles glistening in the light, Sophie looked every inch the New York woman she was. Her hair was twisted high on her head, and diamonds glistened on her ears. He watched as a trail of male eyes followed her. She seemed almost regal, this gal with the sharp tongue and quick wit. She had moxie, more than was good for her. He watched her scan the crowd, searching for him. When her eyes locked with his, a jolt ran through him. He'd never married, never wanted a woman wondering when he left for work each day if he would return in a body bag. Seemed unfair to him.

For the first time in sixty-five years, Sophie felt elegant. Not because she practically strutted through the five-thousand-square-foot Moulin Rouge Ballroom decorated in deep reds, shimmering taupes, with luxurious fabrics, tiered seating, and a stage to re-create the feel of a turn-of-the-century cabaret. She felt relaxed. She'd attended many conventions with Walter throughout his short-lived banking career, knowing at the end of the night, when they came home, there would be hell to pay. Tonight, however, when the festivities ended, she would simply retire to her suite, order room service, and enjoy every single minute of it. If Goebel was a gentleman, she might invite him up for a drink, but nothing more. After all, she was recently widowed.

Goebel was grinning from ear to ear as she approached him. "Wipe that smirk off your face right now," Sophie admonished. "You look just like a dirty old man." She was smiling, her brown eyes twinkling with mischief.

"I am a dirty old man," Goebel said. "Sadly, tonight I won't be able to take advantage of the most beautiful woman in the room, because we have work to do. I haven't spotted Nancy. The picture from the Department of Motor Vehicles was six years old. Women can change their appearance on a dime."

"Is that supposed to be an insult, a compliment, or what?" Sophie asked.

"None of the above, just a fact. Women change their hair color, makeup, clothing. It confuses a guy. For the record, you look stunning, Sophie," Goebel said.

"Thank you, Goebel. You've cleaned up nicely yourself." Sophie averted her eyes, scanning for the woman whose picture she'd seen in a fax two hours ago. Though she had an eye for recognition, Goebel was right. Women changed their appearance so often these days, they could look like completely different people.

"Let's stroll over to the bar. Bartenders always seem to know who's who," Goebel said. "And thanks for the compliment. It does an old guy good to hear that once in a while."

"Well, don't think I like you . . . I mean in *that* way, because I don't. We're just pretending, remember?"

Goebel chuckled. "I'm sure you won't let me forget."

They walked past flocks of people, hearing bits and pieces of conversation, the occasional shout, a burst of laughter, the clinking of glasses. Dinner was to be served promptly at eight thirty. Tables were scattered throughout the huge ballroom, each holding a tapered candle and vases of fresh flowers. The place settings had small, attractively wrapped gifts for the guests. At ten thousand dollars a pop, Sophie hoped whatever was inside the box was something that glimmered and shined, but she doubted it would be anything more than a memorable trinket engraved with tonight's date and type of function. She did love presents, especially presents with red or silver bows.

As they approached the bar, Goebel placed a protective arm around her waist. He leaned in and whispered in her ear. "Pretend I'm nibbling your ear. I think I just spotted Nancy. Behind you, my nine o'clock. I'm going to let go of you, and I want you to turn around and wrap your arms around me." Sophie did as instructed. "Tell me if you think that's the woman in the picture I showed you."

A sense of doom so great cascaded down and around Sophie that she was suddenly glad she had Goebel to lean on. The woman Goebel referred to was in her thirties. Dark and smarmy, yet quite pretty. She didn't resemble Thomas at all, and had it not been for her dark complexion, she wouldn't have recognized her. In the DMV picture, her hair was short as a boy's, and giant hoops dangled from her ears. Tonight her hair almost reached her waist. She wore a cream-colored lace dress that fit snugly against her voluptuous curves. Crimson chandelier earrings hung to her shoulders. She might've passed for a young version of Cher had she been thinner. Still, she was an attractive woman.

"That's her. I'm sure of it. What next?" Sophie said, surprised that she was actually enjoying being in Goebel's arms. It'd been so very long since she'd felt wanted and desired. Walter, bastard that he was, had been a louse in the romance department. She'd packed that part of her life away, never giving it much thought until that moment. She wanted to kick herself for the thought, too.

"Let's just watch her for now. If she goes to the ladies' room, follow her. Try to strike up a conversation with her. Don't you gals always chitchat in the ladies' room? It seems like when you all have to *go,* you go in pairs."

"I could act like I'm upset. My husband just died. I'll say something to that effect, see if she takes the bait. And I always go to the ladies' room *alone.*"

"I'll try to remember that. Now, let me get us a drink while you keep those pretty brown eyes on our mark. What would you like to drink?"

Sophie watched Nancy, fearful that if she looked away, the woman would disappear. "I'll have whatever you're having."

"Okay, we're having two soft drinks," Goebel said, then turned toward the bar.

Sophie nodded as she continued to watch Nancy. She needed to get close to her, needed to understand why, when she'd first laid eyes on her, she'd felt such a sense of doom. Her abilities as a medium, psychic, whatever you wanted to call it, were beginning to scare her. Nancy was evil. She could feel it in her bones.

Goebel returned with two small glasses of ginger ale. "These cost me ten bucks each. Drink up."

"Cheers," Sophie said, clinking her glass to Goebel's yet never taking her eyes away from Nancy, who was now speaking with a group of men who were ogling her breasts. *Perverts, no matter how rich,* Sophie thought. *Give a man a set of knockers, and he's putty.* Lord, she was beginning to sound and think like Ida. This was not good, not one little bit.

"Look, she's leaving," Goebel said. "Let's follow her. If she goes to the ladies' room, remember what I told you to do."

They dropped their glasses on the tray of a passing waiter, quickening their pace so as not to lose sight of their quarry. Just as Goebel had expected, Nancy was headed to the ladies' restroom.

"Cry if you have to. Women are always suckers for a teardrop," Goebel instructed.

Sophie rolled her eyes and replied, "I'll handle this." She abruptly turned around, heading straight for the restroom.

The ladies' room had pink, gold, and

cream marble floors. Plush mauve lounging chairs with side tables equipped with telephones and laptop computers had been placed strategically throughout the ladies' room. It looked more like a plush spa than a restroom. The commodes were discreetly hidden behind dark wooden doors. There was no chance of Sophie walking the length of the restroom, peeking beneath the stalls. She sat down on one of the plush chairs, took out her cell phone, and dialed Toots's cell phone number.

As soon as Toots picked up, Sophie talked as though her life depended on it. Ida's life or liberty might. That was the frightening part, Sophie thought.

"I'm in the ladies' room with Nancy. I'm going to act like I'm crying over my dead husband. Then I'm going to hang the phone up. Goebel wants me to try and gain her sympathy, get a little one-on-one girl talk going on. See what I can find out about her." She said this in a hushed whisper.

Sophie heard the commode flush, her signal that it was showtime. She started to cry loudly into the phone. "I just can't believe he's dead," she cried. "Murdered! It's terrible. Yes. Yes. I will. Of course. Robert was dedicated to finding a cure for AIDS. Okay, I will. I have to go now."

Sophie replaced the phone in her bag, watching Nancy as she reapplied her lipstick. She went to stand at the sink next to her. Sophie blotted her eyes with a tissue, making sure to smear her mascara. "Oh, look what I've done! I'll never be able to sit through dinner looking like this."

She waited for Nancy to respond; when she didn't, that feeling of doom grabbed hold of her, forcing her to shove it aside. *Not now, Sophie. Not now.*

She dampened a paper towel, rubbed a small amount of liquid soap onto it, and began to scrub the eye makeup from her eyes. If this didn't get her attention, nothing would. Nancy continued to primp in front of the mirror.

Okay. It was now or never, Sophie thought. "Miss," she said, looking directly at Nancy as she spoke.

The evil brunette turned to face her. In a deep, throaty voice, she asked, "Are you talking to me?" Anger burned in her eyes.

Sophie was momentarily stunned at the sharpness in her voice. She wanted to tell her to kiss her ass, that soon she'd be in a place where there were no makeup mirrors, no Chanel tubes of lipstick, and no privacy when you had to pee, but declined as this wasn't her gig. This was for Goebel and the police. She was here simply to pick the woman's brain. It was more than obvious she didn't like unwanted attention, but tough shit, Sophie thought.

"Yes, I was. I'm sorry I interrupted you with your . . . lipstick. I just wondered if you might have a tube of mascara I could use. I've . . . Well, my best friend just found out her father was murdered! He was supposed to be here tonight." Sophie called forth the tears, and thank heavens the soap was burning her eyes as this made it easier to tear up. Her eyes stung so badly. Sophie sneaked a look at Nancy. Her dark skin looked ashy and gray.

Good, Sophie thought. She'd hit a nerve. The little bitch. When she thought of all Ida had suffered, she wanted to jap-slap this witch but held herself back, knowing justice would be served in due course. It was one thing for Sophie to torment Ida; it was another to face the woman who was responsible for sending Ida into her dark days with OCD.

"I don't lend my mascara. Sorry," Nancy said, still sounding like a smart-ass.

"Really?" Sophie pretended ignorance. "Why is that?"

Nancy shook her head, a hateful grimace distorting her features. "Are you serious?

You work at Cryotech? If you're in the lab, you better start looking for another job. Seriously."

Again, Sophie wanted to jap-slap her but couldn't. "I don't work for Cryotech. My —" She was about to say that her husband did, but caught herself. If Nancy were to ask for a name, she'd be screwed.

"Just so you know, don't ask to share makeup. There's all kinds of germs that can spread that way." Nancy tossed her lipstick in her clutch purse, gave one last look in the mirror, then headed toward the exit.

Shit, Sophie thought. "Wait!"

Nancy stopped, her hand on the door handle. "What now?"

More images of jap-slapping, only this time Sophie envisioned kicking, too. Right in her mouth. Mentioning her best friend's father's murder hadn't affected her. Maybe she could get somewhere with a common interest. God, this was so lame.

"Uh, I was wondering . . . What kind of germs? I, well, I just started wearing cosmetics a few months ago."

"What do you think I am? A frigging scientist? Get a life, lady," Nancy said, this time swinging the door open and making her escape before Sophie had a chance to reply.

True evil, personified, Sophie thought as she followed her out the door.

Like a true gentleman, Goebel had been waiting outside the ladies' room while she supposedly tended to her private business. When he saw that she was following Nancy, he synced his step with hers. "Anything?"

"Just that she's a true bitch, and an evil one, too. I don't like the vibes she's sending."

"One of the reasons we're here. I don't want to lose sight of her until I receive those lab results from Ted. I sent it to arrive by six in the morning tomorrow, so he said he would be there waiting and, with any luck, he'd have something for me to take to the authorities by ten o'clock in the morning."

"You plan to follow her home?" Sophie asked, eyes still watching Nancy.

"Of course. You don't think I came here for the rubber chicken and some inedible ricelike gunk they'll try to pass off as gourmet food, do you?"

Sophie laughed. "Put that way, heck no. So where does that leave me?" Sophie asked, visions of luxuriating in her suite going straight down the tube.

"That, my dear, is up to you," Goebel said, a wicked smile making his chubby face almost handsome.

Sophie had a flashing thought: Mavis could turn this man into a hunk. The goods were there. Just too many.

"We'll see. Right now" — Sophie nodded in Nancy's direction — "she's about to sit down for dinner. Since there doesn't seem to be assigned seating, let's see if we can sit at her table. I've already established somewhat of a repartee with her."

"I'll take your word," Goebel said as he cupped her elbow in his hand and guided her to Nancy's table.

"And you aren't my husband, remember? Say you're a distant cousin if asked," Sophie explained, her brilliant smile reaching eyes that were flaming like tigereye gemstones.

Their "mark" sat at the table along with two men and one woman. The tables were set for parties of eight, so there were still four seats left when Sophie and Goebel joined them.

Seeing the look of shock on Nancy's face, Sophie piped up, all smiles and giggles. "Oh, I'm so glad I found you. You never finished explaining where those nasty germs come from."

Under the table Goebel patted her upper thigh. Sophie shot him a killer look.

The night was turning out to be very, *very* different from what she had expected.

CHAPTER 34

Sophie was so tired, her eyelids were starting to droop. Goebel, on the other hand, was as chirpy as a newly hatched chick. It was after 7:30 AM on Saturday morning, and they were still in the Moulin Rouge Ballroom, where at least a dozen guests still lingered, Nancy being one of the dozen.

Goebel explained that if they were lucky, Nancy would stay until he heard from Ted, but Sophie couldn't imagine staying awake much longer. He could follow Nancy; she'd go along for the ride so she could nap. She was too old for this all-night stuff. She had a flight to catch that evening. She would at least like time for a quick shower and a change of clothing. She could only imagine the kind of stares she'd get if she hopped on the plane while still wearing her evening gown and looking like she'd been ridden hard and put away wet.

Ida really owed her for this. Big-time.

One of the men who'd sat at the table with them cornered Sophie. "We're about to go to Aria for some breakfast. Would you and your cousin like to join us?" This man had been giving her the once-over all night long. At this point, if it helped to move things along, she'd do just about anything. Well, almost.

"Goebel and I would love to go," Sophie responded. So as not to reveal her or Goebel's interest in Nancy, she asked, "Will I be the only girl attending?" continuing to pretend that she was the demure and coy bimbo in her forties, instead of the sixty-five-year-old widow she really was.

"Nancy is still here. I'm sure she's coming along. Why? You don't like being with a group of distinguished gentlemen?" he teased.

Not caring that she sounded sarcastic, Sophie said, "I'm not so sure I would use the word *distinguished*."

After the formal dinner and ceremony last night, the group at her table had ordered drink after drink, becoming quite rowdy. Any trace of sophistication and politeness was washed away by the alcohol. Sophie had observed Nancy throughout the night. She wasn't a heavy drinker, sticking mostly to cranberry juice and water.

They all agreed to meet at the front entrance to the restaurant at nine, allowing those who were staying at the hotel time to run to their rooms to change out of their formal attire.

Once she and Goebel were out of earshot, Sophie asked, "What's your take on Nancy?"

The elevator doors swished open. Goebel placed a hand on Sophie's waist, guiding her inside the small space. Fortunately, they were the only two in the elevator and could speak freely. "Are you asking me as a man or as an investigator?"

"Both," Sophie said.

"As a man, I think she's quite attractive. As an investigator, I think she reeks of foul play. Did you notice how her eyes darted throughout the ballroom all night? Every time someone entered or made an exit, she was aware of it."

"I did. The woman gives me the creeps, pure and simple. If she were to get her hands on Ida, that would be the end of her. Ida's no match for that woman."

"Succinct and to the point. I agree. Now, let's get out of these clothes, and I'll meet you in front of the restaurant. We have plenty of time. Ted should have the swab now. From here on in, it's a waiting game."

"I'll meet you in an hour," Sophie said.

They went their separate ways, she to the left, he to the right. Inside her suite, which she'd spent only a couple of hours in last night, getting ready for the big event, she really hadn't had time to take in all the bells and whistles. Sunken tub. A shower that would fit at least ten people, a full array of bath products. Thick towels on a warming rod. Damn, she could've spent the entire night in the bathroom alone. This hotel was almost as ritzy as the Beverly Hills Hotel in Los Angeles.

Sophie took a nice hot shower and washed her hair. She dressed in a pair of beige Ralph Lauren trousers with a matching navy and beige sweater set. Cream-colored pumps added to her height. She applied a swipe of mascara, blush, and her new favorite, black honey Almost Lipstick, as the label read. She grabbed her purse and room key, then grabbed the elevator. She looked at the time. She had five minutes to spare. *When you're good, you're good,* she thought as she waited for the plush doors to open.

Goebel was waiting exactly where he had said he would. He wore khaki slacks with a black polo shirt. He didn't look half bad. Now, if he could get rid of the gut, she just might view him in an entirely different light. Maybe. What was the accepted time to mourn? Ten days if you were Toots. Sophie laughed out loud.

"I'm dying for a cup of coffee, but I swear if I'm seated next to that awful woman, I'm not going to take my eyes off her while I'm eating. I sure as hell don't want to end up six feet under like Thomas."

"I seriously doubt she's got any vicious plans for you. Just keep acting like the bimbo you pretended to be all night, and you'll be fine. Trust me."

"I never trust a man who says 'Trust me,' " Sophie said as they weaved their way through the dining room to the table where one of the two men was already seated.

When he saw them, he motioned for them to take seats. "I took the liberty of ordering coffee and tea. I thought we would wait and place our orders when the others arrived," the man, whose name Sophie couldn't recall, said.

"Works for me," she said. Then, staying in her role of bimbo, she added, "I wonder if they have Froot Loops here?"

Goebel laughed out loud, and the man looked away, as though her request was an embarrassment to him.

"We'll ask. I wouldn't mind having a big

ole bowl of cereal myself," Goebel said, patting his stomach. "That crap they called food last night didn't do the job for me." He turned to the man. "What about you?"

Again, the man looked as though he was offended by their crudeness. Sophie loved it. The stuck-up snot. Reminded her a bit of Ida.

"It wasn't the best meal I've ever eaten," he had to concede.

A murmur of voices from behind caused Sophie to turn around. She leaned close to Goebel and whispered in his ear, "She just walked in."

He looked at his watch, then checked to make sure his cell phone was turned on. It wouldn't do for him to miss Ted's call. Goebel had called in a few contacts with the Chicago Police Department, informing them there might be something going down today. He'd given one of his buddies a quick rundown on the events that had led to his trip to Chicago. He promised Goebel that the Chicago PD would back him up. Goebel had programmed their number into his cell phone. In a case like this, seconds could matter.

"Put a smile on your face, kiddo. It's gonna be showtime real soon," Goebel advised.

Nancy and the others approached the table, all but Nancy wearing casual clothes. Strong-smelling cologne wafted from Rex, the one man whose name Sophie did remember. She wanted to gag but refrained. After they were all seated, a waiter hefting a trayful of coffee cups, two pots of coffee, and a large pot of tea served them quickly and efficiently. They placed their orders, and the conversation picked up where it had left off earlier that morning. Of course, politics came into the equation, and Sophie acted dumber than a box of rocks, but when they changed the topic to a local woman who'd recently been murdered, Sophie figured this was her chance.

"It's so terrible! I can't imagine hurting a flea, let alone a real, living, breathing person. My friend's father was murdered two days ago. He was supposed to be here last night, but for obvious reasons, he wasn't," Sophie announced, hoping to get the reaction from Nancy that she hadn't last night.

"That's tragic. How was he killed?" Nancy asked, a morbid smile on her face.

Here goes, Sophie thought to herself. "They think he might've been poisoned." There. She'd said what she'd wanted to say last night. She took a sip of coffee, watching

Nancy turn three shades of white.

"Are there any suspects?" Nancy asked, more than curious now.

Sophie wasn't sure what to say but figured she was on a roll. "They think his stepdaughter might be involved. Apparently there was an issue over his will. I'm not sure, but whatever happened to that poor man, I hope the person responsible rots in a prison cell for the rest of their life." Sophie's eyes never wavered from Nancy's as she spoke.

Just as Sophie finished, Goebel's cell phone rang. He excused himself and stepped away from the table.

Back in bimbo mode, Sophie knew she had to get Nancy's attention focused elsewhere. Ida's life depended on it.

"That's probably his boyfriend calling to check up on him. He's gay, you know. It's supposed to be a secret, but I told Goebel there was absolutely no reason under the sun for him to hide his lifestyle. His lover, that's what they refer to one another as, Bruce is his name, he sells antiques in Georgia. I know poor Goebel wants to come out of the closet, but he's afraid he'll be banished from the family." Sophie couldn't believe the line of trash that tumbled from her mouth. If Goebel heard what she was saying, he might not like her. She smiled, continuing in the vein of family bimbo. "Now, myself, I could never, well, you know" — she looked at the man whose name she just could not remember, hoping to embarrass him further — "kiss another woman, let alone have a romantic relationship. What about you, Nancy?"

Sophie glanced over her shoulder, saw Goebel's serious expression, and knew the ax was about to land in Miss Nancy's face.

"What did you just ask?" Nancy said. "Are you implying or asking if I'm gay?"

"Oh, heaven's no! I'm sorry. I just wondered what your thoughts were on the subject, that's all. I certainly didn't mean to imply anything at all," Sophie said sweetly.

Nancy shifted her attention to the man seated next to her. "What's your opinion? Do you support same-sex marriages?" she asked, avoiding having to give an answer to Sophie's question.

Sophie threw a glance in Goebel's direction. He was gone. Now she knew it was up to her to keep the conversation focused, and whatever she did, she couldn't let Nancy leave the table. Their food arrived just then. That would give her a bit of a reprieve.

After the waiter served their breakfasts, Sophie picked up where the conversation had left off. "If it's your way, then I believe same-sex marriages are okay. It's not for me, thank you very much, but it works for some. Look at Ellen. She has her own talk show, and that beautiful wife. They seem very happy together." Something had best happen soon, or Sophie was going to run out of bimbo talk. She could only act like an idiot for so long. The truth was, she felt that same-sex partners should have all the rights that heterosexuals had.

Once again, she turned around in search of Goebel. He was still nowhere to be seen. Sophie hoped he was out front, ready to bring in Chicago's finest. She couldn't wait to get out of here. Nancy's evil was starting to get under her skin even more.

Rex and the other man discussed the pros and cons of gay marriage. Each was fiercely opinionated. Rex seemed to think that if it was your thing, go for it. The other guy thought it was extremely distasteful. *Surprise, surprise,* Sophie thought.

A commotion at the entrance to the restaurant caused them to turn around. Goebel, along with six men in blue and another man wearing a gray suit jacket and navy slacks, probably a detective, hustled over to their table.

Without further ado the man wearing the

gray suit jacket read Nancy her Miranda rights, then proceeded to handcuff her hands behind her back and lead her toward the exit. The attention of every single soul in the restaurant was riveted on the sight of a woman still dressed for a charity ball being led from the restaurant in handcuffs. And Nancy's loud protests did nothing to make her any less conspicuous.

"What the hell do you think you're doing? Take your hands off me! Did you hear me? Take your hands off me! Don't go spouting that gibberish to me, either. I'm not listening to you," Nancy shrieked so loud that Sophie thought her eardrums ruptured. "You've got the wrong person!"

Goebel stood next to Sophie. "We got her. Ted's report said the brown stuff on the swab I sent was definitely ricin. Our part is done. Now we'll have to let the legal system take over."

"What was that all about?" Rex asked.

"Yeah," said the guy he had been arguing with. "What just happened? What do the cops want with a nice lady like Nancy?" Which only went to show that some people still thought you could tell a book by its cover.

"That *nice lady,* guys, murdered one of my best friends' husbands and intended to kill my friend. Would probably have done so already if she had known where to find her. Just count yourself lucky that you didn't say or do anything that might have gotten her mad at you. Who knows? Maybe she would have poisoned you, too. My 'cousin' and I will be leaving now. You all have a nice day."

Sophie couldn't believe it was over. In less time than it took to prepare a soft-boiled egg, Nancy had been removed from their table and the restaurant, as though she'd never been there. She did leave a few overturned chairs as she was dragged kicking and screaming out of the room. Sophie removed her cell phone from her purse and called Ida.

"It's over, sweet cheeks. You're gonna live, after all. And when you hear what kind of garbage I had to feed a group of people, you are going to faint." Sophie clicked the END button. She had a few hours before her flight to Charleston was due to take off. She was going to soak in that damned tub if it was the last thing she did. "I'll see you around, big guy," she called to Goebel before heading to the elevators.

"You can count on it," he said, then turned back to the cops surrounding him.

And she damn well would.

CHAPTER 35

Six weeks later, Los Angeles, California . . .
Toots almost cried when they left Charleston, but knowing she would be seeing Abby and Chris soon was enough to hold the tears at bay.

The day before they left for Los Angeles, she and the girls had spent the day at The Sweetest Things, helping Jamie with her Grand Reopening. Toots had taken out full-page ads in every publication connected to the dessert and baking industry. People started to line up at the door at 4:00 AM to purchase the pralines and cupcakes. Jamie was in her glory. She'd promised to send Toots a weekly e-mail update. Since Sophie's cleansing, she hadn't felt anything strange or cold in the old building. Sophie explained this was nothing to be frightened of, should it happen again. Then she promised if it did, she would simply return and perform another cleansing.

Bernice wasn't as sad this time, as she had a new project to keep her busy. Jamie and the bakery. Bernice had volunteered to help out whenever Jamie needed her, and they had bonded immediately. Pete would continue to work in the gardens, and Toots made sure he knew that whatever Jamie needed, he was to see that she had it. She'd picked up on his mistrust of the young woman and set his mind at ease when she told him her story, and how she'd practically had to force her to take her up on her offer of a partner. Pete was good with this, telling her he didn't want anyone taking advantage of her.

Mavis's clothing line, Good Mourning, continued to receive orders daily. That was another reason for their return to California. The factory Mavis had hired to sew the patterns while she was in Charleston needed more cloth, more patterns, more workers. Mavis's idea for a line of clothes for those in mourning had taken off like a rocket. Ida was starting to take an interest in the dead, too, but not in the wardrobe department. For her everything was about color. Why did people have to look like they'd been smeared with Coppertone when they were laid to rest? She was considering a line of cosmetics for the deceased.

So here they were on a bright, shiny day, back at the Malibu beach house, sitting out on the deck, where Toots and Sophie returned to their constant habit of puffing away.

"Abby needs something for her column. She said she's milked every living source she has for something related to the afterlife and has come up with zilch. I think you and Ida need to tell her about Thomas solving his own murder," Toots suggested.

Sophie drew on her cigarette. "It's fine with me. It's Ida we have to convince. Remember that when we left here, she and that old, perverted fake were headlines. I'm not sure that she even wants to relive this. Nancy is awaiting trial. That alone will be a challenge when Ida is called to testify. I can just imagine what the headlines will be this time around."

"Goebel seems to think there won't be a trial. Said he heard Nancy was offered a sweet plea deal, and her attorney advised her to take it. For Ida's sake, I hope she does."

Curious, Sophie asked, "When did you speak to Goebel?"

Toots smiled. "I called him last night. Just to say hi, see how the case was progressing. He mentioned something about taking a vacation."

Sophie's ears perked up even more. "Did he say where he was going? When?" she asked, suddenly excited at the thought of seeing the old coot.

"Not really. Though he did mention something about how he'd always wanted to go on one of those Hollywood home tours," Toots said. "I would guess he's thinking about a trip out West. You know, California." Toots pronounced the state like their previous governor, Arnold Schwarzenegger, did. *Cal-ee-for-ne-uh.*

"Did he ask about me?" Sophie questioned.

"No, he never mentioned you. Why?" Toots asked with a giant grin on her face.

"Kiss off, Toots. Finish telling me about Nancy's trial." Sophie wasn't about to let Toots know she was interested in Goebel, or at least any more than she already knew. She sure as hell didn't want to be in the headlines.

"That's it, really. It will take months, maybe years, for this to make it to the courtroom. The fact that it's made it this far is a true miracle. I can't wait to see the look on her face when she discovers that Thomas revealed her crime during a séance."

"I don't want to see her face again. She totally creeped me out."

Mavis chose that moment to make an appearance on the deck. Normally, she would've had a trayful of sliced fruit and healthy food. Today she had several e-mails she had printed out. "You have to see this! I need both of you to advise me on what to do. Read these," Mavis said, handing half of the papers to Sophie and the other half to Toots.

"Mavis! This is fantastic. I think you should do it," Toots said. "You know I will do whatever I can to help."

Sophie shook her head. "We're a bunch of sick bitches, you know that?"

Mavis had a stack of e-mails from funeral parlors all over the country inquiring about her line of clothing for the living. Now it seemed morticians, undertakers around the country, thought a line of clothes for the dead would be successful, too. Several of the e-mails stated how they had to slice clothing in the back from top to bottom, many times having to stuff the clothing with plastic and paper to absorb the bodily fluids that often leaked from the body.

"This is gross, Mavis!" Toots exclaimed.

"Remember that story I told you about Pearl Mae Atkins?" Mavis asked.

"I do," Toots said. "That's the saddest story. Leaving this world without anyone to tell you good-bye. I think you should consider this. Maybe you could even dress them yourself for a while, teach others how to do this. I truly believe you're onto something."

"That's what I think, too. I've already sketched a pattern for women. And I thought instead of the usual macabre colors, we could use peaches, lavender, and maybe a mint green. I have an idea for lining the clothes with a material, almost like a disposable diaper would feel. That could help absorb the body fluid. Plus, it would fill out the areas that needed . . . you know, *plumping.*"

Sophie looked like she was ready to lose it. "I can't believe you're even considering something that . . . that bizarre."

"It's no worse than your séances. Aren't you reading tarot cards now? Abby said Chris was going to send over one of his clients to you for a reading. A midlist actress whose career is about to take a nosedive," Mavis said.

"That's not the same thing," Sophie said. "Dressing dead bodies! Just think about it, Mavis. You'll smell like formaldehyde. And you know, people that dress the dead usually wind up doing the hair and makeup, too. Did you know that?"

"I've heard that, yes. But look at it this way. If I can make someone pretty on their way to the hereafter, when they come to you through a séance, at least they won't look . . . tacky, if you know what I mean."

"I'm going inside. You two can continue discussing the dead while I speak with Ida. I've got to convince her to tell Thomas's story to Abby so she can use this for her column. Whatcha think, girls?" Toots said before slipping through the sliding glass doors.

Both Sophie and Mavis just shook their heads.

CHAPTER 36

Two weeks later . . .

Again, they prepared to gather in the dining room, now referred to as the official séance room. Sophie hadn't performed a séance since Thomas's last appearance in Charleston. She'd been aching to perform another one. Again, she was going to ask Toots to assist with the psychic writing since Ida was still out of town. It had worked before, and she hoped it would work again. This time, though, she had a purpose. A goal she hoped to achieve. This time around, she wanted to make contact with Walter. Though she'd made contact with his presence before, she wanted a face-off with him. For thirty years, she had wondered why he treated her like a broken-down dog. In order for her to move on, she needed answers. She was no longer fearful of anything he could do to her. He had better be worried about what she could do to him. It didn't matter that Walter was already dead. She'd send him to the fires of hell for eternity if she could. Well, maybe she didn't have *that* much power, but the visual was nice.

Ida and Mavis were in San Francisco, taking training to learn how to dress the dearly departed. Abby and Chris would be attending tonight's séance in their place. So Sophie and Toots prepared the dining room just as they always did. The purple silk bedsheet covered the old wooden table, and a drinking glass was in the center. Candles were placed in their usual positions. In front of Toots's chair, Sophie placed a pencil and a pad of paper. Chris and Abby were due to arrive any minute. Sophie wanted to get started as soon as they arrived, didn't want to waste a minute on anything that was unnecessary.

She glanced around the room one last time before going out on the deck to smoke a cigarette with Toots. Everything was as it should be.

Outside, in the early evening air, a warm breeze blew in from the Pacific, seagulls cawed, and waves rushed against the shoreline. Voices and laughter from the beach below drifted up to the deck. Sophie wasn't sure which place she liked more, the back porch steps in Charleston or the deck opposite the beach in Malibu.

"You're way too quiet tonight. What gives?" Toots asked.

Sophie lit a cigarette and sat in the lounge chair next to Toots. "I'm going to try to make contact with Walter tonight. It's something I feel like I need to do."

"Does this have anything to do with Goebel?"

"Why would you think that?" Sophie asked.

"I can see the signs. Remember, I've been married eight times? I'm quite an expert at putting one relationship behind in order to move on to another. At least I think I am. If John hadn't died, I would still be married to him. He was the true love of my life, but he wasn't my only love. You and Walter, on the other hand . . . Well, let's just say we both know there was no love lost between the two of you. I don't see why you stayed with him all those years. Why you took his abuse. I never took you for the type of woman who would put up with a man's abuse, not to mention his many indiscretions, but the past is prologue. You're ready to move on, Sophie, and that's okay. More than okay. It's great. If anyone deserves it, you do."

"Call it what you will. It's just something

that I need to do. I think I just heard a car. I'll go see if it's Abby and Chris."

Coco's fierce growl announced their presence. Abby must have brought Chester along. Coco's true love.

Sophie arrived at the door at the same time Abby and Chris prepared to knock. Chester, Abby's German shepherd/ bodyguard, danced up and down, excited because the canine knew what awaited him on the other side of the door. Inside, both dogs ran to their favorite spot in the kitchen, licking and barking at one another. Both would be content for the rest of the evening.

"Sophie, you look fantastic!" Abby gave her godmother a tight squeeze, then stood back to rake her in. "You've changed."

Chris stood off to the side, grinning from ear to ear. "She says the same thing to me every time I see her," Chris said.

"Well, I don't know if I've changed or not, but I'm certainly not the woman I was a year ago. I smoke less. I don't eat near as much garbage as I used to. I've all but given up saying the F word, so I guess you could call that change."

Chris and Abby both burst out laughing.

"What's so funny?" Toots said as she entered the room.

Abby practically raced to her mother's

open arms. "Sophie said she's smoking less and giving up the F bomb," Abby said laughingly, her clear blue eyes lighting up like diamonds. "So, what's on tonight's agenda?"

"Sophie wants to try to make contact with Walter."

When they'd returned to California, they had told Abby about Thomas's coming through and how successful Sophie was becoming in her new career as a medium. Chris had not told her, because Toots had asked him not to. Ida had just given Abby permission to use her story for *The Informer*. Their story would run in tomorrow's edition.

Ida said she didn't really care about publicity anymore. She wanted to put that part of her life behind her, as she and Mavis were working together to make dying a beautiful experience. At least in the clothing and makeup department. Don't ask and don't even go there. It's their thing . . . their . . . calling late in life or some such thing.

"If you guys are ready, I say let's get this show on the road. I can't wait to tell Walter to go straight to hell," Sophie said, a fierce expression on her face.

They all laughed, but the laughter was

nervous, edgy-sounding.

Five minutes later, they were seated around the wooden table. The lights were dimmed and the candles were lit. Toots held the pencil in her hand, ready to do its bidding.

Sophie started with her usual prayer. "Oh, great one, bless this dump and those who inhabit it, living or dead. Everyone, relax. Think of something pleasant. Let's all take a deep breath."

Toots, Abby, and Chris did as instructed.

"We are here to communicate with the other side. We are friendly. We mean no harm." Sophie said this at the beginning of every séance she conducted. Who knew what kind of evil lurked in and among them?

"Place your fingertips around the glass very lightly," Sophie instructed.

Chris, Abby, and Toots placed the tips of their fingers on the glass.

"Is there anyone here who wishes to make contact tonight? Roll the glass toward the window for yes and the other way for no."

All focused on the glass. Nothing happened.

"Toots, start making circles on the paper."

"Walter Manchester. In life you were a cruel, wicked man. In death, you may have a chance to redeem yourself," Sophie intoned in a solemn voice.

Before she could utter another word, tiny orbs of light filled the room. They flew around like miniscule shooting stars, up and down, right and left, until they formed one giant glistening orb. Suddenly, the temperature in the room dropped by several degrees. Sophie watched as Toots's hand raced across the paper. She strained to read the words in the dim light, but all she saw were dozens of tiny circles.

"Walter, are you here with us?" Sophie asked.

Abby and Chris were focused on the glass. Ever so slowly, it inched to the right, toward the window.

Intakes of breath filled the room.

"Yes, you are here," Sophie continued. "Do you know who I am?"

The glass rolled to the right again.

"You are Walter Manchester, former husband of Sophia Manchester?" she clarified. She needed to be sure.

For the third time, the glass rolled to the right, stopping when it reached the edge of the table.

"Are you in hell, Walter?" Sophie inquired, making it sound as if she were simply seeking information the way a neutral observer might. She sneaked a glance at the others.

They were staring at her as if she were out of her mind.

Nothing happened for several seconds. Then Toots's hand began to slash words across the paper. Over and over. Left to right.

Sophie wanted to see what, if anything, she'd written and stretched to make out the word she'd repeatedly written across the paper.

Forgive? Forgive? Forgive?

"Walter, are you asking me to forgive you?" Sophie asked, obviously stunned by the words, her voice no longer anything like that of a neutral observer.

The glass finally rolled off the edge of the table, crashing to the floor.

Toots's hand went crazy across the page again.

Please! Please! Please!

"You wicked son of a bitch! I said those very same words to you over and over again for thirty long and painful years! Did you listen to me when I begged you to stop hitting me? Hello! No, you didn't! Did you listen to me when I begged you to stop drinking? Hell no! I hope your soul cries out in pain as you burn in the deepest, hottest flames of hell! I hate you, Walter! Can you hear this?" Sophie all but screamed the words.

"Leave, Walter! Never make your presence known to me again, in this life or in the afterlife! Begone with you!" Sophie swung her arms out to the sides, toppling one of the candles. Abby quickly grabbed it and placed it back on the table.

As suddenly as the temperature had lowered in the room, it returned to normal. The giant orb was no longer visible, and the pencil fell out of Toots's hand, dropping to the floor.

Sophie stood up and flicked the light switch on, bathing the room in bright light. "That bastard! He's returned from the grave, asking for my forgiveness! I can't believe this. I need a cigarette." Sophie walked out of the room, leaving Toots, Abby, and Chris sitting in the séance room, totally stunned.

Outside on the deck, the breeze whipped the ends of Sophie's hair around, tossing them in the air. She'd wanted to make contact with Walter tonight, and she had. She didn't plan on his spirit asking her to forgive him. *Once a bastard, always a bastard,* she thought. Why should she forgive him?

Toots, Abby, and Chris stepped outside

on the deck.

Toots stood beside her. "You can forgive him, you know? That doesn't mean you'll forget the terrible things he did to you," Toots said, placing a hand on her arm. "It's the right thing to do. He's the past, Soph. Don't let your memories of him ruin your future."

Sophie nodded. "You're right, as usual, old gal." Sophie looked up at the stars, then leaned over the deck, looking down at the grayish tan sand. "Walter, if you can hear me down there, kiss my ass and the dog's ass, too! You got that?"

Toots, Abby, and Chris bent over in a fit of laughter. Sophie gave an aggressive flip of the bird to the beach below.

"Rot in hell, Walter!"

CHAPTER 37

Mavis turned white as a ghost, and Ida could barely keep her lunch down. Mavis swallowed several times, took a few deep breaths, then sat back in the chair as close to Ida as humanly possible.

San Francisco's Society of Morticians was holding its annual weeklong classes on how to dress the dead for their final departure. Since Mavis's idea to design, manufacture, and sell clothes to send departed loved ones off for their final good-byes had launched last week, she now wanted to learn how to instruct her clients on how to use them. She'd made a pattern using Sophie and Toots as her "bodies," and the rest was quite simple. Mavis made the front of a dress/jacket or skirt/jacket for women and slacks/shirt/jacket fronts for the men. Her designs came with an absorbent cotton liner since she'd learned that after embalming, there could be leaks. These designs were selling faster than she'd ever dreamed, so much so that she'd had to hire ten more seamstresses just to keep up with the orders. When the body was placed in the casket, no one needed to see the back side of the body, and this made dressing the dead much easier. Mavis had dressed her first body last week, with minimal training from a local mortician in Los Angeles. He loved her idea so much, was so impressed with her skill, that he recommended she attend these classes in San Francisco this week. Ida had been working with a chemist to produce a line of cosmetics strictly for those who were about to be laid to rest.

"I thought they were just going to instruct us on how to lay out the body after it's placed in the coffin," Ida whispered to Mavis. "You forgot to mention we'd have to watch an actual embalming."

"Shh," Mavis said. "He's speaking." She focused on the guest speaker.

"Once the body has been cleaned, the next step is to make a small incision here in the neck." He used a small knife to make an incision in the jugular vein. A small hose was inserted into the incision, and all body fluids were flushed from the body and drained into a large glass container. The guest speaker, a mortician, explained each step of the procedure while performing it. Ida held a tissue over her nose. Not only could she smell the formaldehyde, but could actually taste it.

The speaker continued, "Once the body is empty of fluid, then we clean the body. If there are injuries, such as a gunshot wound, any visible markings on the body, we try to cover them with flesh-colored bandages. Eye caps are placed under the lids of the eye." He opened the corpse's eyes as he did this. Several people turned away.

"Next, we will stitch the mouth in a closed position, and we try to keep it as natural looking as possible. See this?" He took a fine needle and a sturdy, thin thread. In three movements, the cadaver's mouth was no longer slack, hanging open.

Ida audibly gagged, but she wasn't the only one in the room who did so. Mavis wasn't quite as queasy. With each step she learned, she told herself she was making it better for those to whom she would be attending. Once she became certified, she would instruct others on how to dress the dead. Of course, using her designs would just be a matter of a few adjustments to the body once it was placed inside the casket. Mavis looked at it as though this were a final performance, and who wouldn't want to look their best?

When the session was over, Mavis and Ida went down to the wharf, where they watched the sea lions. Neither one of them felt they would be able to eat after what they'd just witnessed, until they saw a small open-air seafood restaurant. They bought fish and chips served in a cone and doused in malt vinegar.

"This is not figure flattering," Ida said.

"Just eat half. We'll walk these rolling streets, which is guaranteed to burn off any extra calories," Mavis said.

When they finished picking at their lunch, they strolled up and down San Francisco's streets. They walked as far as Presidio Boulevard, then tromped up Russian Hill to Lombard Street, one of the most winding and crooked streets in the world.

"I'm glad I didn't wear heels," Ida said.

"I've always wanted to do this, though I didn't think to add it to my 'life list.' As soon as we get home, I'm going to do just that, then cross it off," Mavis said. "What about you? Is there anything you want to add to your list?"

Ida's pace was slow as they turned around to walk back up the hill. "I'm not sure yet. Being normal is a big accomplishment for me. I like helping you, too. At first, I thought I would be frightened, but I find that I'm not at all, though I didn't like watching that poor man's embalming. Did I tell you I've come up with a name for my new line of cosmetics?"

Mavis gushed. "No, and I, for one, am so proud of you for taking this step. Tell me, what are you going to call them?"

"Don't laugh, but I thought it appropriate. How does Drop-Dead Gorgeous sound to you?"

As they strolled through some of San Francisco's most famous streets, Ida felt lighthearted, more carefree than she had in years. Like Toots said, she would know when the time was right to make changes in her life. She glanced at Mavis, who was complete and total proof that you could do and be anything you wanted to be.

"I think it's perfect. We can work together. I'll dress the dead. You can apply their makeup." Mavis was so excited over their new venture together.

"I've even thought up names for the colors of the nail polish and eye shadow, though I'm not sure if that matters. But if my cosmetic line is as successful as your designs, I like to think those in this business might want a name for the products they use. What do you think?"

"Of course they will. Now, tell me what they are. This is just so exciting to me!" Mavis exclaimed.

"Don't laugh. I'm calling the new peach-colored nail polish and eye shadow Pulse-Less Peach and the lavender Life-Less Lavender. Does that sound too disrespectful to you?" Ida asked.

"Not at all." Mavis looked at her watch. "It's time to go back. Just think. When we get back to Los Angeles, we'll be official dressers to the dead."

CHAPTER 38

Ghostly Encounters
By
Abby Simpson

New York City millionaire medical-supply tycoon Thomas McGullicutty is truly a hero even though he died two years ago. The New York County Medical Examiner originally reported the cause of his death as food poisoning. Though deceased, the wealthy playboy was not happy with the results. In a rare and most unusual event, Thomas spoke from beyond the grave during a séance, explaining to the medium that he had not died from eating tainted meat, as was reported. Those attending the séance were stunned when McGullicutty led authorities to his killer. Another odd twist in the story was that the victim died at the hands of a daughter whose existence he had only just learned of. In an operation orchestrated by society widow Ida McGullicutty, evidence located in the basement of the alleged killer's Chicago home led authorities to reexamine the cause of death. Ricin, a protein extracted from the castor bean and toxic when ingested, proved to be the real cause of death, and Mr. McGullicutty's death was reclassified as a homicide. His daughter has been charged with murder in the second degree in his death and is being held on a five-million-dollar bond.

"I plan to run the rest of the story next week, but I thought Ida would want to see this first. I'm not reporting it as I normally would. Not that this isn't spectacular as it is. I just didn't add all the paranormal stuff. Might even gain *The Informer* a few new readers," Abby said.

Ida placed the copy of *The Informer* on the table. "I knew you would handle this with as much discretion as your paper allows. Thank you for that. With any luck, the other tabloids will not do any sensationalized follow-ups."

Toots refilled their coffee mugs. "I told you so. Now the world will know about Nancy, not that it matters. You never suspected that Thomas was cheating on you, did you?"

Ida shook her head. "No, I didn't. Looking back now, I see there were signs, but I chose to ignore them. He traveled so much for his company. It would've been easy to do. I was so busy with my own life, I didn't take time to stop and examine my marriage. I'm sorry that Thomas died the way he did, but sadly his death has opened up a new chapter in my life. I never had any desire to go into business. Though I still love photography, I wouldn't want to traipse around the world, taking photographs of war zones. I do believe my sense of light and color can assist me when I prepare the dying. Did you tell them, Mavis?" Ida asked.

"Tell us what?" Sophie piped up.

"No, I thought I would wait and let you have that honor," Mavis said in her usual sweet voice.

"Do we need a drumroll?" Toots asked.

"Mom! Go on, Ida. Don't pay any attention to her. What's your news?"

All eyes were focused on Ida. They'd come so very far this past year. Each one of them had created a new and exciting life for her golden years.

"Tonight Mavis and I are going to do our first paid official layout. That's what we call it. With the certification we spent a week getting, we can do this at any funeral home, hospitals, wherever. Actually, we're thinking about making up brochures and sending them to funeral parlors and morgues all over the country. Of course, I'll take the photographs and do the makeup. We're going to need a few volunteers for this."

"What?" Sophie cried out. "Volunteers! Are you nuts?" She held her hand out in front of her. "Don't answer that. You've come way too far."

"I think she meant to say models," Mavis added.

"As in living and breathing models?" Abby teased.

"Exactly, dear," Ida said, then went into further detail. "I thought you girls could pose. You know, wear Mavis's designs. I'll do your makeup, hair, and nails, snap a few pictures. A catalogue really. We plan to list Good Mourning, clothes for the living, so it wouldn't be like this is a complete death . . . thing. I'll be using colors from the Drop-Dead Gorgeous line. Having live models will increase my sales, I'm sure."

When they had digested Ida's words, they all doubled over with laughter.

"Yeah, it's not like your client can say, 'Hey, I don't resemble that woman in the brochure,' and ask for her money back,"

Sophie joked.

"True, but her family members can," Ida said. "I want them to recommend my services."

More laughter from the women as they clustered around the table.

"Why don't Toots and I come to the funeral? We can view your work firsthand, act like we're long-lost friends or something," Sophie suggested.

Mavis looked at Ida. "It's up to you," she said.

"I think it's a fantastic idea. If we're going to do this right, Mavis, we need to get a move on. The viewing starts at seven o'clock tonight. I want to have enough time to work with our . . . client."

"Yes, I agree. I need to stop by the factory and pick up a small peach dress. This poor little woman we're sending off only weighed ninety-eight pounds. I'm sure we'll have to stuff her a bit." Mavis said this as though it were completely normal.

"Why don't you drive the Thunderbird? Take the top off, but remember, Ida, Mavis has to drive. You are not to get behind the wheel of any vehicle, and I mean any vehicle, until you have a driver's license. I don't care what state it's from as long as it's legal. Are we clear on that, Ida?"

"Crystal." Ida saluted Toots. "I haven't had time to study that horrible manual I got from the Internet when we were in Charleston, but I promise to get to it as soon as I have this business established. So, Mavis, let's go. I can't wait to see what the family thinks."

Mavis and Ida gave Abby a hearty hug, then gave the girls the name of the funeral home and directions.

"I can't wait," Sophie called out as they stepped out the front door.

Toots, Abby, and Sophie relocated to the deck as soon as the two left.

"We're obsessed with the dead, each and every one of us, don't you think?" Sophie said fretfully.

"We're simply trying to make things better for the living. At least that's the way I look at it," Toots said.

"Mom's right, Soph. No one, at least no one I know, thinks you guys are totally deranged, whacked out, off your rocker, or whatever you want to call it," Abby joked. "If you're doing something you like, and it's helping others in some small way, what more could you want?"

"You're such a smart daughter," Toots said.

"Yeah, she is. Takes after me," Sophie added.

"Bull," Toots said.

"Shit," Sophie finished.

"Enough," Abby stated.

They spent the next hour reminiscing, and planning, going in all directions at the speed of light and at the same time knowing their future could turn on the spin of a coin.

CHAPTER 39

Upon arriving at Parker's Funeral Home, Mavis and Ida were a bit nervous, yet excited, too. They had more than five hours to prepare Mrs. Wilkinson for viewing.

Mavis picked out the peach dress for the elderly woman.

Upon seeing her, Mavis's eyes filled with unshed tears. "She was such a tiny woman. The family said she simply died in her sleep of old age. She was ninety-six. This is how it should be," she said as she prepared to remove the plastic from under her body.

"She's so cold," Ida said, a trace of fear in her voice.

"Yes, poor dear, she is. But that's where you come in. You're going to make her look like she's just gone to sleep."

"Did the family leave a picture?" Ida asked.

They had learned in their class to ask the family, whenever possible, to provide a recent picture of their loved one. This would enable them to create as close to a natural appearance as possible.

"Yes, it's here somewhere," Mavis said, searching the small room reserved for laying out the body. She spied it next to Mrs. Wilkinson's dentures. "Oh no! They've forgotten to put her teeth back in her mouth. Look at this!" Mavis exclaimed.

Ida stepped behind the casket, where Mavis held upper and lower denture plates in her hand. "Let me see the picture." Mavis handed the five-by-seven color photo, something probably taken for the woman's church roster, to Ida. "This is awful. She doesn't look presentable without her teeth in place."

"What do you think we should do? I don't know if there is enough time to call someone to fix her mouth. Mr. Parker said he would be gone for a few hours."

Ida took a deep breath. "We'll have to do this ourselves. We don't have a choice. If the family sees this little woman's mouth looking like she's sucking on a lemon, they're not going to recommend our services. We have to make this first showing our best. Let me look at her," Ida said, returning to stand at the head of the coffin. She put on a pair of latex gloves, and with her thumb and forefinger, she tried to open Mrs. Wilkinson's mouth. "She's not cooperating," Ida said to lighten the mood.

"Don't you remember, Ida? At the demonstration in San Francisco, the mortician sewed up the mouth so that the corpse would not look slack-jawed. Here, take this pair of scissors, snip the thread, and insert the dentures. Then I'll resew what was snipped off."

Mavis smiled but remained at her side while Ida snipped the thread and attempted to insert the poor dear's dentures in her mouth.

Carefully, Ida pried Mrs. Wilkinson's mouth open, then tried to place her bottom dentures in her mouth. "She must've had a large mouth before, because these aren't going in as easily as they should," Ida said. A few adjustments later and she was able to force the bottom plate in Mrs. Wilkinson's mouth. "Okay, hand me the top dentures."

Mavis, acting as Ida's new assistant, placed the upper dentures in her outstretched gloved hand. Mavis had a flashback to the time when Ida wore a latex glove as part of her attire. Hopefully, those days were long gone and would never return.

Holding the bottom denture, Ida tried to slide the upper denture in place. She wiggled it a few times and managed to force the upper dentures into her mouth.

"I'm glad I have all of my own teeth. Herbert had his teeth, too. He was such a stickler about flossing at night."

"That's wonderful to know, Mavis," Ida commented dryly. "I'm not sure I could live without that extra tidbit of knowledge."

"Ida, for Pete's sake, I was just talking. Your hands are shaking like a leaf."

Ida looked up at Mavis, snapping, "Do you want to do this?"

"Uh, no thank you. It was your idea."

"Then be quiet," Ida said.

"You don't have to be hateful, Ida. Are you sure you can do this?"

Ida removed her hand from Mrs. Wilkinson's chin. When she did, her mouth hung open like a dark hole leading to a cave. "Mavis, something is not right here. Look at this."

Mavis stepped up to the head of the coffin again. She looked at Mrs. Wilkinson's mouth, and it did appear to be rather . . . well, stuffed.

"Unless her mouth was twice the size in life, I don't think we're going to be able to hide these extra-large teeth. They must belong to someone else. Possibly Mr. Parker switched them with another . . . client's?"

Ida stated.

Mavis's eyes quadrupled in size. "It can't be! It says right here . . ." Mavis scurried around, searching for a paper from the funeral director; when she found it, she skimmed its contents. "It states right here that she specifically wanted to be buried with teeth."

"Let me see that," Ida said. She read through the instructions, then passed the paper back to Ida. "Yes, it does, but it doesn't say they have to be her dentures. We can't screw this up, Mavis. We'll be has-beens before we've even started. I think I can make this work." Ida snapped off her latex gloves. Carefully, Ida maneuvered the dentures until Mrs. Wilkinson's mouth was closed. Then Mavis resewed the mouth so that it would not pop open.

Ida propped a pillow under Mrs. Wilkinson's neck. Hands shaking, Ida carefully outlined Mrs. Wilkinson's lips with Pulse-Less Peach lip liner. She stood back to view her work.

"There," she said, feeling quite proud of herself. "Hand me that tube of lipstick."

Again, Mavis did as instructed.

Using a lip brush, Ida carefully filled in Mrs. Wilkinson's lips with the peachy lip-stick. She added a touch of clear gloss, then blotted her lips with a tissue. When she was finished, she stepped back to admire her work. "Well, what do you think?" she asked Mavis.

Mavis stood at the foot of the casket. "I think poor Mrs. Wilkinson looks like she's wearing someone else's dentures. Remember that show with the horse . . . Mister. Ed? I think she looks like that horse."

Ida huffed, "If you can do any better, then I suggest you try. I've still got to do her eye makeup. Do you think you can paint her nails with the Pulse-Less Peach? It matches her dress perfectly," Ida said, still admiring her handiwork.

"Of course."

For the next two hours, Ida and Mavis tended to Mrs. Wilkinson. When they were finished, she looked a bit more colorful, and a bit more . . . lively. The only imperfection: the teeth were still two sizes too large. If they were lucky, the family would be so overcome with grief, they wouldn't notice.

They packed up their cosmetics, with enough time to visit the ladies' room so they could touch up their own makeup, though they didn't use anything from The Drop-Dead Gorgeous line. It was almost time to meet with the family and the mourners.

Mavis fussed with her lipstick, added a bit

more blush to her ever-thinning face, then spritzed her wrists with Joy perfume. Ida reapplied her own lipstick, tucked her pageboy in place, and washed her hands. Twice. She saw Mavis watching her with a worried look on her face.

"Before you ask, no, I am not having a germ issue. My hands just felt extra yucky from touching those dentures. Who would've thought me, of all people, would touch a set of dentures, then cram them into someone's mouth?" Ida asked, looking quite pleased with herself.

She hadn't painted a pretty visual at all, Mavis thought. She was becoming like Sophie. That wasn't a bad thing. Well, not that bad.

"I'm so proud of you, dear. But there's something I've been meaning to say. Do you remember how you told us about that shrine room Nancy had and what Goebel heard her say? I've been thinking about it, and if she intended to kill you all along, then why did she end up waiting until more than a year had passed? We know that's what happened because of when she hired that detective to find you. I now think I have it figured out. It was your OCD that saved your life."

"What are you talking about, Mavis? That's nuts."

"No, listen to me. Suppose Nancy came to New York to poison you and found out how you were living, that you were always wearing protective clothing, et cetera. How was she supposed to get to you? You weren't seeing visitors. You didn't go out. You certainly didn't eat in restaurants. So, she went back to Chicago and hoped she would get another shot at you. But the next thing she knew, you had disappeared. Voilà. You may have that fake Dr. Sameer to thank for curing you of your OCD, but you probably have the OCD to thank for keeping you alive until Toots rescued all of us."

Ida was still thinking over what Mavis had just said when they stepped out of the ladies' room and into the hush of the funeral parlor's main room. Murmurs of condolence could be heard throughout. As though they were in a formal receiving line, Ida and Mavis stood off to the side while the family members each took turns viewing poor Mrs. Wilkinson. Some dabbed at their eyes; some simply patted her thin hands. One woman commented on the color of her nail polish, saying she wished she knew where she could find such a color. Ida wanted to jump up and tell her, but manners dictated that now wasn't the time.

They spotted Sophie and Toots as they

made their way toward the casket. Each wore one of Mavis's Good Mourning gray ensembles. As soon as the family members stepped away from the casket, Sophie and Toots came forward, not to say a final good-bye to a dear friend but to see Ida and Mavis's handiwork.

Ida and Mavis observed them as they inspected the body of the little old woman. Toots's smile seemed a bit forced, and Sophie's eyes bugged out of her head like those of a character in an old cartoon.

They joined them in the corner. As always, Sophie was the first to speak. "My God, Ida, Mavis, that poor woman looks like Marlon Brando in *The Godfather!* Did you stuff her jaws with socks, or was she just naturally homely?"

Ida cleared her throat several times to distract Sophie. When she finally caught her attention, Ida whispered to them, "See that elderly man with the walker heading our way? He's the husband. Be nice."

It seemed like it took the old man an hour just to walk to their side of the room. Talking among themselves, they guessed his age to be in the midnineties.

"Poor old man," Mavis said.

"Why do you think everyone is poor? The old coot could be loaded," Sophie said.

Mavis wrinkled her nose. "I didn't mean it that way. It's just a term of endearment."

"Sounds more like a financial conclusion if you ask me," Sophie shot back.

"No one asked you, Sophie, so be quiet," Toots admonished. "Here he comes. Act like you have manners."

The four women waited patiently as the elderly man approached them. He was hanging on to his walker as if his life depended on it.

When he finally managed to drag himself and his walker within speaking distance, the old man, not much bigger than his dearly departed wife, dug into his pocket and pulled out a handkerchief.

He leaned on his walker for support, took a deep breath, then gummed the words, "I gave you the wrong teeth."

Ida and Mavis looked like they'd been kicked in the mouth; Toots was stunned; and of course, Sophie, being Sophie, cackled so loud the funeral director came to see if she was all right.

"Yes, I'm fine. I think my friends might have some explaining to do."

Mavis looked at Ida, and Ida looked back as if to say she hadn't a clue.

"Yes, the family asked me if we forgot to remove some medical apparatus from her mouth," Mr. Parker said.

"No, they didn't. They simply got the wrong set of dentures, that's all," Sophie informed him.

The old man gummed a smile. "Well, isn't that something. Old Martha said that when she died, I was to make sure to bury her with teeth."

Apparently she hadn't specified they had to be *her* teeth.

EPILOGUE

Six months later . . .

Gushing with excitement, Sophie said, "Toots, you're not going to believe this, but Chris called again and said he's being flooded with requests for more private tarot readings. It seems that last tartlet I did a reading for told all her friends, and they told their friends, too."

"That's fantastic. Now maybe you can open up your own shop. I think the neighbors suspect I'm running a house of ill repute, with all your nighttime clients popping in and out during the wee hours," Toots said.

"I may have to consider doing just that," Sophie said, tongue in cheek.

They were sitting on the beach in their two favorite beach chairs, only this time they had both wrapped themselves in one of those newfangled Snuggies that were all the rage. Late fall in California was chilly

410

this year.

"I think this is going to be a thriving business for you. It's funny how we've all managed to branch out on our own these past eighteen months. First, Mavis and those damned mourning clothes. Ida and her Drop-Dead cosmetics. And now you, giving advice to the stars. Who woulda thunk it?"

"And you forgot to mention you're now half owner of Charleston's hottest new bakery. Don't forget that. And what about the number one tabloid in the nation? You can't forget that, either."

"No, I can't. I would kill for one of those pralines right now, but with Mavis and her constant nagging, I don't think she will let me get away with eating too much junk. I saw her adding granola to my box of Froot Loops the other day. You do realize I created a monster when I decided to help her? In a nice way, of course."

"And it was for your own good," Mavis said, sneaking up behind them with two folding chairs. "I want you to be around for a long time. I certainly would hate it if I had to lay you out. Oh dear, I don't think I could stand to do that!"

"Keep putting granola in Toots's Froot Loops and she'll kill you. You won't have to worry about laying her out," Sophie said, a puff of smoke coming from her mouth with each word.

Ida tromped down the steps leading to the beach, then sat in the chair next to Mavis. She'd brought a thermos of coffee; Mavis had the cups.

"I was just wishing for a cup of coffee," Toots said. "You must be a mind reader."

"That would be Sophie," Ida said.

"You're all wrong. I'm not a mind reader. Just highly intuitive, that's all."

A chill breeze blew in from the ocean, waves splashing back and forth, the scent of wood smoke wafting in the air while they each relaxed, enjoying the moment.

"I have a surprise for you all," Mavis said. She retrieved a large paper bag that she'd managed to bring down to the beach without anyone noticing. She emptied its contents on her chair.

"Please don't ask me to model for one of your death brochures again." Sophie grimaced. "I was the laughingstock of every funeral parlor across the country."

And she had been, just not in the sense she was alluding to. Morticians and undertakers from across the country wanted to know exactly how Mavis had managed to make a dead woman look so beautiful, and so alive. Mavis had confessed that her model was very much alive. Once that became known, Mavis had started receiving e-mails from all over the world, asking her the name of her model. In response, she said that she would forward them to the model, which she did, allowing Sophie to do as she pleased. Sophie had eyes for one man only. Goebel. He'd been to California twice since they'd caught Nancy.

"I saw this at the grocery store this morning and thought it would be perfect for a night like tonight." Mavis revealed a disposable charcoal grill. Next were the makings for s'mores.

"This is perfect. I can't remember the last time I had s'mores. Mavis, you're a good egg, you know that?" Toots said. "How did I ever get so lucky to find the three greatest friends, and godmothers for Abby?"

"You're really including Ida in the equation?" Sophie smarted off, though she was laughing when she said it. She wasn't quite the smart aleck of times past.

They all laughed.

"Yes, I am including Ida in the equation, and you, too," Toots singsonged.

Mavis followed the directions on the mini-grill, and within minutes they had their own fire burning. Using forks, they all stuffed a giant marshmallow on the tines, each toasting her own. Toots passed out squares of chocolate, and Ida snapped graham crackers in half. When their forks held a mess of sugary goo, they pressed it between the chocolate and the cracker.

"Damn, this is to die for," Toots said, biting into the delicious sweetness. "Not as good as Jamie's pralines, but good."

Sophie nodded, munching with her mouth full. "I can't think of anything I've enjoyed as much today. Foodwise."

"Are you implying there is something else you've enjoyed that we don't know about?" Ida asked, raising her perfectly manicured brow. "Surely you're not having thoughts of having a fling with Goebel. I thought you hated men."

"I do, most of them. Not that it's any of your business, but Goebel and I are just friends. For now. I told him right up front that I did not want to get involved in a romantic relationship. Then I told him what happened with you and that phony doctor. He said he was perfectly fine to be friends. For now."

A buzzing from Sophie's pocket put a halt to further conversation. She held up her hand, indicating she needed a minute.

"Yes, this is Sophie Manchester. Yes. Well, I did help Lana Lowery with her career, or rather my tarot reading led her to make the right career decision. Yes, I'll hold." Sophie placed her hand over the cell phone's mouthpiece. She shrugged her shoulders, letting them know she didn't have a clue who she was speaking to. "Yes, I'm still here." Sophie paused for several seconds. "Are you trying to yank my chain? If you are, I'll cast a . . . What? You're serious, aren't you? Yes, ma'am. Of course. I would be honored. I can leave and be there immediately. You'll do *what?*" Sophie turned ten shades of white. "Yes, ma'am. You can count on it. Uh . . . good-bye." The cell phone fell out of Sophie's hand, landing in the wet sand.

"Sophie, you look like you're going to faint. Are you?" Toots asked, scooting to the edge of her chair. "If you are, let me know so I can get out of the way."

"You're not going to believe who just called," Sophie said, her voice a hoarse whisper.

"You're probably right, but tell us, anyway," Ida said.

"That was the governor's mansion in Sacramento. It seems that the first spouse of California has requested a reading from me. It seems like my fame has spread. Oh my God! The personal secretary said they'll send for me, and they would appreciate it if I would not blather. . . . That's what she actually had the nerve to say, *blather* about this to . . . the tabloids. Pinch me, girls!"

All four women were truly stunned. Several minutes passed before any of them could talk, and when they did, it was the most natural thing in the world for them to place their hands on top of one another's, lift them to the sky, and shout, "When you're good, you're good!"

LADY BALTIMORE CAKE/ BERNICE'S DEATH CAKE

Ingredients

Cake:
1/2 cup butter
1 1/2 cups sugar
1 cup water
3 cups flour
2 teaspoons baking powder
4 egg whites, stiffly beaten
1 teaspoon vanilla extract

Frosting and Filling:
1 1/2 cups sugar
2/3 cup water
2 teaspoons light corn syrup

2 egg whites
1/8 teaspoon salt
1 teaspoon vanilla extract
1/4 cup chopped pecans
1/4 cup chopped figs
1/4 cup raisins
1/4 cup candied cherries
1/4 cup candied pineapple

Preparation

Cake:
In a mixing bowl with an electric mixer, cream butter and sugar. Add water gradually, and then add flour and baking powder. Fold in stiffly beaten egg whites and vanilla. Bake in three buttered and floured cake pans in a 375°F oven.

Frosting and Filling:
Combine sugar, water, and corn syrup in a saucepan. Cook, stirring, over low heat until sugar is dissolved. Bring to a boil and boil to 240°F. Meanwhile, when syrup reaches about 234°F, beat egg whites until stiff peaks form. Add salt. Remove syrup from the heat when 240°F is reached and immediately pour a very thin stream over stiffly beaten egg whites and salt, beating constantly. Add vanilla. Continue beating

until frosting cools and is of spreading consistency, about ten minutes.

Add chopped fruits and nuts to about a third of the frosting mixture to use as a filling between the cake layers. Frost the sides and top.

ABOUT THE AUTHOR

Fern Michaels is the *USA Today* and *New York Times* bestselling author of *Betrayal, Home Free, Southern Comfort, Deadly Deals, Exclusive: The Godmothers,* and dozens of other novels and novellas. There are over seventy million copies of her books in print.

Fern Michaels has built and funded several large daycare centers in her hometown, and is a passionate animal lover who has outfitted police dogs across the country with special bulletproof vests. She shares her home in South Carolina with her five dogs and a resident ghost named Mary Margaret. Visit her website at www.fernmichaels.com.

We hope you have enjoyed this Large Print book. Other Thorndike, Wheeler, Kennebec, and Chivers Press Large Print books are available at your library or directly from the publishers.

For information about current and upcoming titles, please call or write, without obligation, to:

Publisher
Thorndike Press
10 Water St., Suite 310
Waterville, ME 04901
Tel. (800) 223-1244

or visit our Web site at:

http://gale.cengage.com/thorndike

OR

Chivers Large Print
published by AudioGO Ltd
St James House, The Square
Lower Bristol Road
Bath BA2 3SB
England
Tel. +44(0) 800 136919
email: info@audiogo.co.uk
www.audiogo.co.uk

All our Large Print titles are designed for easy reading, and all our books are made to last.